# SEEKING EDEN

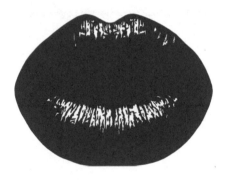

# BEVERLEY HARVEY

**URBANE**
Publications

urbanepublications.com

First published in Great Britain in 2017
by Urbane Publications Ltd
Suite 3, Brown Europe House, 33/34 Gleaming Wood Drive,
Chatham, Kent ME5 8RZ
Copyright © Beverley Harvey, 2017

A CIP catalogue record for this book is available
from the British Library.

ISBN 978-1-911331-89-6
MOBI 978-1-911331-91-9
EPUB 978-1-911331-90-2

Design and Typeset by Michelle Morgan

Cover by Michelle Morgan

Printed and bound by CPI Group (UK) Ltd, Croydon, CR0 4YY

urbanepublications.com

# SEEKING
# EDEN

DEDICATED TO RODNEY
CURLED AT MY FEET FOR EVERY WORD:
SLEEP WELL MY FAITHFUL DOG

SEEKING EDEN

# PROLOGUE

An emergency locksmith arrived bringing a whiff of fried food and an air of futility into the flat with him.

'If they're coming in – they're coming in,' he said, before scribbling an eye-watering invoice and handing it to Kate.

Two police officers had made a big deal of pretending that burglary was a rarity in their street. Kate and Neil exchanged cynical glances. Several of their friends had been burgled already - break-ins were one of life's inevitabilities in their corner of South East London.

They'd only been gone for two hours. To the Moon & Stars - the same pub they went to most Thursday evenings after work; a pre-weekend livener that Neil had begun and Kate had run with, enjoying the easy interaction with neighbours and locals.

Arriving home at ten, they'd found the street entrance unlocked and their own front door yawning open.

Silenced by shock, Kate and Neil entered the flat, stumbling on things that should not be there. Kate switched on an overhead light; what had lined the edges of their living room, on shelves and cupboards, had become a hideous centrepiece - a chaotic tangle of books, CDs, paperwork and cables strewn on the floor.

A muffled buzz led them into their bedroom, where Kate's vibrator lay maggoting around the duvet - god alone knew what they'd done with it. Mortified and wearing rubber gloves, Kate had dispatched it to the wheelie bin outside before calling the police (nobody needed to see that).

She looked around, taking in the scene of ransacked carnage; at photo frames knocked from the dresser and smashed, at drawers hanging open, their contents scattered like confetti.

Materially at least, they hadn't lost much, but even after Kate and Neil had tidied up, vacuuming the broken glass and rubbing away the smeary mess left by the SOCOs' finger print powder, the flat felt sullied. Because someone faceless and uninvited had been there, rifling the relative order of their home - of their lives.

It took three days for Kate to discover that her eighteenth birthday ring, its heart-shaped ruby dulled by soap and age, had gone the way of her laptop, their iPod and Neil's watch collection. Losing the ring hurt like hell. After her parents had died, it became symbolic, a talisman. Now it had gone – and for what purpose? So that some low-life scumbag junkie could get his next fix?

Queasy at the thought, Kate searched her reflection in the hall mirror. Looking back at her; blue eyes, etched with laughter lines that were empty of joy now. Her mouth, usually full and mobile was pinched with anxiety, and furrows competed with the tiny scar on her forehead – a legacy of falling off her bicycle aged six. Was this what a victim of crime looked like?

Kate boiled the kettle for the umpteenth time, knowing that an ocean of tea couldn't wash the bilious taste from her mouth.

# PART
# ONE

# CHAPTER 1:
## NO PLACE LIKE HOME

### KATE

'Katie, remind me again; why exactly are we doing this?' Neil said, the car's ailing air-con making him fractious.

'Darling, just think of it as a day out – there is life beyond London, you know,' Kate said, fanning herself with the property brochure.

She remembered taking the London underground a week earlier; the tube had been rammed and stifling, with people pole-hanging in the aisles. Wedged into her seat, Kate had picked up an odour of sour socks coming from the man next to her as sweat prickled between her own shoulder blades.

Since she'd been freelancing, Kate had been careful to swerve rush hour, but this time she'd timed her meeting all wrong. *These poor sods do it every day*, she thought, eyeing a thin blonde, swaying unsteadily on four inch heels.

Picking up a discarded Standard, she'd opened the property section, her eyes drawn at once to an image of a village green flanked by weather-boarded, picket fenced houses.

'Eden Hill; 55 minutes from London', boasted the ad. Kate tore out the page and stuffed it into her bulging handbag.

Now they were inching through Saturday morning traffic, barely leaving second gear, until the motorway signalled a change of pace, and they were speeding through the Kent countryside, past rolling hills dotted with sheep and deer, interspersed with small towns of sand-coloured brick and grey concrete.

They'd expected an estate, but as the SatNav led them past shops and gleaming offices, along tree-lined boulevards bordered by grassy banks where children played and rode bicycles, they realised that Eden Hill was a whole new town.

'Hey, this is it!' Kate said as they rounded a bend to find a red and white bill board: 'Wicklow Homes Welcomes You' it said, as a cluster of New England style houses shimmered before them, mirage-like in the midday sun.

They could see by the array of shiny new cars parked in driveways, and other tell-tale signs of life that most of the homes were already occupied. But as they stepped from the car, the only sound was the tinging-clang of the developer's flags tolling in the wind.

'Quiet, isn't it?' Kate shivered despite the heat.

Then from the site-office, a woman dressed like a flight attendant came bowling towards them, beaming.

'Hello! Mr and Mrs Farleigh? I'm Jackie – we spoke on the phone. You picked a super day for it,' she said, before Kate and Neil had even introduced themselves.

Jangling a bunch of keys, Jackie steered them into a gleaming white house, her tan tights whispering as she walked.

'This is the last one - and that's only because a couple pulled out last week; couldn't get their finance sorted in the end, bless them. Anyway, welcome to your new home.'

'Bit presumptuous,' Neil hissed as they stepped into the coolness of the oak-floored hallway.

Kate shot him a look; 'Hey, I like it - I like it a lot. It's hard to believe that this four bedroom house costs the same as our flat, and with all these bathrooms, we can have people to stay every weekend.'

'And this,' Jackie said, pausing for effect, 'is the kitchen.'

Taking in the sleek granite worktops, prep-island and double-oven Range, Kate's heart leapt in her chest. She imagined hosting chic candlelit dinner parties, and being showered with compliments.

'Darling, I think this could be it,' Kate said, eyes shining.

Neil nodded; 'It could be. Why don't we go and get a coffee and talk about it?'

ď

'But can you imagine our friends in London coming down for the weekend? Most of them would come out in hives.' Kate said, stirring her flat white, whilst eyeing the Boden-clad mums stuffing cake into apple-cheeked infants.

She tried to picture the two of them living in the white house, but the image was fuzzy. Could they really live in Eden Hill? In a neat little cul de sac, within this vast estate of street after street of the kind of homes they'd always scorned?

'The thing is Katie,' Neil said, 'we wouldn't be buying it for our friends, and anyway, screw what people think. We're done living our lives for other people. Before we know it, we'll be fifty – maybe this is the change of pace we need...you know, communing with nature – taking up hobbies and sports...what do you think?'

'I think we'd feel safe here. It probably makes the local news when a window gets broken around here,' Kate said, nodding slowly.

'I know what you mean,' Neil drained his Americano. 'It's like the bad people don't know this place exists. It's kind of...what's the word? Wholesome.'

'Okay, let's have another look and make a list of pros and cons,' Kate said, standing up.

As they reached the door, a young mum with aubergine hair called out to them.

'You left your handbag, love,' she said, holding it towards Kate. Kate thanked her.

'First point for the 'pros,' she said 'excellent community spirit.'

♋

By October the blousy colours of summer had made way for autumn's mellow palette. The fields around Eden Hill had taken on a golden hue, while the streets in the neighbourhood were slick with rain and fallen leaves. A relentless wind whistled round the developers' flags, so that they clanged and flapped, like ships in distress. Kate hardly recognised the place.

'God, Neil. This isn't how I remember it from the viewings...it all looks so different.'

'Katie, give it a chance – that was summer,' Neil said, drawing her closer to him.

'What are we doing here?' Kate's voice wobbled with rising panic.

'Love, ever since the break-in, all we've talked about is getting out of London, and making a fresh start. Give it time, baby, please.'

Kate watched the removals van belch out fumes before chugging away, thinking how incongruous and shabby their eclectic Londoners' possessions seemed against the stark white walls and gleaming appliances.

On the door step, they found a flowery tin, with a card taped to it:

Wishing you good luck in your new home (it said) all the best from Clifford and Moira at No 17.

The neighbouring house on the right looked established. Bright curtains hung at the windows and ceramic pots sat either side of the front door, the last knockings of autumn colour still blooming. Miming delight in case they were being watched, they went back inside and broke off chunks of yellow sponge, the sugar-fix a temporary distraction from Kate's disappointment.

'It's delicious, and so kind of them. At least we know the neighbours are nice,' Neil said, through a mouthful of crumbs. 'When was the last time someone in London baked us a cake? We'll pop round and thank them this evening. We'll be fine here, you wait – it's just different, that's all.'

'Who are you trying to convince?' Kate said.

♂

If someone had told Kate that she would weep for South London, for their old flat - its view of the common partially obscured by the bus terminal with its stink of diesel and hotdogs from a van – she'd have laughed her tights off. But here she was, crying tears of self-pity and regret.

For one thing, she couldn't seem to get warm, however many layers she put on.

She missed the chaos of London, the steamy coffee shops, the mish-mash of delis and grocery stores with their exhaustive supply of spices and muddied weirdly-shaped vegetables; the newsstands on every corner that sold Vogue in a dozen languages, the thrift shops where she'd found the odd designer gem, and spent hours looking at books for a pound – she even missed the drone and stench of traffic as life surged from every direction.

By contrast, Eden Hill had an odd stillness to it, and felt two-dimensional, giving Kate a sense of detachment. She couldn't imagine belonging, however long they stayed.

But Neil had been right about the neighbours. They'd introduced themselves to the couple at No. 17. Clifford, hard of hearing, had retreated to his study as soon as the pleasantries were over, but Moira had welcomed them into the kitchen, which was stuffed with family photographs, including several of three gap-toothed grandchildren – and there were chickens everywhere; ceramic chickens, glass chickens, and chicken motifs on mugs, plates and tea-towels.

'We like chickens,' Moira said.

Kate relaxed. There was something reassuring about this ash-blonde, curly haired woman, who smelled of L'Air du Temps; even her Earl Grey tea was gentle.

On the other side, they'd met Rachel, but a loud wail that erupted just as they rang the doorbell told them their timing was off.

'Yes?' A woman in leggings and Ugg boots answered, arms folded across her thick little body.

'Hi, I'm Kate, this is Neil. We-'

'Oh, sorry, yes! You've just moved in next door, haven't you? I'm Rachel – my husband Rob's at work. We've got two little ones, Jordan and Ellie – god, they're a handful! We've only been here six weeks ourselves. Sorry...just a minute. Ellie! Ellie, come here please.' There was a bump, followed by a high-pitched scream. Rachel grimaced.

'You must pop round when the kids aren't trying to kill each other – I'd better go. Bye.' Looking harassed, she shut the door.

'And breath,' Neil said; Stressed or what? Okay, that's done. We can meet some more people another day.'

☪

Driving back from the smart gym she'd joined, or coming home from one of the out of town supermarkets, Kate would see the estate, high on the hill, like a film set waiting for the cast and crew to show up and it gave her a leaden feeling in her stomach.

If she was going to survive, in this suburban Truman Show of a town, drastic measures were called for.

'Darling,' she began, one evening in March, as the days were becoming longer and the temperature had begun to rise, 'Let's get a dog.'

Neil was sprawled on the sofa, limp with contentment after an excellent midweek roast dinner.

'Where did that come from? Go on, sell it to me, baby,' Neil said, trying to pull Kate onto his lap.

Kate resisted - all the better to negotiate.

'Babe, my biggest problem here is that I'm alone all the time. I've hit a drought with work and my so-called friends can't be bothered to come out here. Darling, I'm trying to make new ones, but it's tricky...it's not like I'm at the school gates with all the mums, is it? And the ladies at the gym are so bloody serious and committed – not a squeak from any of them since I joined. But a dog...' she paused for dramatic effect; 'A dog would make us a family and get me talking to other dog walkers.'

Kate knew Neil was worried about her; he'd watched her shrink into herself at an alarming rate since they'd arrived. Coming home, eyeballs burning from eight hours spent in front of a Mac, Neil had found her in tears more than once. But when she tried to hide her feelings of despair, somehow it came out all wrong – fake and hearty - which was just weird.

'I reckon a few dog hairs on the furniture is a small price to pay for getting the old Katie back, so if it'll make you happy, let's go to the local rescue home this weekend,' Neil said, as if reading her thoughts.

Ten years earlier, Kate might have said; 'Let's make a baby.' Except that ten years ago, they hadn't known each other, and on Kate's part, being a mum had never been on her To Do list.

She didn't care when people thought her hard or selfish, and she'd been accused of not wanting to ruin her lithe figure on more than one occasion. What rankled was when people felt sorry for her. Like the time she'd run into an old colleague, Jessica, in a shopping mall.

Swarmed by three pairs of sticky, grabby hands, Jessica - who had produced three babies in quick succession - was evangelical.

'Oh my god, Katie! How long has it been? You look so well,' Jessica gushed, fending off jabs and kicks, without missing a beat. 'Any little ones of your own?' The question had bubbled up, instant, uninvited.

'Er, no ... life is quite full enough, what with work and-'

'Never give up! Miracles do happen.' Jess said, inclining her head and patting Kate's arm in sympathy.

Kate had been furious, desperate to set her straight. Instead she made her excuses and escaped; how fucking presumptuous, she thought, as rage powered her around Marks & Spencer's food hall.

The simple truth was that the ache – the yearning – that other women described had never arrived. There had been one short window – one broody moment, when her niece Natalie was born and Kate had held her; inhaled her warm biscuit smell and touched her perfect tiny fingers and toes. But the mood had soon passed.

She'd been forty when she met Neil, so had tackled the subject head on.

'I'm already the luckiest man alive to have found you,' he'd said, 'So I'm fine with being just us. It would be greedy to ask for more.'

☩SEEKING EDEN

A year later, Kate Stone had become Mrs Neil Farleigh, and it hadn't come up again. But sometimes she'd catch him looking wistfully at friends' kids, and would feel a wave of guilt and sadness.

Oh, but a dog.

A dog would allow them to be parents - of a kind - and now it seemed ridiculous not to have one.

Kate stripped the duvet cover off, poked it into the machine and set the dial to 'hot'. Muddy paw prints were a dead giveaway and Neil would be home by eight.

'I love him too, but we can't have Ludo in bed with us, Katie – it's just not right. There's not even enough room. If you wanted a lap dog, you shouldn't have got a whippet; those joints are bloody sharp!'

She'd pretended to suck it up, but on the three nights that Neil stayed in London, Ludo slept beside her.

Kate was overwhelmed with tenderness for the bony, quivering creature; their bond was instant.

Ludo forced her out in all weathers and made her get up by seven, even on the days when she had no copy to write, or gym classes to attend – days when, without him – she'd have stayed in bed, her energy sapped by lethargy and self-pity.

As spring arrived, Kate began to remember why she'd been attracted to the place, as cherry trees popped with blossom along the avenues and people began to emerge from their houses, light of step, and with ready smiles.

She found herself walking longer and further with Ludo, just for the joy of being outside. Fast as a bullet, he would hunt rabbits and squirrels but never to the kill, and when Kate called, he'd trot back to her side and stick close, until the next unseen rustle in the scrub would send him tearing off again.

By May, the woodland paths had hardened underfoot but Kate still wore wellingtons. Snakes were rumoured to live in the tree roots and coppiced wood piles. A fear of reptiles was striped through her DNA. Even in Primary school, she'd cried when Lucy Jones had produced a newt in an ice cream tub during show and tell.

She took no comfort from Neil's assertions that only adders were poisonous and that they were a protected species; the prospect of Ludo getting bitten terrified her beyond reason.

One bright morning, experimenting with a new – and reptile free – route to the orchards, Kate found herself in front of high wrought iron gates shielding half a dozen or so grand looking houses. As she paused, a Chihuahua came steaming across the courtyard, like a wind-up toy, through the maze of polished limos and 4x4s, bound straight for Ludo, who'd begun to wag his tail and bounce on the spot.

'Nellie! Come here, girl.' A tanned blonde in white jeans and a chiffon top came click-clacking towards the gates after the dog.

'Nellie, come!' But Nellie had other plans. Passing easily through the bars, she pranced at Ludo's feet, yapping with excitement. Ludo, delighted by his micro playmate, was trying hard to slip his lead, desperate to play.

'Nellie – you get back here!' the woman shouted, 'Sorry about this – she does exactly what she likes. It's my fault – she's spoilt rotten.'

'I don't blame you, she's so cute. I spoil mine, too. My husband's always saying the dog gets more attention than he does,' Kate joked.

Beautiful in an obvious way, with perfect teeth, high, round breasts and bottle-blonde hair that fell past her shoulders, the woman looked immaculate despite it being barely nine-thirty.

Un-showered, and with hair scraped back into a claw, Kate looked down at the jeans she'd worn all week, feeling like the hired help.

By now the woman had scooped up the little Chihuahua and was nuzzling her around her face, like a powder puff.

Kate giggled.

'She's like a toy – I'd be scared of treading on her.' Close up, the woman looked familiar; the penny dropped.

'Have I seen you at the gym? Do you do boxercise on Tuesday afternoons?' Kate said.

'Yes. I thought I'd seen you somewhere. I'm Lisa – so good to see a friendly face. I've only been here a few months and I don't know anybody yet.'

'I'm Kate...I know just what you mean. We moved here in October – and it's felt like a long old winter...still, everything's better when the sun shines,' she added, conscious not to whinge.

'We should do something,' Lisa said, 'we can meet for coffee, or get a juice next time we see each other at the gym.'

'You're on,' Kate said, smiling broadly and feeling ridiculously upbeat as the women swapped numbers.

Ć

'Ludo's my lifeline, Alice. I think I might have topped myself, otherwise,' Kate said into the handset.

'How can you even joke about that? It's not funny.'

'Who's laughing? Look, you're my sister – don't make me edit my life. You're the one person I can be truly honest with. I mean, it's a bit better now the days are longer and the flowers are out. But, you know...I think it was a knee jerk - we gave up on London too soon.'

'Katie, have you forgotten how upset you were after the flat got turned-over? Please, love - give it time. It will get better, I promise – especially when you've made friends.'

'How's that going to happen? Blogging from home is hardly a team sport, is it? Al, I'm so pissed off with my friends; Meredith has bailed on me twice - and Ian and Sarah came down last weekend and they hated it! I could read the contempt in their eyes. They thought we were bonkers and couldn't wait to get away,' she said, going pink at the memory.

'I got Ludo because I thought I might meet people out dog walking, but so far, no joy. Well, until today when I met a total glamour-puss called Lisa; we swapped numbers,' Kate said, unable to keep the excitement out of her voice.

Alice laughed; 'You make it sound like a date.'

'Yeah...daft, isn't it? We've probably got nothing in common but it was nice to talk to someone. It's been eight months, Al, and apart from the odd chat with the neighbours, I don't speak to a living soul here. Oh, I'm sorry for moaning; me, me, me. How are things with you, darling?'

There was a pause at the end of the line.

'I'm okay, but Pete's been acting weird. More bad tempered than usual – and he's so tired all the time. I'm worried about him.'

'It's probably stuff at work; it won't be anything you've done. I think forty is a funny age for blokes. It's like they finally have to grow up – and they kind of resent it...although to be fair, Pete's always been a grown-up, at least since Natalie was born. How is she?'

'Oh you know, moody; stays in her room half the time. I caught her shaving her legs the other day – with my razor – she's thirteen!'

They rattled through what Kate called 'The Weekly Twaddle'. Maybe she and Neil should have moved to Brighton – at least then she'd have had her sister and niece for company, rather than upping sticks to somewhere totally alien, where neither of them knew a soul.

But who was she trying to kid? Neil didn't live in Eden Hill; he still lived in London, sleeping on Jonno's futon three nights a week, a pattern he'd slipped into, complaining that the commute was just too exhausting. Kate had wheedled and cried – and then let it go, tired of bickering. After all, Neil's aversion to getting up before six every morning was entirely reasonable.

Fridays were spent in a frenzy of cleaning and pampering so that by the time Neil arrived home on the 19.40 train, the house gleamed like a new penny and Kate would greet him cocktail in hand, and ready to party. But too often, Neil would return morose with exhaustion, unable to do anything but snore in front of the television until bedtime.

Over time, the ache that Kate had felt so acutely when Neil was away in London faded - to the point where by Sunday, annoyance would bubble up instead. She was irritated by his man-crap everywhere, by his need to watch TV and be a sofa-slug, when they could have been outside with Ludo, or exploring cosy pubs and restaurants, or visiting sleepy, pretty villages across the county. And after one weekend's particularly bad bicker-thon, Neil had looked at her as though noticing something for the first time.

'Kate, sometimes I think you prefer it when I'm not here,' he said.

# CHAPTER 2:
## CREATURES OF HABIT

### BEN

Ben Wilde didn't worry too much about husbands. He'd never found them an obstacle to getting what he wanted. Discovering that Kate was married had been a shock, although it shouldn't have been – of course someone had snapped her up. Regardless, if hubby needed to be dispatched at some juncture, then so be it.

It felt like a sign that they'd washed up barely an hour apart after all these years. Well for now at least, living at the coast suited him. The ugly pebble-dashed bungalow was cosy inside and all the essentials worked well enough. Better still, there was plenty of space to store his collection of guitars, keyboards, recording equipment, books and CDs.

Nestled behind the dunes, it was a place where he could breathe, think and write. It was incredible; the songs were flowing like Prosecco at a wedding – and far more freely than in Almeria, where he'd lived with Gabriela.

In hindsight, the white-washed villa, with its crimson arch of bougainvillea around the door, had been conducive to little more than getting stoned on cheap local hash and drinking sangria in the afternoons.

Now, most mornings, Ben was on the beach by eight, sneakers rolling on the pebbles, picking a path through the dunes. Dragging on a Marlboro Light, he'd walk for a mile or so, enjoying the silence, except for the sea as it inhaled and exhaled its lacy foam.

He'd stare at the carrion; dead things fascinated him - the way they created their own macabre eco-system, with parasitic lifeforms that vacuumed everything up and made it all go away. Today's grisly body count included a maggoty cod's head, a dumped catch of sprats, and a rotting seagull, pterodactyllian in its proportions.

It would be different in the winter, when the sea became a churned-up brown soup, and the waves would crash and roar – but with that came another type of savage beauty, so maybe he'd stick around. And by then, perhaps Kate would feature in his plans.

☾

'Kate? It's me.'

Would she recognise his voice after eighteen years of radio silence?

He'd found her number online: Blogger & Corporate Copywriter her website said. There was a smiling black and white photo - she hadn't changed much. After that, he'd cyber stalked her for a bit – and found out she'd married an ad-man called Neil. Ben wouldn't have found her at all if she hadn't kept her maiden name for work.

'Ben? Is that you?' There was shock and incredulity in Kate's voice, but recognition, nonetheless. 'Where are you?'

'About an hour from you, as it happens...near Dungeness.'

'Really? What are you doing there? Why aren't you in Spain?'

'I'm very well, Kate – thanks for asking.'

'I...I'm just a bit surprised...how long has it been?'

'Too long. Look, I've been back a while. Me and Gabriela are history – and it didn't end well...'

'You don't say. Did you wreck her life, too?'

'Katie, don't be like that. Look, it just wasn't the right time for you and me...you know that – and anyway, it's ancient history. I was hoping we could be friends. Fancy meeting up? I want to hear all about you...and your new feller of course.'

'Not so new now - we've been married for five years. We left London last autumn...some weird stuff happened... so we moved out.'

He could hear sadness in her voice – or regret.

'Kate, I'd like to see you. I'll come over to you, shall I? We can just go out for coffee.'

Three days later, Ben filled his battered Mercedes with petrol and was on his way.

☙

Christ, did she really live here - in this suburban hell-hole? It was offensive, a shrine to materialism. He could almost smell the desperation from the blinged-up, maxed-out residents who'd sold their souls for two SUVs, three en-suits and a hot tub. Nobody needed all this stuff, the sad fuckers. This wasn't real life - and if this was Kate's bag now, perhaps it had been a mistake to look for her.

Not that Ben had been immune to the lure of creature comforts, back in the day.

He'd never liked the term one-hit-wonder, but that was about the long and short of it, and his one master stroke of song-writing genius, Seagull, had bankrolled him for years - thanks to a Radio 1 DJ, who'd spun the hell out of it during the summer of '97.

And with success he'd bought freedom, escaping to the Andalusian sun – until the royalty cheques began to dry up.

Now, there was a very real danger he'd have to get a proper job; not easy staring down the barrel of the big 5.0.

Or maybe – and it seemed so obvious to him now - he just needed to get his muse back. He'd loved Kate when he'd written Seagull. It had made her cry – because it was about her, with simple lyrics, a beautiful melody and a haunting guitar riff. He wondered if she ever listened to it now.

Checking the address Kate had given him, Ben pulled up outside a big white house, which would have been impressive, had it not been flanked by half a dozen others just like it. Play nicely, he thought, ringing the doorbell.

Then she was standing there, as if frozen by time, except that her hair was less lustrous than he remembered, and her face looked a little thinner. But Jesus – she still had that lanky frame and killer rack – hadn't got all soft and mumsie like so many women did after forty.

She was smiling at him, arms open, so that he caught a whiff of the same perfume that had driven him crazy all those years ago. He wanted to drag her upstairs for some skin-on-skin action there and then.

'Bloody hell, girl, you look amazing. You haven't changed a bit. So good to see you...we've got years of catching up to do.'

And then a skinny mutt came bounding towards him, looping around the hallway wagging his tail and quivering all over.

'Ah, you're beautiful, aren't you boy?' Ben said, meaning it.

Ben took the house tour and feigned an interest - even managing not to say anything rude or negative about her new digs. And he had to admit there was a stylish cool about the place, with its shabby furniture, and its delicate scent of tea-rose. Kate had always been a great homemaker – even in their first flat together, when they'd lived on love and lentils and every scrap of furniture they owned had been a hand-me-down or fished from a skip.

In a silver frame above the fireplace was a photo of Kate snuggling up to a good looking guy, all even teeth and broad shoulders.

'Is that him? He's a handsome bugger, isn't he? Are you two happy?' Ben said.

He was rewarded by a moment's hesitation.

'Most of the time, but we have the odd spat. Right, shall we head off then? I can't wait to hear all your news.'

He could see she was nervous, eyes wide and smiling too hard - tell-tale signs of anxiety that Ben knew so well.

◌

## MARTIN

Some of the locals thought it old-fashioned of him to close the shop on Wednesday afternoons, that nobody should do half-day closing in this day and age. But then, Martin was a stickler for routine and anyway, the demand for flooring wasn't so fierce that he needed to open six whole days a week.

Nevertheless business could be brisk; sometimes Martin and Trina would be run off their feet, ordering from suppliers, booking fitters, and visiting prospective clients to measure up and provide quotes; then things would go quiet again, it was a cyclical trade.

Martin was grateful for the estate two miles away. Without business from Eden Hill, he'd have closed down long ago, he was sure of that. Like most locals, he still referred to it as the 'new' estate, and it was still spreading (like a cancer, the country set called it), but many of the houses were at least fifteen years old, and the residents came to replace tired carpets battered by family life, or to upgrade hard floors scuffed with age, or out of fashion.

He could spot the estate dwellers a mile off; they were shinier somehow, with brighter clothes and smarter shoes than those worn by people from the neighbouring villages - as if they'd been invited to a country theme park for the day, and were wearing fancy dress. They marched around in their new waxed-jackets, and spotless wellingtons - even the 4x4s they drove were grime-free.

Many of the families in Eden Hill had moved from London, swapping urban two-bed flats for four bedroom detached houses overlooking green spaces.

Martin didn't care where his customers had come from, or where they were going next. What he cared about was people giving him their business, rather than going to the out of town carpet giants on one of the identical soulless retail parks, with their perpetual phoney sales and free car parking.

'Remember, Trina,' he said, at least once a week, 'Our customers have a choice. We may not be the cheapest, but we aim to be the best.'

Bevan's Flooring had been on Crabton High Street for twelve years and was wearing pretty well, considering. So, for that matter, was Martin - thanks to a preference for what his wife called rabbit food, and a keen interest in racquet sports. In his early forties, he'd even played badminton at county level for a while – but his sporting career had been short-lived. Travelling to tournaments around the Home Counties had proved a commitment too far - what with the way things were at home.

For a while, he'd stopped playing, when Jan was first diagnosed and put on medication, but these days he managed a knock-about most weeks.

Not that Jan cared much about his whereabouts. No amount of counselling and anti-depressants seemed to break through the fog that had plagued her for years. Pale and blank eyed, she read, watched television, dozed in the daytime and went to the supermarket with Martin on Wednesday afternoons, shuffling beside him, mono-syllabic. Occasionally, for two or three days at a time, a rare burst of energy would galvanise her to cook a meal from scratch, or bake a cake. Once, she'd planted a blaze of petunias and geraniums in the garden and watered them every day for a week. Another time, she'd had her hair cut and highlighted at one of Crabton's four salons, and bought makeup in Boots. Martin had found it two days later, smashed in the kitchen pedal bin.

Not a flicker of intimacy stirred between them now. Jan recoiled if he so much as stroked her arm and Martin knew better than to stray on to her side of the old pine bed they'd shared for almost twenty-five years.

ඊ

'Dad,' Hayley said, one night, after Jan had gone to bed early, 'Don't blow a gasket, but I'm moving out. Me and Si are renting a flat in Brighton – right next door to where he works. It's small but we've got to start somewhere, haven't we? Oh, and I've been offered an HR job in Hove. It's what we want, Dad; it's what I want.'

It had not been a point for discussion, but an announcement. Then it was just the two of them in the Edwardian semi, rattling around like peas in a drum.

Martin's chest grew tight when he thought of his daughter, cooking and cleaning in her own home - and much worse, letting that boy touch her, although he seemed a decent enough lad and a grafter, too.

'I'll come every weekend,' she'd promised, through the window of Simon's hatchback as they pulled away. But when the visits went down to once a month, Martin rang Hayley from work so that Jan wouldn't overhear.

'Love, your mum and me would like to see more of you and you know that Simon is always welcome, don't you?'

'Dad, it's her,' Hayley said, after a considerable pause during which Martin could picture her nibbling her thumb nail while she searched for the right words.

'Mum doesn't care whether we come or not, does she? She just stares into space and doesn't say anything. It's awkward. Honestly Daddy, I don't know how you cope.'

'Oh, don't you worry about me, love. Anyway, I must go - I've got a customer waiting,' he lied.

Choked, Martin turned the shop sign to Closed, while he composed himself in the back room.

He'd been at a low ebb when Lisa Dixon had blown into the shop, one gusty spring day, wearing a fake-fur hairband and tortoiseshell sunglasses. Typical of Eden Hill, he thought, not unkindly.

'Hi. I'm replacing my carpets – can you help me, please?' she said, dazzling Martin with bright-white teeth and removing her sunglasses to reveal heavily made-up eyes the colour of a lagoon. She'd be beautiful if she washed some of that muck off, he thought.

If Martin had been a betting man, he'd have set her at around forty. Laughter lines creased her lovely heart-shaped face and her long honey-blonde hair looked too vibrant to be natural.

He watched her pacing around the shop floor with a restless exuberance, her manicured finger-tips brushing swatches of soft woollen pile.

'I've just bought a house in Eden Hill and I love it, but the carpets are a bit...' she wrinkled her nose. 'What I want... is...ooh,' she strode over to a stand displaying luxurious piles in shades of ivory and cream; 'This! I love it.'

Martin was about to take her through an array of similar options, providing the pros and cons of each, but she cut him short.

'Thank you, but I want this one. It feels so lovely and squishy,' she said, hugging herself.

His eyes travelled to her open blazer, where ample breasts strained beneath a thin ribbed sweater.

'I'd be delighted to measure up personally, and provide you with a no-obligation quote,' he said. 'How's the day after tomorrow for you? Would ten-fifteen suit?'

That night, Martin couldn't stop thinking about her, remembering those intense sea-green eyes, and the feline way she had prowled around the shop.

On the day he was due to measure up at Mrs Dixon's house, Martin dressed carefully in a soft charcoal suit and spritzed on aftershave which prompted a hostile glare and some extra banging about in the kitchen from Jan.

'Morning boss,' Trina said, through a mouthful of croissant. 'Coffee's made – you look nice and what's that lovely pong?'

Ignoring her comments, Martin looked at her hair. Good god; what had she done to it this time? It was just as well she was blessed with a long thick mane, for all the punishment it took. Today, it was conker brown, except for the last six inches, which were of a vivid tangerine hue.

'It's called dip-dying. I got it done last night, over the road – models' night. I only paid eight quid for it,' she said, sounding delighted.

An hour later, Martin left Trina in charge – dip-dye job, and all – and set out to see Mrs Dixon.

# CHAPTER 3:
## THE EX-FACTOR

### LISA

Lisa marvelled that she'd managed to stay married for so long. Fifteen years together – thirteen of them wed; where had all the time gone?

Justin wasn't a bad man – just the wrong man – and had been all along, in hindsight. Rita had warned her about marrying a footballer – but then, her mother had always had her own agenda.

To his credit, Justin had been generous enough. They'd sold the big house in Chislehurst and split the equity straight down the middle. On top of that, he'd given her a hundred thousand pounds, which was more than he needed to. Hush money, a couple of friends had mooted at the time; for keeping quiet about the drinking and the rehab. Not that anyone cared now; Lisa could scarcely remember the days when a small army of paparazzi would be camped outside the house day and night.

A flash of genius, three seasons in the Premiership, talk of a Spanish side - and then Bam! The injury. Even now, just remembering the angle of Justin's tibia and fibula made her feel sick – and he had been, vomiting right there on the pitch, in front of a capacity crowd, as his blood pressure plummeted with shock and excruciating pain.

A year of agonising surgeries followed; recovery was slow. Then came the weight gain, followed by depression, which only made Justin binge more. And then the bourbon hit like a hurricane, and left him spewing foul blackness most nights for a month – until his body found a way to process it. And as the months turned to years, Justin shut down; from Lisa, from his parents and from his brother and sister, Sean and Debbie.

'Babe, you have to fight back - for god's sake!' Lisa cried in despair, 'You'd be a great coach, even a manager. Or...or...we can start a business together, or a charity. But you keep this up and you'll kill yourself. Well, don't expect me to stand by and watch.'

'So fucking what? There's nothing for me now.' Self-pity had sucked Justin under, closing over the space where he used to be, like water after pebbles chucked in a pond.

She'd married a twelve stone soccer star, and divorced a fifteen stone drunk; all things considered, it was a miracle she'd stayed so long.

♋

Sunlight streamed across the big French bed - a bed Lisa had no intention of sharing with anyone but Nellie.

'Good morning, angel puppy – kiss mummy!'

The sandy Chihuahua gambolled across the pillows to oblige as Lisa reached for her robe.

The decorators and the carpet man were due today and she needed to jog, shower and walk Nellie before the house was invaded by tradesmen.

It had taken a couple of months to get her bearings. Lisa had unpacked, joined the gym, found a doctor and a dentist, and now she was ready to transform the house into her own style.

Jeremy Hunter, the smooth (verging on oily) local estate agent had insisted there was nothing to do.

'Ten years old – one careful owner,' he'd said at the viewing, adding 'Of course custard walls aren't to everyone's taste, nor are powder-blue carpets, but everything works, the build quality is excellent and the location's a dream; you're buying into the most exclusive development in Eden Hill.'

The house was the smallest of six faux-Georgian homes set behind wrought iron gates - it was good to feel safe.

'This is perfect for me and Nellie,' Lisa said at the viewing.

'Ah. How old is your daughter – the primary schools here are excellent.'

Lisa giggled; 'Nellie's my dog. It's just us.'

It was time. Lisa had stayed with Rita for three hellish months, and then rented for a year before finding the house online, and judging by the rave review one of her oldest friends had given the neighbourhood, Eden Hill was one of the safest and friendliest places to live in the county.

'Mrs Dixon, if you like this house, I urge you not to deliberate for too long. It's well-priced because the family are going abroad and are very motivated to sell,' Hunter said, adding 'I'm conducting other viewings here this afternoon.'

So after a final trawl of *MoveNow.com* on her smart-phone, Lisa had offered three thousand pounds under the asking price.

'Cash,' she'd added, to clinch the deal. She'd still have a little money in the bank; enough to stall getting a job for a year or so – if she could resist blowing the lot on interior decorating.

⚲

Now, as she waited for the carpet man, Lisa wondered if it was unseemly to be so happy. She pushed Justin to the back of her mind – she couldn't go there; they weren't married now and he was not her problem. The last she'd heard, Justin had relented and gone to Sean for help – and by all accounts, he was making his brother's life an utter misery instead of her own.

♌

## MARTIN

'You can tell a lot about a person by how punctual they are,' Martin had said to Trina, more than once. He checked his watch for accuracy every week – although the Rotary he wore had never been found wanting.

Parking in front of No 3 Regents Square, after being buzzed through the gates, Martin checked his shoulders for dandruff and short, sandy hairs. Then clutching his brief case, he walked up Mrs Dixon's drive.

She looked different today, wearing less make up – she was smaller too, without the high heeled boots.

'Would you like some tea? The kettle's on already,' she said.

Martin followed Mrs Dixon into the sun-filled kitchen, setting his bag down on the granite-topped island.

'Smashing décor, Mrs Dixon.'

'Call me Lisa. D'you think?' she laughed, 'I'm not keen – I've got decorators due any minute – soon all this yellow will seem like a bad dream.'

Lisa reached for mugs on a high shelf, her thin V-neck sweater leaving little to Martin's imagination. He wondered if her breasts were real.

'Right, I must get started,' he blustered, opening his bag and taking out a laser meter, before moving from room to room nimble as a cat, and making notes in his journal.

She wasn't short of a bob or two, he thought. Not too much furniture (which would please the fitters), and most of it brand new in delicate shades of grey and cream.

Upstairs, there was no mistaking her room. The bed was fancy - French perhaps. He pictured her lying there, hair splayed out Princess-style, fudge coloured limbs peaking from a silk slip.

An array of perfume bottles stood on an elegant dressing table. Against the opposite wall was a taller chest, its top drawer protruding.

Martin could hear her on the telephone – still in the kitchen. He slid the drawer out further and gasped. Jan's underwear drawer looked nothing like this! He plucked out a scrap of teal coloured silk and lace, bringing its softness to his face, inhaling the delicate scent. Then hearing her on the stairs, Martin thrust the underwear back into its drawer, closing it as Lisa reached the doorway.

'How are you getting on?' she asked smiling.

The doorbell rang.

'That'll be the decorators...call me if you need anything.'

Crikey. What he needed was a cold shower. What he'd just done...was grubby...and cheap...and just wrong! Martin hadn't felt so turned on in years.

The sky had clouded over and rain threatened. Martin got into the car and took a few deep breaths before starting the engine, feeling his self-control return.

On a whim he called Trina and asked her to hold the fort, then drove straight home. He'd surprise Jan, and take her out for coffee and cake.

Putting his key in the door, Martin felt the same twinge of trepidation he always felt on arriving home these days. Still in her dressing gown and a pair of Martin's fishing socks, Jan was in the kitchen, exactly where he'd left her. Beside her was a mug of coffee which had skinned-over on top. Martin wondered how long it had been since she'd washed her hair.

'Not having a good day, my love?' he said.

Jan scowled.

'When do I ever have a good day?' It was the beginning of the same conversation they had on a loop several times a week.

'Have you taken your tablets today, my love?'

'Of course I have - for all the good they do. Anyway Mart, why aren't you at work?'

Martin ignored Jan's question.

'Shall I run you a quick bath, love, while you pick out some clothes? I thought we could go to the new coffee shop in the high street. The cakes in the window look delicious.'

Jan brightened at the prospect of an outing and cake.

Inside the café, three or four tables were already occupied and they sat in the window. It was raining hard now, shoppers had their umbrellas up and heads down.

With chocolate cake and steaming lattes, Martin knew they must look like any other middle-aged couple. Jan had put on grey trousers and a denim shirt that Martin was partial to. She'd twisted a blue and white cotton scarf around her neck and had put on lipstick. Only her hair, hanging limp and unwashed, prevented her from looking pretty, he thought.

'I do love you, Jan. You know that, don't you?' Martin said, covering her hand with his.

Jan withdrew her hand and ate her cake in silence.

Ć

## KATE

When Ben Wilde came looking for her, he didn't knock on the door, he kicked it in. At least that's how it felt to Kate, so discomforting was his sudden appearance in her life. Who the hell did he think he was, showing up after all these years? And after the way he'd stiffed her with the flat in Balham, just as he got a whiff of success.

She'd supported him on a PR account manager's salary for years, while he'd sit at home, getting stoned and playing guitar, chasing the perfect ballad. And when it came to him - when he wrote Seagull, which she had inspired, and it became a top ten hit for six weeks, he'd fled to Spain without her; Wilde by name and wild by nature.

It was some small satisfaction that he had aged more than her. The cigarettes, the spliffs and the red wine had all taken their toll - not to mention years of frying under an Andalusian sun. Ben looked every day of his fifty years, from the deep laughter lines around his eyes, to the modest paunch he was sporting, and the greying of his unruly hair.

And yet she'd still felt butterflies as big as bats in her stomach, and despite her fury, Kate had found herself grinning like an idiot, and wanting to run her fingers through that spoilt-brat mop of curls, which hadn't thinned at all; god alone knew what was holding it all in – bloody mindedness would be her guess.

 

'So, tell me again where you're living,' Kate said, once they'd found a shady table in the beer garden at The Fox & Hounds.

'Near Dungeness - St. Peter's Bay, it's called. I've rented a place right on the beach for the rest of the summer. It's not much but I love it down there – it's wild. I can go days without speaking to anyone.'

'So can I – but I don't see that as a good thing. So you're not working then?'

'Yeah, every day. I've written some epic songs since I left Spain... it's like I'm back, you know?'

'I was talking about paid work...a job, even.'

'Like what? I'm going to spend the next few months getting the old crew together – go into the studio – see what happens.'

Kate sighed - same old Ben.

She hated herself for thinking Ben still looked good, in his own bad-boy way, although it was weird to see him drinking orange juice.

'This is new,' she said, pointing to his glass.

'I'm driving, Kitty – and anyway, the booze was getting out of hand.'

Kitty; he'd always called her that - or Kit - but how dare he now?

'Ben, sorry, but what are you doing here?'

'Maybe laying some ghosts to rest. You've been on my mind a lot. I wanted to know if you were happy. I mean, you look great and everything, but I never had you down as a Stepford Wife.'

Ouch - she could add judgemental to Ben's long list of flaws.

'You can't just rock up here, slagging off my lifestyle, Ben. What are you doing that's so great, anyway? From what you've just said – you're living alone in a rental, having screwed up another relationship.'

Ben was nodding, his expression resigned.

'I know...I know, guilty as charged – but I'm writing again, Kate – and I feel alive, you know? Like I'm on the cusp of something. Kate, I miss you – I was such an idiot...do you ever think about-'

'No – I don't,' Kate jumped in. 'Ben, I'm married – and Neil and

I are just fine, thanks. Okay, so where we're living is not entirely me – or him – but we had to get out of London...find some space... some peace.' Kate drained her glass. She'd need another drink if she were to listen to anymore of Ben's drivel.

'You're right. It's none of my business. I just wanted to see you again – and say sorry...for everything. I'm not proud of how things ended, and god knows I've regretted it for long enough.'

Ben seemed subdued as he drove Kate home; there were no more smart comments, and no more digs.

'I miss you, Katie,' he said, as she got out of his car.

&#x0263;

Kate's mobile tinged; 'Hi. Are you free for coffee today/tomorrow at mine? Lisa. X'.

When the text arrived, Kate's first response was to look in the mirror; no way could she arrive at the home of a high-maintenance woman like Lisa with a pasty face, ragged nails and grey roots.

Since seeing Ben, she'd been neglecting herself and hiding away indoors – which needed to stop. But that was the thing about Ben – he'd got to her, he always had. The fact that he'd disapproved of her – sneered at her lifestyle and implied that she'd somehow sold out, had left a bad taste in her mouth.

She'd lied to Neil by omission, to the extent that she hadn't mentioned seeing Ben at all – and now it was too late. So Kate had retreated into herself and apart from walking Ludo, hadn't left the house for a week. Coffee with a potential new friend was a gentle but much-needed kick up the backside.

After finishing a client blog on the baffling subject of pension-splitting, Kate set out for the gym where she swam hard in the outdoor pool. Then, muscles tingling, she spent a blissed-out hour sunbathing, letting the warmth caress her pale limbs.

On a whim, she booked a manicure and a facial, luxuriating in the deft strokes of the therapist. Feeling back in the game, her thoughts turned to Lisa, who was totally unlike any of her London friends, who would have mocked Lisa's artifice and considered her overt sexiness vulgar; *as I would have done*, Kate thought, with a degree of shame.

The next day, wearing her best skinny jeans and a halter-neck top that showed off her toned arms, Kate walked the couple of blocks to Lisa's house, where the smell of new paint vied with the aroma of freshly ground coffee.

'Great to see you, Kate; you should have brought your doggie - they could have played,' Lisa said, as Nellie trotted at her heels, pleased to have company, on four legs or two.

'It's so nice of you to invite me,' Kate began, taking in Lisa's spotless shaker-style kitchen, with its cultivated rustic vibe. Lisa herself looked anything but rustic. Her honey blonde mane was tousled to perfection, and her face was camera ready. It was the first time Kate had noticed her incredible blue-green eyes. Despite her makeover the day before, Kate felt dowdy beside the younger woman.

But two hours and a packet of stem-ginger biscuits later, Kate had quashed any niggling rivalry; Lisa's warmth was infectious and when Kate got up to leave, it was with reluctance.

'You're popular this morning,' she said, eyeing Lisa's mobile phone, as it lit up for third or fourth time.

☾

## LISA

Lisa picked up her mobile just as it stopped ringing. There were three missed calls; two from her former brother in law and one from Rita. Her mother was always ringing with some spurious complaint, but why would Sean be calling?

The phone rang again.

'Hello?'

'Lisa, it's Sean.'

His tone set off alarm bells at once. Something was wrong.

'Lisa, I'm so sorry – it's Justin. He's gone,' Sean said, his voice cracking with emotion.

'Gone? Where?' Goose-bumps were rising on her arms.

'He's dead, Leese – I'm so sorry to tell you...'

'Dead? Sean?' He'd made a mistake – Justin wasn't dead.

'He's been doing great, he hadn't touched a drink for months... he's been going to the gym and, you know, he was very positive.' Sean cleared his throat which sounded thick with snot and tears.

'Last weekend, he went on a stag-do; do you remember Ian Ray from County? Well he's getting married again - so they went to Marbella and when he got back he was off his head. But then he sobered up - and got back on the wagon. Lisa, last night, we went to bed early – and he was sober. But this morning - I found him, with an empty vodka bottle and some migraine tablets by the bed. It looks like he'd been sick and choked. The police are still here and the coroner is on his way. I didn't know...I had no idea he was...'

'Sean, stop it. You're not to blame – but what about me, eh? I should have been there for him. Oh my god. My poor baby... I'm so sorry...Christ, Sean...I'll ring you later.'

Lisa jumped to see Kate still in the room, her expression anxious.

'My god, Lisa!' Kate said. 'Here, drink some water, and sit down for a moment – you've had a massive shock. I got the gist of that, I think – and I'm so sorry. I'll wait with you while you call someone.'

'There's no one,' Lisa wailed. 'My sister lives in Portugal, and my mum hated his guts. I've only got one friend here, Tanya – and she'll be at work. I've just got to get on with it, haven't I?'

'Your mother may not have liked your ex – but she's still your mum. You can't be on your own today. I'll stay with you until she gets here.'

'I used to worry about him – falling asleep pissed, and not waking up. And now it's actually happened,' Lisa said, wiping away the tears streaking her make-up.

'It's obvious how much you still cared about him,' Kate said. 'You'd just been speaking so fondly about him - before you took the call.'

'Yes...oh, I did love him, but the booze and depression...it wears you down, you know? I just needed to get my life back...but now I feel so guilty.'

Lisa knew Kate was right; she would call Rita - give her mother the chance to look after her.

'Kate, you should go...I'll be okay, promise. Let's meet again soon...take the puppies out... or something. Thank you for being so kind – I'll ring my mum the moment you've gone.'

After Kate left her, Lisa sat on the stairs and wept. Poor, poor Justin; what a mess. The tabloids would have a field day.

#  CHAPTER 4:
## RISK

### BEN

Ben could tell at once Kate wasn't happy. How could such a free spirit thrive in a dead zone like that? All those cookie-cutter houses, and with people to match; she didn't belong there.

Her husband sounded like a right selfish prick. Ben had pulled some strokes in his time, but staying in London all week – rather than getting on a train every day – well, boo-hoo. It smacked of him having some other gig lined up, and just biding his time. It all sounded dead in the water already. He picked up the phone.

'Hey baby,' he said when Kate answered on the third ring. 'Fancy a day at the seaside? Bring your bucket and spade – we'll go crabbing.'

'How are you Ben?' Kate was guarded.

'I'm amazing, Katie – the sun is shining, the sea is blue – come on down. I'll treat you to a knock-out seafood lunch. Anyway, I need you to hear some tunes – all new material. Please - I know I'm on to something big.'

'Ben, I can't just drop everything – I have stuff to do at home. I'm meant to be writing a newsletter for an insurance company today. And what about the dog?'

'Bring Ludo with you. He can play on the beach – has that dog even seen a beach?'

He heard her giggle; progress.

'The weather is due to break tomorrow – write your...thing then, when it's raining. Come on, Kit, treat yourself to a day off. Summer will be over before we know it.'

It had taken a bit more wheedling and persuasion, and then she'd warmed to the idea.

At noon Ben heard Kate park up outside, and then Ludo was running at him.

'He likes me, what can I say? He's only human!'

Kate smiled at his joke.

Man, she looked hot in faded jeans and a little striped top, with her hair pulled back into a pony tail. Her face was lightly tanned today and she seemed energised, laughing at Ludo as he explored, bouncing from one room to another.

'Welcome to my hovel,' Ben said, kissing her lightly on the cheek.

'Well, it's not nearly as bad as you described; the light's good and the view is dazzling. And you've tidied up, I can smell lemon cleaning spray,' Kate said.

'Yeah, rumbled. Hey, I know a shady spot in the dunes where we can walk Ludo before we have lunch - he can come with us.'

She was watching him, noticing that he looked good. He'd washed his hair and used some of that incredible French conditioner that she used to buy for him and which turned his usual nest of chaos into glossy, tendrils. And he was still off the sauce – which had had the effect of opening up his eyes, trimming down his waist and making his skin glow.

In the dunes they fell in step, while Ludo ran ahead barking at seagulls. It was taking every ounce of Ben's will power not to pull her to him, and crush her pink lips with his own.

'I've got a new friend,' Kate announced. 'She's called Lisa. Have you heard of a footballer called Justin Dixon?'

'Of course. He's been in the news recently. Poor sod snuffed it from the old rock stars' demise, didn't he? He played for County for a few seasons, when they were a premier side – but after that terrible accident, he was finished.'

'Yes – it's sad, isn't it? My new pal Lisa was married to him.'

'No shit! I'd hate to be in her shoes...the tabloids are trying to pin it on her. Saying he topped himself because she left.'

'Which is bollocks. They'd been divorced for a year. And it was an accident – he'd started to drink again. Anyway, I thought you might have heard of him and-'

Ludo was bounding towards them, a rotting fish glistening in his jaws, making him look comical and gross at the same time. Kate screamed.

'Ben! Get it off him, please - GET IT OFF HIM!'

'Drop it, boy,' Ben said, in an attempt to be masterful. Ludo ignored him, trotting like a circus pony, delighted with his trophy. It took several minutes to wrestle the mangy fish away from him.

'I'm glad you think it's so bloody hilarious,' Kate said, before howling with laughter.

The Wicked Whelk was buzzing. Several tables were taken up with holiday makers and day trippers, and a few office-workers had driven round the bay from Rye, their shirt sleeves rolled up and top buttons open.

Sitting on the faded decking, with Ludo curled at their feet on his little blanket, Ben knew they could pass for a family and was puffed up with pride.

'Here you go, boy,' said the waitress, setting down a bowl of water for Ludo, who lapped gratefully.

'That's him sorted; what are we having? Glass of vino, gorgeous?'

'I'm driving, Ben. Coke's fine for me.'

'Not for hours yet – and we'll be eating...go on, just a small one.' Without waiting for an answer, Ben ordered a bottle of Chablis, crab linguine for two, and some crusty bread.

'My treat,' he said. She was giving him that look again. Be cool, Ben.

Her phone buzzed.

'It's Neil,' she frowned. 'I'll call him later.'

Inside, Ben was punching the air.

⌘

## KATE

Marshmallow-limbed, Kate contemplated the drive home. She hadn't noticed Ben refilling her glass so perhaps it was the sunshine, or the fact that she felt more relaxed and happy than she had in months. It was three o'clock – where had the last three hours gone?

As if in a time-warp, Kate listened as Ben talked about his new material.

'Come and listen, Katie, please. I need your input. You get my music - like no one else ever has. Remember when I first wrote Seagull? And I played it to you on my oldest guitar...you knew at once...you just knew it was the one.'

She had known. It was beautiful, simple – the kind of love song that people would be playing at weddings and funerals for decades.

'Of course I remember. I loved it from that first time.'

But it had been Ben's escape route, too – and she hadn't even known he was looking for the door. Seagull was a bitter sweet memory, painful to recall. Couldn't he see that?

There was no point stirring up the past now. Her life was with Neil, who was pretty damn wonderful – and a completely different animal to Ben.

'Please Kate. Come and listen to some tunes.' Ben said.

'I have to go...I need to get back.'

'To what? I'll make us both a coffee while I play you a couple of demos. I feel a bit pissed to be honest – it's been a while since I had a drink.'

'Okay, one quick coffee. And Ben - thanks for lunch.'

They walked back along the beach, under a cloudless sky, Ludo prancing at the water's edge, Ben still babbling, about his mate Steve, who had a contact at a record label that was open to new talent.

'Aren't you a bit old for all that, Ben?' She hadn't intended to be mean; it had just slipped out, thanks to a couple of glasses of truth-serum.

'Kate – this is what I do. What, you think I can just get a job in a bank, or a supermarket? Believe it or not, Seagull still opens doors. I just need to come up with another hit, Katie – and you're going to help me,' he said, putting a tanned arm around her shoulders.

But the cool shadiness of Ben's bungalow had an instantly sobering effect. Kate gazed out at the beach, while Ben busied himself in the kitchen.

When her mobile rang again it was Neil. How could she tell him where she was? She hadn't even admitted to being in contact with Ben. The lying had to stop. She'd tell him everything at the weekend, face to face; that Ben had called her out of the blue, that they'd met up twice and that he was living nearby.

But the thing was, she'd enjoyed having a secret, something that was just hers and telling Neil would break the spell. The last few weeks had made her feel more alive - because Ben had managed to break through the numbness that had weighed her down for months.

Even before Ben had reappeared, she'd felt the connection with Neil beginning to fray, missing him less all week, and then at weekends, she'd try too hard – when before, she'd never needed to try at all.

When exactly had she become one of those awful women who 'let' her husband make love to her? Because that's what she'd been doing for the last six months. Acquiescing to sex, rather than wanting - needing – the intimacy that had been the backbone and the glue of their relationship from the first time they'd slept together.

This was serious stuff. She needed to get out of Ben's orbit and go home and work on her marriage.

'White, no sugar – and jammy dodgers; what more could a girl want?' Ben said, setting down a tray.

He was such a child.

Then Ben struck a few keys on his laptop and the room was filled with a soft low guitar, before his voice emerged, as strong and haunting as ever.

He was looking at her, waiting.

'It's beautiful, Ben. What's it called?'

'As yet untitled...I was hoping you could help me out with that.'

Ben cranked the volume a notch; for such a crude demo the sound was breath-taking. Kate's heart swelled. She felt inexplicably tearful.

'I'm going into the studio next week - to make a really good cut – Kate, I think I've got something here. What do you-'

But then he saw the emotion in her face, and was crossing the room with big strides, kissing her and cupping her hots cheeks with his hands.

Kate stepped back; 'Ben, don't!'

'I'm sorry – it's just...you are doing my head in! I think about you night and day. I was a total fucking idiot to leave the way I did.'

'Ben, you went away for two weeks and never came back! Don't tell me you're sorry. All those phone calls...with me in tatters, begging you to come home. You weren't sorry then!'

'I was a reckless fool - and it all got too cosy. I knew you wanted to get married and all our friends were having kids and I panicked - I just spun out. And by the time I met Gabriella – it was all too late for us.'

He lit a cigarette and looked out at the sea.

'I wanted to come home, but I knew by then you'd never forgive me. Me and Gabby were a train wreck. I never loved her...not properly. The woman was a maniac - she tried to top herself once... sometimes I wished I'd let her.'

The music had stopped and the only sound was the seagulls wheeling overhead.

Kate couldn't trust herself to speak. Grabbing Ludo and her bag, she left without another word.

ত

## MARTIN

'Boss, have you seen this?'

Martin wished Trina would empty her mouth before speaking. It turned his stomach to glimpse bits of sausage and white bread rolling around her masticating jaws, like clothes in a tumble dryer. She was holding a copy of the Gazette, a look of surprise on her doll-like face.

'Former football ace, Justin Dixon, was found dead at his

brother's home in what Police are calling an alcohol-related incident,' Trina read aloud.

'Police are not looking for a third party, but cannot rule out suicide at this early stage in the investigation. Sources close to the family have revealed that Mr Dixon, who had battled alcohol abuse and depression, was devastated by his recent divorce and unable to accept that the relationship had ended...'

'Oh dear, that's sad,' Martin said. But why was she so interested? He hated this type of salacious tittle-tattle. That poor family – the man was someone's son after all – and it could hardly be called entertainment, nor was it...what was the phrase they used in the media...in the public interest?

'No, look Martin. Look at the photos,' Trina thrust the paper right under his nose so that it blurred to a sea of grey dots. Lowering the page, he looked at the photographs; one was of Justin Dixon in his glory days, handsome, mugging to camera, resplendent in home strip. The other was of a blank-eyed blonde in a bikini, breasts skyward and lips parted, in an ad for a low calorie drink.

Martin was becoming exasperated: 'And? Trina, we're very busy today, love - we've got a delivery this afternoon.'

'Boss, look at the lady. She's a customer; Mrs Dixon, from Eden Hill. Look, that's her, isn't it? She still looks the same, just older and less of a tart if you ask me.'

'Well nobody did, Trina. Look it's none of our business, is it? Anyway, it's not like she's the first celebrity who's come through that door.'

'Who else then?' Trina said, picking at her nails.

'The chap who does all the double-glazing ads for one – and the taxi driver that was on Dinner Dates... it doesn't matter; the point is, we shouldn't gossip about something like this – it's not decent.'

He looked more closely at the photograph.

So Lisa Dixon had been a footballer's wife - a WAG. She was more beautiful now; less hard-looking and with nicer teeth. The poor woman must be distraught - especially if Justin had killed himself because she'd dumped him.

He closed his eyes and remembered the teal lace knickers. He thought about them – about her – at night, lying beside Jan as she snored and ground her teeth.

Who would Lisa turn to now, with the press on her back, spreading rumours and lies like they always did?

'I'm just popping out, Trina,' he called over his shoulder, feeling for the car-keys in his pocket.

It was ten o'clock and Crabton was already in full swing. By now, shoppers were sharking around the car park that served the high street. Sunshine glinted off car bonnets, bleaching out all but the silhouettes of people going about their routine. Martin walked to the far corner, past the row of stinking dumpsters, to the dozen or so spaces reserved for shop owners. Someone had written COCK in the dust on his rear windscreen. Annoyed, he rubbed it out with his hand; he'd call in at the car wash later - the Vauxhall estate had rarely been so filthy.

Without the slightest notion of what he was going to do or say, he began driving towards Lisa Dixon's house, where a dozen or so journalists were lurking by the gates. Martin was reminded of hyenas waiting for a deer to wander by a watering hole.

Lisa's car was there, but the house blinds were pulled down.

They really are vultures, thought Martin; either they've chased her off - or she's in there hiding.

A lone hack strode over and peered into his open window.

'Are you a resident, sir?' said the wiry-haired guy, sweat stains visible on his pale shirt.

'No comment,' Martin said, like he'd seen people do on television.

The reporter stepped back, smirking. 'He's nobody,' he called to the others.

Suddenly the pack jostled forward as Lisa's front door opened, and two women emerged. Lisa, hair scraped under a cap, face puffy and covered by large sunglasses, and another woman, older and thicker around the middle, with coppery, candyfloss hair, also wearing dark glasses.

Ignoring the rabble, the two women got into Lisa's metallic blue sports car and roared off as the gates swung open.

Now what? Martin's left temple pulsed. He wanted to tear after her – but she might mistake him for one of those bloody parasites, which would upset and frighten her. No, he'd go back to work, give it some thought...figure out what he could do to help. Because one thing was for sure – that poor woman needed someone in her corner, somebody reliable, and with their feet on the ground.

ර

By early evening on the Saturday, Jan was in tears of rage and frustration. Every dress she owned was strewn on the bed in a tangled heap. In the last hour, Martin's primary objective had shifted from helping Jan to pick an outfit for Jeremy Hunter's party, to the more pressing one of calming his wife down, because any ill-chosen words would only inflame the situation, and he couldn't afford to let that happen.

He'd felt discombobulated all week – the stuff in the papers about Lisa had been playing on his mind and as if picking up signals, Jan had seemed more erratic than usual.

Midweek, the day after his brush with the paps, Trina had

answered the back office phone while Martin was with a customer.

'Phone call for you, boss; I think it's urgent – I'll take over here,' she said, saucer-eyed, causing Martin to sprint across the shop floor.

'I can't find them!' Jan wailed, 'I've looked everywhere but they've gone missing. Someone has taken them!'

What was she talking about? Gently, Martin asked Jan what had gone missing.

'Hayley's baby photos of course – what do you think I'm talking about?'

Martin sighed.

'What do you need them for, my love? I'm pretty sure they're indoors. I'll be home in a few hours and we can look for them together.'

She was getting worse, obsessing about nonsense – it was too much.

'Can't you come now? I need them.'

'Jan, I am with a customer at the moment – you know I have to work, darling, but I'll leave Trina to lock up and knock off a bit early. How's that?'

He'd speak to Trina about a pay rise and an extra day a week. From behind the grimy back-office window, he watched her helping a man in a padded checked shirt. Even from twenty feet away, Martin could see the guy was mesmerised by Trina's nose-ring. At least today it was the silver hoop and not the ruby stud, which resembled an angry spot.

A fortnight earlier, after a rash of weird phone calls from home, he'd confided in Trina about Jan's deteriorating mental health.

'Ah, bless her,' she'd said, head tilted, 'And bless you, boss - must be hard seeing her like that. My Auntie Joanne's the same; some days she doesn't get dressed...other days, she doesn't even get up.

You just let me know if there's anything I can do.'

Arriving home around five, Martin found the house in a near state of ransack. In the kitchen, the pine dresser drawers hung open, their contents spilled all over the table and floor.

Suddenly Martin knew exactly where to find Hayley's baby albums. He remembered having a sort-out six months earlier, and moving them all (including Jan's favourite with the ducklings on the cover) to Hayley's old bedroom. They'd done it together, but when he showed Jan, she had no recollection; the fog must have been particularly dense that day.

It took an hour to tidy up and smooth things over. When Jan had calmed down, Martin went out for fish and chips, where he sagged in the queue as the staff shouted above the roar of the deep fat fryers and the smell of grease sullied his clothes.

He wondered if anyone would notice if he sat down on the pavement and wept. Deciding that they probably wouldn't, Martin walked home to find Jan warming plates in the oven.

'Thank you for finding the photos, Martin; sorry I got into a pickle about it...it was just... I'd looked everywhere and they're precious to me. You and me, first married...Hayley as a little tot - happiest time of my life.'

The following day, Jan had barely acknowledged him, turning her head when he tried to kiss her before leaving for work. On Friday morning, they had breakfast together at eight o'clock.

'You've remembered that we've got that party in Eden Hill tomorrow night, haven't you love?' Martin said.

'What party?' Jan said.

Oh god.

'The Hunters' party, you know...they own the estate agency in town...I play badminton with Jeremy most Thursday evenings.'

Jan shook her head. 'I'm not going - you never said.'

Martin corrected her, 'Jan, I did. The card's still on the mantel piece and we said we'd go. It's his wife's birthday – it'll be a smashing occasion. I've checked the forecast and the weather's set to be lovely, so we'll be outside in the garden. It'll do us good to get dressed up and chat to some people. You know, a bit of mingling and a glass of bubbly? Good for business, too.'

Martin reached into his wallet and pulled out a bundle of notes. He'd counted out £150 the night before.

'Why don't you go into town and have a look around the shops. Pick something nice to wear – and not jeans, buy yourself a summer dress – it'll perk you up a bit.'

Surprised, Jan took the money.

'Thank you, Mart. I'll make a day of it...I might even look for some shoes as well.'

But when Martin got home on Friday evening, there were no carrier bags on the kitchen table, just the cash.

'I didn't get anything,' she said. 'I tried on five dresses and about fifty tops - everything looked horrid. I looked fat in all of them – huge – in every single one.'

Please god, not this again.

'Jan, you've only gained a couple of pounds and as I've said before, it suits you – makes you look younger. The problem is not with the scales – it's in here,' Martin tapped his forehead with his index finger.

He took a deep breath; 'Love - you'll look good whatever you put on. Why don't you wear my favourite dress tomorrow? The short black one – your legs look knock-out in that. There, all sorted.'

Jan nodded meekly. Crisis averted.

With an hour to go until the taxi arrived - necessary because Martin was determined to have a glass of wine or three, Jan was in the midst of a full meltdown. The black linen dress had been jettisoned for making her look 'like a complete tart' and for numerous and complex reasons known only to Jan, everything else had been rejected, too. Martin surveyed the jumble of clothing on the bed.

'Come on love – let me help...you've got lots of pretty things...' he said.

'I'm not going,' she raged from the bathroom. 'You go – they're your bloody friends.' I DON'T HAVE ANY!'

Neither do I, thought Martin, exhausted but doing his best to be conciliatory. After negotiating through the closed bathroom door for another ten minutes, Jan emerged blotchy-faced and red-eyed.

'Martin, I'm sorry, but I'm staying in. All those women on the estate... glammed-up to the nines. They just make me feel worse. You go – have a drink with Jeremy and talk about shuttle-cocks or whatever it is you lot talk about, and I'll watch a DVD. You need a break and I'd rather be on my own. Honestly, I'm fine.'

Jan didn't look fine, but he'd lost the will to argue. Grabbing his best linen jacket and the sparkling rosé and chocolates he'd bought in the supermarket, Martin got in the cab.

'Eden Hill estate, please,' he exhaled the words. 'And put your foot down, mate – I need a drink.'

# CHAPTER 5:
## NEW ASPIRATIONS

MARTIN

The Hunters' driveway looked like a car-park, with vehicles spilling onto the neighbouring plot and along the street. The house was bathed by uplighters, with potted laurels either side of the glossy black front door. Martin could hear INXS pumping into the night, and was thrown back to 1987 and Janet Ward, who'd given him his first blow job; not the kind of thing a guy forgets, he thought, blushing.

He felt awkward now. Jeremy could hardly be called a close friend; badminton was their only connection. He'd been flattered to get an invitation. After all, Jeremy Hunter was a big noise in town; he owned the estate agency in the High Street – and he'd just opened up a second branch three miles away at Woodley Green. People said he owned the coffee shop, too – but nobody seemed to know that for sure. Martin clasped the bottle of pink bubbly he'd brought for Claire's Birthday, wishing he'd bought real champagne, instead of Spumante.

He'd met Claire once when she'd picked Jeremy up from the club in her white Merc. He remembered her as being sleek and blonde – young looking for her age.

The door opened.

'Hi! Welcome, Martin. Glad you could make it. Flying solo?'

Jeremy said.

'Jan's had a migraine all day, but wanted me to come anyway,' lied Martin, 'First time I've been here, what a lovely home.'

He followed Jeremy through to a kitchen that looked more like an operating theatre than a place to cook and eat, he thought, taking in the white lacquered surfaces and cream tiled floor. A few people smiled at him as he passed by. Through open bi-folding doors, Martin could see at least another twenty-odd people in the well-lit garden.

They were a well-dressed crowd; he thought of Jan and the contents of her dowdy wardrobe strewn on the bed. At least they had both been spared that particular humiliation.

After gratefully accepting a glass of champagne, Martin spotted Claire standing on the terrace with two other reed-thin women. In a moment's exuberance mixed with guilt at leaving Jan behind, Martin drained his glass and hastily refilled it. He was here now, and he was going to have a bloody good time.

It was likely, he realised, as the champagne began to percolate, that he wouldn't know a single soul, so for once, he could be anybody he wanted. He waved to Claire.

'Happy Birthday, Claire – I'm Martin. I play badminton with Jeremy. You look lovely, by the way – and your home is fabulous.'

'Thank you,' Claire smiled. 'We've met before. Is your wife here?'

'She's not very well I'm afraid, but she insisted I come anyway. She says 'hello' and I'm under strict instructions not to return without a piece of cake. I know how much you ladies love your cake,' he said, pleased by his own ice-breaker.

'Ha-ha! Indeed. This is Tanya – and this is Carrie,' Claire said, indicating her friends.

Martin was surprised when Tanya lent forward for an air kiss, her long black hair swinging across his face.

'Ooh, lucky me,' he said, wondering if he should kiss the other woman, too. In for a penny, he thought, pecking her on the cheek.

'Ah, bless – here's our girl,' Tanya said, waving to the tanned, toned blonde walking towards them. And then Lisa Dixon was standing beside him, the heady smell of her perfume hitting him like vertigo.

'Hello darling,' gushed Tanya, 'Well done you for getting out – I hoped you'd come but, you know… what with you being under siege all week.'

'I needed to escape to be honest, but I'll soon be old news. I haven't said a word to any of them…they're full of shit these people – what do they know?'

Martin saw Claire and Carrie exchange glances and tight smiles.

'Sorry – don't mind me,' Lisa said, offering her tanned, be-ringed hand while introductions were swapped.

'Lovely to meet you, Claire – and Happy Birthday,' Lisa said. 'It was your husband who invited me – he sold me the house a few months ago. But me and Tanya go way back, don't we, hon? And I know you, don't I?' Lisa said, turning her attention to Martin.

'We've met, yes. How are you? I read about your husband in the papers – I'm so sorry, must have been a terrible shock,' Martin said.

'Ex.'

'I'm sorry?'

'Ex-husband…we split up a couple of years ago. But thank you… yes, it's all been very distressing as you can imagine.'

'What you need,' Claire said, 'is a big glass of bubbly and to let your hair down for a few hours.'

'Allow me,' Martin said, steering Lisa towards the kitchen, where several bottles of champagne were on ice, alongside rows of sparkling glasses.

'I'm sure we've met somewhere,' Lisa said.

It occurred to Martin to make something up but he feared being found out and made to look ridiculous.

'I'm Martin Bevan. I own the carpet shop in town – well, a chain of shops really,' he lied.

'Of course. Sorry Martin, my head's all over the place at the moment – I remember you now. Yes, my carpet's fab... transforms the whole place. Where are your other shops?' Lisa asked.

'I've one in Guildford and I'm opening up in Tunbridge Wells in a couple of months.' *Liar, liar, pants on fire.*

'Ooh that's nice,' Lisa said, taking a gulp of champagne.

By the time it was dark, people were attacking the buffet, keen to soak up excess alcohol.

Then somebody turned the music up and half a dozen people, Claire and Jeremy among them, began dancing on the terrace, shuffling awkwardly at first before getting into their stride.

'Let's have a bop,' Martin said, taking Lisa's arm.

It was an old fashioned expression and he'd said it to make her laugh.

Several couples were strutting and twirling now, moving rhythmically as the Scissor Sisters burst through the night sky.

Martin sang along, hamming it up in a jokey falsetto.

After two or three more tracks, people were egging him on and one or two guys were goofily copying his moves, playing to the gallery. When had he ever had so much fun? This was the life!

He looked at Lisa; face flushed, arms raised, shaking her hair with abandon to Tom Jones's Sex Bomb.

'It's great to hear all the old ones again,' Martin said, twirling and dipping Lisa as she shrieked with laughter.

'I'm so glad I came out tonight – I nearly didn't you know... the last couple of weeks have been hell.'

'I'm glad you did, too,' Martin said, holding Lisa's gaze. 'Shall we have another drink?'

'Are you single, Martin?' Lisa said when they were seated, eating poached salmon and salad laced with mint and basil.

'I'm separated.' *Bong!* Where had that come from?

'I'm sorry to hear that,' Lisa said, not sounding sorry at all. 'It must have been a hard decision - but I bet it was a relief, too. It was the same with me and Justin. One day, I just couldn't stick it any longer, you know? I never knew what I was going to find when I walked through the door...' her expression clouded; 'Oh, god – I didn't mean...'

'You mustn't feel guilty about what happened. The way he passed away - he was just very unlucky. More people than you think die like that - choking, I mean.' Martin said.

'I'm sorry, this is meant to be a party, let's not talk about it. And anyway, it's not your problem. Look, I need to catch up with Tanya – we've hardly spoken all night – and then I think I'll go home.'

Martin watched Lisa's bottom jiggle in her thin dress, as she walked away. Two muscular young men with high quiffs and full beards were laughing, enjoying a conversation about wild-life. For the life of him, Martin couldn't think what was so funny about cougars; a lot of wild cats were endangered species – which was no laughing matter at all.

'That's very interesting,' Martin said, edging his way into the conversation. 'My daughter used to love the big cats at Howletts Safari Park – do you know it? The tigers were always her favourite.'

The two men fell silent before letting out a machine-gun volley of laughter.

'You crack me up, man,' said one. Bemused, Martin laughed along.

'You look like you've been having a riot, Martin,' Jeremy said from his blind side.

'Oh yes! I've had a fantastic time tonight. You and Claire are brilliant hosts – thanks again for inviting me. Jan and I don't get out much. She's not that well, and it's rare for us to let our hair down.'

'Sorry to hear that,' Jeremy said, looking over Martin's shoulder; 'Will you excuse me for a moment? I just need to catch Mikey before he goes. Michael! Where do you think you're sneaking off to....?' And he was gone, leaving Martin alone, watching the stragglers in the garden, where a cool breeze began stirring the women's filmy dresses. Lisa was walking back towards the house, hugging herself against the sudden chill.

'Martin, I'm off,' she said.

'You look cold – where's your jacket?'

'I didn't bring one,' she shivered.

In one seamless movement, Martin reached for his blazer, and draped it around Lisa's shoulders.

'I'm leaving now, too. Why don't I walk you around the corner – and you can borrow my jacket. All set?'

☙

Martin was in a parallel universe. He'd gone to the party alone, where he knew nobody but the host; had danced all night with a group of attractive women, and now he was leaving with the most beautiful girl of all, and a celebrity to boot. He wondered if the journalists would still be hanging around Lisa's gates but none were in evidence as they approached Regent's Square.

'See? They're bored already,' Lisa said. 'I'm surprised Anson's given up though - he's always there.'

'Who?'

'Andrew Anson; he gave me his card - and stuck a note on my car; he's desperate to interview me. But why should I talk to him? Who'd be interested, anyway? It's not like I'm famous...so it can only be about digging-up dirt on Justin. Well, they can all go to hell... it's none of their business - they should have more respect.'

Lisa tapped the keypad on the gate four times; it played Rule Britannia.

'Do you want to come in for coffee?'

*Ping!*

'Go on then, just a quick one,' Martin said following her inside and through to the kitchen, where Lisa opened an American-style fridge-freezer crammed full of fruit and vegetables and several bottles of wine and Evian. He thought of his own fridge at home and the jumbled assortment of leftovers covered with cling-film.

'What can I get you? You don't have to have coffee - I've got plenty of wine and beer.' Opting for wine, Martin peered through the French windows. A square covered object crouched in the semi darkness.

'Oh, I say – is that what I think it is? Do you know...this'll make you laugh...I've never been in a hot tub.'

'Seriously? Not even on holiday?'

'My ex-wife and daughter aren't into that sort of thing...it just, never...'

'Well, you'll have to come round and have a dip sometime,' Lisa said.

'That would be nice. Ooh – I hope you don't think I was inviting myself.'

'Of course not!' Lisa said, but he could tell by the tightness in her voice that that was exactly what she'd thought. She'd taken her shoes off and looked small and vulnerable beside him.

Martin drank his wine, desperate for words of wit or wisdom to come to him; Lisa stifled a yawn.

'Ooh, sorry,' she said, giving in and stretching like a cat. 'I am suddenly so tired...'

'Of course. I should go,' Martin said.

On the doorstep, they embraced awkwardly, noses bumping as they kissed on each cheek. On impulse, Martin hugged Lisa. She was small in his arms compared to his wife.

Bam! A flash popped in the darkness, then another and another...

'What was that?' Lisa jumped. 'Jesus, that's all we need. You'd better go – don't speak to whoever is out there. I bet it's that idiot, Anson. Good night, Martin – thanks for a fun evening.'

Dazzled by the flash, Martin couldn't see Lisa's expression as she closed the door.

Feeling ten feet tall, he walked right past Andrew Anson.

'You a close friend of Lisa Dixon's, mate?'

'Oh, I'm nobody,' Martin said, swaggering inwardly, until he'd rounded the corner where he took out his mobile and rang for a mini-cab.

For the first time in his life, Martin felt like the star of his own movie.

🍏

The morning after the Hunters' party was a huge comedown. Martin woke at nine, his head throbbing. Jan was already up, sitting at the kitchen table in her dressing gown and his fishing socks.

'What time did you get in last night? Must have been late – I woke up at gone midnight and you weren't home.'

'Just after one I think. Have we got any paracetamol?' Martin said, rooting in the dresser drawer and finding the last two Hedex.

'So, what was it like?' Jan said, studying him.

'I don't know...like a birthday party I suppose.'

'Did you know lots of people?' Jan said.

'Jan, I can honestly say that I didn't know anybody except Jeremy. Oh, and one of my customers was there, too.'

'Well you took your time considering you didn't know anyone.' Jan crossed to the sink and filled the kettle.

'Hayley might pop in this afternoon – she rang me last night,' she said.

'Oh, marvellous. What time?' Martin said, brightening.

'She didn't say, and it's not definite.'

So despite the cotton wool in his head, Martin cleaned the car, swept the front path, and pushed the vacuum round downstairs, before walking to Tesco in Crabton with Jan.

'She's not five,' Jan said, as Martin loaded the trolley with biscuits, cakes and pop, 'She'll want a glass of wine.'

'My daughter does not drink and drive,' Martin was indignant.

'Simon might be driving,' Jan said, 'she's not long passed her test.'

Jan had a point, so Martin put back the fizzy drinks and bought a bottle of Pinot Grigio instead – everyone drank that.

But at two o'clock, Hayley phoned to say that Simon's brother had turned up unexpectedly.

'Sorry, Dad. Next weekend should be alright though – if you and Mum are home of course.'

'Where else would we be?' Martin said.

ॐ

'Well, that's that then. How about we go for a drive and a shandy in a pub garden?' Martin said.

'You know I don't like beer,' Jan's tone was peevish. 'Anyway, I'd have thought you'd be happy to be indoors after last night,' Jan said, 'I'm not bothered, you go for a drive if you like.'

So Martin drove for a while, with the windows down, letting the sunshine and summer scents pour into the car as he sped along country lanes. He thought of Lisa, home alone, possibly nursing a hangover.

They'd had such a laugh, dancing and talking nineteen to the dozen – and after what she'd been through, too. His own wife couldn't bear to look at him and yet somehow, he'd monopolised the most beautiful woman at the party for the whole evening. He wondered if she'd been thinking about him today, hoping he'd get in touch.

On a whim, he looped back and headed towards Eden Hill through the main entrance of the estate, past the rows of starter-homes and shops, towards Lisa's. No journalists were in evidence - even that clown Andrew-what's-his-name wasn't there.

Martin had Googled Justin Dixon. It was a sorry state of affairs. He'd been a star player; burning bright but then burning out. Who could blame him for hitting the booze after a terrible injury like that? But then who could blame Lisa for walking away? Drunk people were hard work; all that self-pity and being sick. It made him shudder to think about it.

Martin got out of the car. The pedestrian gate was open so he walked in and rang Lisa's doorbell. He was about to turn away when the door opened and there was Lisa in sweat pants and a vest top, her hair in a ponytail.

'Martin! What a surprise. How are you?' She looked flustered.

'Hello, Lisa. I was just passing and I thought I'd make sure you were okay; not too hung over after last night?' Martin said.

'I was a bit fuzzy first thing, but I'm fine now.'

'Ah, well...' Martin rocked on his heels.

'Do you... do you want a cold drink? I was just going to take the dog out, but she can wait a bit,' Lisa said.

'I'd love one – thank you. Where is the...er...' Martin followed Lisa inside.

'Nellie? She's asleep on my bed keeping cool.'

'Alright for some, eh?' Martin said.

The house was cool and shady, and the lack of clutter added to the calming effect. Martin thought of his own house – mismatched stuff everywhere, surfaces covered with biros, rubber bands and Post-It notes. He'd found a half-sucked mint welded to the dresser last week that he'd had to pry off with a butter knife.

'I can offer you apple juice or fizzy water. Shall we sit in the garden?'

She'd got it nice, he thought; simple, classy - a few terracotta pots of colourful flowers on the decking near the Jacuzzi, and a small area of lawn; he wondered who cut the grass.

'So, have you had a good day?' Lisa said.

'I've been out enjoying the sunshine. I've just been for a drive and I was passing your house – well, passing the estate anyway. I was due to take my daughter out for lunch but she cancelled this morning.'

'Oh, that's a shame,' Lisa said. 'You're so lucky to have a daughter. I'd have loved a little girl.'

There was a pause.

'Great party last night,' Lisa said. 'I wonder what time it finished. I'll have to ask my friend Tanya...'

The conversation was stilted and Lisa seemed tense. He'd drink up and leave her to it - some people didn't like visitors unannounced.

'Well I'll love you and leave you,' Martin got to his feet.

'Oh...thanks for popping in Martin.'

'We must meet up soon – for a drink, or for a meal in town.' Martin said.

Lisa hesitated; 'I'm quite busy at the moment; I've got some sorting out to do...with Justin's family and so on. I'm sure I'll see you around though.'

'Yes indeed,' Martin said, 'See you later then.'

See you around? He didn't much like the sound of that. On the other hand, she was dealing with a grieving family so perhaps it wasn't appropriate to have male friends. He'd be patient and sensitive. There was no need to rush into things.

☪

'You sound perky, whistling away,' Jan said.

'I've just had a drive and a lemonade at the Fox. There were lots of people there, enjoying the garden...families and so on.' It was easy to make stuff up, Martin realised – as long as it was based on truth.

It had gone four o'clock but the sun was still high in the sky.

'Put the kettle on love, and let's get that cake open. We can take a tray outside...get some sun on our faces.'

Jan obliged, changing into a flowery sundress.

'There are going to be some changes around here,' Martin said, eyeing the dated crazy-paving and the rash of weeds sprouting through it.

'Like what?' Jan said.

'The whole place needs smartening up – can't you see that?'

And I'll still be polishing a turd, he thought, as he cut into the Victoria sponge.

# CHAPTER 6:
## HOME TRUTHS AND LITTLE LIES

KATE

It had only been a kiss, and an uninvited one at that, but since the day at the beach, Kate had fallen into a Ben-shaped reverie - because although he could be crass and irritating, he was endearing, too.

She'd dreamt about him; about making love, hidden away at the beach house, with the roar of the waves and the cry of seagulls for a soundtrack. She'd woken up sweating and breathless.

Then at the weekend, Kate had been vague and short with Neil, pushing him away in bed.

'What is it, Katie? We don't see each other all week – our weekends mean everything to me...what's wrong, darling?'

She'd shrugged the question off, said she was tired. Hurt, Neil had slunk off downstairs and watched some recorded football.

The next morning, feeling contrite, Kate got up early and made banana muffins and freshly ground coffee.

'I'm sorry,' she said, breaking open a still-warm muffin. 'It's not you – it's this place. I get so stir crazy. It's only Ludo that stops me from going completely round the bend.'

At the mention of his name, Ludo hopped up on the bed beside them; for once, Neil let it go.

'Sweetheart, I know it can be lonely, with me away so much.

If things are no better next year, I think we should go back to London.'

'What! God, no! We can't do that. For a start, property's gone up so much – we wouldn't even be able to buy back our old flat. Anyway, I'm used to all this space and having a garden for my boy. No, going back to London is not an option.'

'Kate, there's something I want to talk to you about,' Neil said, rubbing his stubbly chin. 'Get dressed – I'm taking you to the Blue Bear in Tunbridge Wells.'

Then Neil had refused to say any more about it until they were sitting in the smart brasserie, sipping gin and tonics, waiting for their starters to arrive.

'I wanted to tell you yesterday,' Neil said, 'but you were in such a funny mood. Anyway, the thing is... Harrington's is expanding – we're opening a new office in Covent Garden – and Roland wants me to be creative director and well, kind of run things. It's a big pay hike, Katie. And it will be creatively rewarding for me, too.'

'Wow – really? Babe, I'm so proud of you, but honestly, all I can think right now is that I'll see even less of you.'

'No, you won't, it'll be the same. I'll be home once mid-week and we'll have all our weekends together, just like now.'

'Well then, congratulations, darling. That's fantastic! Shall we order a glass of champagne to celebrate?'

They'd toasted Neil's promotion and then taken a taxi home for clumsy, grabby sex, falling asleep with the late July sun streaming across the bed, too sleepy to pull down the blind. Kate woke up to Ludo whining and licking her face.

'Okay, boy – we get the message. Neil, wake up – we need to take Ludo out.'

Pulling on sweats and sneakers they went out into the street reeking of sex. When they reached the fields, Ludo ran free, bounding after butterflies.

In the distance, a blonde woman was walking towards them, waving.

'That's the woman I told you about,' Kate said.

'Lisa!' she called, waving back. By now, Ludo had found Nellie, whose head barely peaked above the long grass.

'Hello Lisa. How are things with you? Oh, this is my husband, Neil.'

'Great to meet you, Neil,' Lisa flashed headlamp eyes in his direction, before adding 'I'm doing okay, thanks - just trying to keep busy. Excuse the state of me; I went to a party last night and I'm a bit jaded. I was just about to shower and change when a guy I met last night turned up at the house...which was all a bit awkward.'

'Well, when you feel up to it, we should do something,' Kate said, 'or come round for lunch sometime – Nellie's invited, of course. Just look at those two...they are ridiculous together.'

They watched Ludo and Nellie chasing each other in circles – Nellie letting out the odd high-pitched yap.

'What do you do, Neil?' Lisa asked.

'I'm an art director, at an advertising agency in London,' Neil said.

Kate felt a surge of pride; 'He's actually the creative director of a brand new agency... and a bloody good one, too,' she added.

'Ooh, that sounds fabulous,' Lisa said, 'and very important. You look the creative type.' She was flirting with him now. Let him have his moment, thought Kate.

☙

'She's nice,' Neil said as they walked home, Ludo panting beside them. 'You two should meet up - have some fun together. Katie, I hate the thought of you being on your own so much.'

'Yes, I like her. Maybe we can have a day out this week – take the dogs to the seaside or something...anything to escape Eden Island for a day.'

The last time Kate had walked on a beach had been with Ben - and Neil had no idea. When had Neil last walked on a beach, or done anything carefree and frivolous?

'I do love you, you know...even if I'm a rubbish wife sometimes,' Kate said.

'You're not rubbish at all – you're just a bit sad. Look...the way things are now...it's not going to be like this forever. You don't think I'll still be working such long hours and going into London every day when I'm fifty, do you? All the extra money I'll be earning now that I'm creative director is for our future. Kate, trust me - we just need to sit tight for a bit.' They walked on in companionable silence.

But what about now? Kate thought.

## LISA

Four hundred and ninety-three thousands pounds; three times she'd read the solicitors' letter and still it made no sense.

It was hard to say which had surprised Lisa the most; the fact that Justin had been worth so much, after the rehab bills and the years of earning almost nothing - except for the odd endorsement here and there – or the fact that he'd left everything to her.

But it was no oversight. The Will had been drawn up after their separation, and along with the baffling legalese explaining Justin's assets, was a letter in a sealed envelope, handwritten in Justin's own childish scrawl:

*To my baby girl, Lisa.*

*If you are reading this, I've been a twat and either drunk myself to death or died of cancer because of the abuse my body has taken.*

*I want you to know that you are the only woman I've ever loved and I'm sorry for being a crap husband. You deserved so much more than life with a self-pitying drunk and I hope now I've gone, you can have a better one.*

*Spend the money in any way that makes you happy – and I hope you find true love with a good man.*

*My love always, Justin. X*

Only Justin would use a word like twat in his last Will & Testament, thought Lisa, laughing through a blur of tears.

It pained her to think that he'd still loved her, even after they'd divorced. And now he'd made her a rich woman, which gave Lisa no pleasure, just a creeping sense of guilt and shame.

She rang Rita.

'You'll never guess what that daft old sod did, Mum. He's only left me half a million pounds! And there was a letter... Mum, Justin still loved me. I had no idea. I feel so guilty. If I hadn't walked out, Justin might be here now... and George and Eileen would still have two sons - and Sean and Debbie would have their brother. I might as well have stuck a knife in him.'

'Well that's ridiculous talk,' Rita barked. 'That man was beyond redemption. I told you when you married him that he'd be trouble – but you wouldn't listen. You could have had your pick of the bunch when you hitched your wagon to that loser. It amazes me that...'

'Oh, give it a rest, mother. Have you heard yourself? I've got to go.'

Lisa banged the phone down and poured herself a large glass of Sauvignon Blanc; it soured in her mouth. She rang Tanya but her call went straight to voice mail.

There seemed no point in calling Andrea - her sister would be working in the restaurant now, preparing for the first sitting; July in the Algarve was peak time for family holidays.

How had she wound up so alone? Divorced, childless and living in a new town where she knew almost nobody?

Lisa looked in the mirror. God, she looked tired – and older. She imagined herself at fifty, at sixty...it would soon come around.

Half a million pounds was a lot of money, but she needed to think hard about how she lived from now on, and the choices she made. Because no amount of money would buy her love or bring her happiness.

She reached for the wine, its earthy taste smacking the roof of her mouth.

Justin had never loved anyone else, had never moved on. He'd died alone, in his brother's spare room with vomit on his pillow after a cocktail of pills and booze. Supposing he'd meant to do it... couldn't hack living without hope.

Re-filling her glass, Lisa dialled Sean.

'Sean - it's Lisa. Can you talk for a bit? Look I just...I just wanted to see how you are - and your Mum and Dad of course. Sean, how was Justin...the night he died?'

'He'd had a good day, Leese. He'd sobered up after the stag do, and had been for a swim and a sauna at the gym. That night we made dinner together but he had one of his heads, so he turned in early. There was nothing on the box, so then I went to bed myself. Lisa, if I'd known Justin had a bottle in his room, I'd have tipped it away.'

⏾SEEKING EDEN

'So, he wasn't upset then? Did he talk about me, Sean – I need to know.'

'Lisa, where are you going with this, love? If it's about that rubbish in the papers, then let it go. It was an accident. He loved you till the day he died, but he was doing okay and talking about getting a place of his own.'

Lisa swallowed hard.

'Did you know he left me a lot of money?'

There was a pause; she could sense the cogs whirring.

'No, but I'm not surprised,' Sean said. 'He paid my mortgage off six months ago. He was a generous bloke. Beats me how the money lasted so long to be honest...'

'Me too. I just wish he'd...that he was...'

'I know,' Sean said. 'I miss my little brother, too. Lisa, no one is blaming you. At least, nobody who knows you - and you know what, love? The rest can fuck off.'

The next day, tidying up paperwork in the study that housed her laptop and correspondence, Lisa came across a crumpled sheet of paper with a business card stapled to it: Andrew Anson; Freelance Reporter. In biro, he'd written 'Lisa. People want to know the truth about being a footballer's wife - a chance to give your side of the story. Please call me. A.'

She'd blanked him so far but perhaps it would be cathartic to give her own version of events. And she could use the opportunity to remind everyone what a star player Justin had been and what cruel diseases he'd battled in fighting depression and alcoholism.

The number on Anson's business card went straight to voicemail so Lisa left a short message and hung up. Within a few minutes her mobile rang.

'Lisa, thanks for getting in touch,' Anson said. 'Kind of you to give me an interview. Let's sort this as soon possible, while Justin's story is still fresh in people's minds. Shall I come to your home? Does tomorrow suit you?'

☾

Beneath cartoonish frizzy hair, Andrew Anson's muddy brown eyes raked over Lisa's body. They shook hands; 'Thanks again for agreeing to chat. I should tell you that I write for a number of different newspapers, but I think the Daily Mail will want the story if I pitch it right, and it could lead to all sorts of opportunities. What's your world these days?'

Lisa hesitated; it had been years since she'd worked - taking care of Justin had been a full time job. And except for the flurry of lads' mags that had come knocking in her twenties, and a couple of press ads, the modelling had never taken off. Now at forty, that ship had sailed.

'I'm on a career break,' Lisa said, as she made coffee and arranged chocolate biscuits on a plate. 'Let's sit outside - shame to miss this weather.'

From a large holdall, Anson produced a tape recorder, notebook and pen, placing them on the rattan table.

'So, how are you feeling, Lisa? It can't be easy for you,' he began gently, 'I mean, if you were still married, people would feel sympathy for the grieving widow. But as things are, a number of people are blaming you, claiming that you abandoned Justin - and that his death was suicide.'

'Which is why I wanted to talk to you,' Lisa said, 'to set the record straight. Justin would never have taken his own life. He just wasn't capable. I have no idea where that rubbish came from – and that's not what his brother thinks. Justin had been living with Sean for the last twelve months and was...recovering.'

Anson took a sip of his coffee, moved the tape recorder closer to Lisa and fiddled with one of the buttons.

'How long were you together,' he said.

'For fifteen years. I was there for Justin...through the drinking and the depression, during the weeks and months of rehab. It's not easy to live with someone in that state of mind, you know. Justin's illness came before everything. I'd have liked children, but that was never going to happen, was it?' Lisa paused, and bit her lip. Anson continued to make squiggles on the page.

'More coffee?' She refilled his cup.

'I mean, don't get me wrong. Justin could be very sweet and loving...when he was himself. I never had any trouble with other women getting to him. He was gorgeous when he was young - he used to get loads of fan mail and girls hanging around on match day - but he was never interested.'

'Leaving Justin wasn't something I did lightly – for one thing, I had nowhere to go. I'd lost touch with all my friends. They couldn't stand being around him when he was on a bender, or afterwards when was hung-over.' Lisa closed her eyes; it was still painful to recall.

'I stayed with my mum for the first three months – which was horrendous. But when he realised I wasn't coming back, he sold the house, and being so generous, gave me half of everything.'

'And how much was that exactly?' Anson said.

'I'd rather not say, but enough that I could buy this house outright.'

'Do you think he was still in love with you, Lisa?'

'No – well, I didn't think that...before. But then I read the letter, saying as much... and I certainly never expected him to leave everything to me.'

'What letter was that, Lisa?' said Anson, leaning forward in his seat.

And before she could stop herself, Lisa was reciting from it, and explaining about the half million windfall. It felt good to talk – she'd been holding it together for weeks, trying not to cry, wondering how to act, what to say. But here was someone on her side – who would write a sympathetic feature, and all the rumours would go away.

'So Lisa; what's next for you? Are you looking for love again? Or should I ask, have you found it? A gorgeous woman like you isn't going to be short of offers.' He was smiling in a way that reminded Lisa of a shark.

'No, I haven't met anyone else – and I'm not looking.'

'Well that's not strictly true is it? You had a man here the other night,' Anson said.

'I thought that was you – taking those photos. Look, that was just a guy I met at a party and he walked me home; I'd borrowed his jacket.'

Anson was smirking, and shaking his head.

'Right, Lisa, that's great. Can I just get a few photographs? Female readers like to see role models of your age, and to check out your personal style. Can I ask you to slip into something a bit more... summery? You've got a stunning figure, Lisa – show it off a bit.' He was smiling again, showing yellow snaggle teeth.

Lisa returned in a fitted blue and white sun dress and vertiginous sandals.

'Great. Now just angle to your left a bit, but look back at me... perfect. And another, yes! Big smile...wow, yes...you've still got it,

Lisa.' He looked across at the hot-tub.

'How about a couple of shots in the Jacuzzi? Why don't you pop on a nice bikini and show your tan off. I wouldn't be surprised if this revives your modelling career; you're looking fab.'

Doubt stirred. It didn't feel right, but he wasn't asking her to go topless and with the jets bubbling away, there'd be nothing much to see.

So wearing a red bikini, Lisa stepped into the foaming water, posing and smiling until Andrew held up his hand.

'Perfect. I've got just what I wanted,' he said. 'Thank you so much. I'll write everything up and let you know when I've sold the piece, and when it will appear.'

Lisa thanked him, shook his hand at the door and ran upstairs to change out of her wet things. For the first time, it occurred to her that there had been no mention of a fee. She'd heard of people selling their stories, but she hadn't sold anything. It wasn't as though she needed the money.

# CHAPTER 7:
## BETRAYAL

### KATE

In August, the temperature fell and the sky darkened. Kate drove home from the airport in rain so fierce that the traffic had slowed to a crawl. She'd been tearful saying goodbye to Neil; ten days seemed like a long stretch and New York was so far away.

'Hey, don't get upset, sweetheart,' he'd said, 'I'll be back before you know it and we can speak on the phone every day.'

It was Neil's second trip away since becoming creative director and New York was a big deal. On a double-hander with Roland Jessop, the senior partner, Neil was pitching to a major soft drinks brand; getting the business would shift the agency into a whole new league.

Kate had made all the right noises but she could feel herself sinking, fearing that too much time alone would crush her. She'd tried to fill her diary; lunch with Lisa, coffee with the neighbours, even an overnight visit to her sister, but these small diversions made her feel like a kid in need of a babysitter.

And then Ben phoned.

'Hey, baby. How's Kent's hottest housewife?'

Kate winced.

'I'm well thanks, Ben, although I was still a copywriter the last time I checked. How are things with you?'

'Never better. When can I see you?'

Kate laughed; 'Try getting to the point, why don't you? Anyway, I'm not sure that's a good idea, is it?'

'I think it's a bloody brilliant idea. But you think that because I tried to kiss you, it would be complicated.'

'Seriously, Ben - do you blame me?' Kate said.

'Katie, I screwed up and I'm sorry. It was wrong on every level and I shouldn't have put you in that position. Let me make it up to you, because - as daft as it sounds - I'd like us to be friends. I really need your input on the music...there's...there's no one else I can ask.'

It was an endearing speech.

'Okay, let's meet for lunch – or coffee?' suggested Kate.

'Oh, sod that. Let's go out for dinner. I'm sick of my own cooking and the novelty of living down here like a total hermit is beginning to wear off. Let's get dressed up and go somewhere posh – I'll pick you up.'

So against Kate's better judgement, they'd arranged to meet three days later. Kate was like a cat on hot bricks until the day arrived and a steely calm came over her. Ben was right; they were both adult enough to conduct a platonic friendship. After all, they were hardly kids being led about by their hormones. And anyway, things had been better with Neil recently, they'd become close again – pushing Ben firmly out of Kate's mind.

She rang Alice.

'Hey, love. How's my favourite sister?' Oh god, I sound like Ben, she thought.

'I'm okay, thanks, Katie – bit fed up with the rain; call this a summer?' Alice sounded flat.

'You're not ringing to blow me out are you? Natalie's looking forward to seeing you – me too.'

'No, of course not. Just checking you're okay with me bringing the dog,' Kate said.

'You have to – Nat's already asked if he can sleep on her bed... she'll want a dog of her own next. You can both stay as long as you like.'

'Thanks, Al. But I have to get used to being alone and I'm meeting up with a couple of friends while Neil's away, so I'll be fine,' Kate said, wondering how to open the subject of her ex-boyfriend. There'd been no love lost between her sister and Ben - not after the way he'd gone AWOL. Perhaps she'd mention it over a glass of wine – then again, maybe she should say nothing at all; Alice would only worry.

'Gotta go, Al – give Natalie a big kiss from Auntie and tell her that Ludo would love to sleep on her bed.'

In the two hours before Ben was due to pick her up, Kate ran a deep scented bath, then buffed, de-fuzzed and moisturised every inch of her body. By the time she'd maxed out her fine hair, applied a smoky-eyed make up, and stepped into a black jersey dress with a deep V at the back, Kate knew she looked defiantly sexy.

Ludo eyed her from his bed, transmitting 'I know you're leaving me' messages in her direction.

'I won't be long, boy,' she said, stroking his silky head as Ben arrived.

'Your carriage awaits, Ma'am,' he said, indicating a sleek German saloon, his own battered Merc was nowhere to be seen.

'I hired it for the night,' Ben said, 'Didn't want to show us up in mine.'

Kate laughed: 'Oh, now that surprises me. I thought you didn't care what people thought of you. Are you getting respectable in your old age, Ben?'

Ben had dressed carefully; in designer jeans, a beautiful white linen shirt and a black jacket that looked suspiciously new. To all intents and purposes, the evening was shaping up like a date, which wasn't Kate's intention; yet something in her wanted Ben to want her – to admire what he'd thrown away. Butterflies fluttered in Kate's stomach as she inhaled the leather interior of the car, mixed with Ben's aftershave.

They purred off in the direction of Tunbridge Wells but then shot off across country to an area that Kate didn't recognise, passing through miles of green common land, and the odd gated country pile.

After half an hour of driving in restrained - bordering on polite - conversation, they swept through gates hidden by a wall of rhododendrons, along a gravel drive, stopping in front of a Georgian Villa that twinkled with soft golden lights.

Kate was stunned. 'We're eating here? Have you had a win on the horses?'

'Nah...I know one of the owners and he's giving me mates' rates. Kate it's not a big deal; I just wanted to apologise and treat you to a nice dinner – end of.'

'Well, thank you. This place is beautiful and so elegant.'

'And so are you. You look perfect tonight,' Ben said, offering her his arm.

A silver-haired Maitre d' greeted them in the grand hall and escorted them to the restaurant. Kate had expected stuffy Georgian splendour, but the interior was cool and contemporary, reminding her of a London Brasserie.

'I love it,' Kate said.

Ben was looking pleased with himself, almost smug as he ordered fizzy water and walnut bread and olives. Kate liked this new, decisive Ben, taking charge, making things happen, and she had to admit he looked handsome tonight, his grey eyes glittering in the candlelight, curls soft and shiny.

'How about a couple of vodka Martinis?' Ben said, without looking at the menu.

'Since when do you drink cocktails?' Kate was amused.

'Since having dinner with a beautiful, sophisticated woman who deserves to be spoilt.'

'Oh, please!' Kate blushed. Why the charm offensive?

They ordered from a menu of fashionable European and Asian fusion dishes. Each course was exquisitely flavoured, but the portions were miniscule and art-directed on the plate.

'Bloody hell, we'll need a sandwich after this lot,' Ben said in a low voice.

By her second Martini, Kate had begun to relax, laughing at Ben's stories and funny voices; she'd forgotten what a great mimic he was.

'Stop it, you'll give me indigestion.' She said, after a convoluted story involving Ben and another musician getting locked inside a studio overnight, and having to break out through a bathroom window. Weird stuff always happened to Ben; he attracted chaos.

'So where's your friend tonight?' Kate said.

'Mmm?'

'You said you know the owner...what's his name?' Kate held Ben's gaze.

'John,' Ben said.

'John? John what?'

'Lennon.'

'The guy who owns this place is called John Lennon?' Kate giggled. 'You just made that up. You don't know anyone here, do you?'

'No, I don't. I've never been here before in my life, but I didn't want you to think tonight was costing an arm and a leg.' Ben shrugged and gave her his sexiest smile.

Disarmed somewhat, Kate felt a familiar tingle in her stomach and was grateful for the table between them, or she might have kissed him there and then.

Ben studied the menu; 'Are we having pudding? Go on, if I get a passion fruit cheesecake, will you help me out?'

While they waited for dessert, another Martini appeared for Kate.

'Uh-oh...I shouldn't...they're too easy to drink – a few sips and they're aaaallllll gone.' Kate giggled; she heard herself slurring a little – it didn't matter, Ben would look after her.

&#9731;

Outside a mist of rain was falling. Kate wobbled on her heels and was grateful when Ben took her arm and led her to the car; something unspoken shifted between them.

When they arrived at Kate's house, Ludo was bouncing off the walls, desperate to get out. 'Walk with us,' Kate said, and after swapping heels for flats and grabbing a mac, they walked through silent streets lit by a crescent moon.

Canine duties dispatched, Kate led Ben into the study at the back of the house and closed the drapes.

Then barefoot and damp-haired, Kate waited for Ben to come to her. He hung back.

'Are you sure about this?' his voice was barely audible.

Kate answered by shrugging off her dress and letting it fall to the floor.

'Jesus, Kit – you're gorgeous,' Ben groaned, clasping her to him before removing her bra and thong so she stood naked and vulnerable.

After hastily shucking off his own clothes, Ben pulled Kate on to the rug, where they lay like spoons for a moment, hearts pounding.

'Oh, baby, I've dreamt about this,' Ben murmured into her hair, before their warm bodies melded into each other. And then they were locked - wary, moving carefully at first, but then spurred on by familiarity as the years dropped away. And as they abandoned themselves to each other, Kate felt the tension rising in her body, up through her core, like a rubber band pulled taut, before she came, taking Ben with her, hard and fast.

Hours later, waking cold and clammy, reality dawned like a slap.

Kate roused Ben then dressed in silence, searching for the right words when there were none.

Ben spoke first.

'My god, that was amazing, but I never thought...'

'Never thought I'd be stupid enough to cheat on my husband?' Kate's temples throbbed and nausea washed over her; 'Jesus, Ben – what have we done?'

'Babe - don't. This changes everything. I want you...I want us to be together, to start over again. This isn't you. Playing house with a man you don't love,' Ben said.

'How dare you? What on earth makes you think I don't love Neil? He's a wonderful person and he deserves so much better. Ben, I don't even know how this happened. You should go. Right now – before it gets light.'

Ben looked shell-shocked.

'It happened because we both wanted it to. You and me? We're unfinished business. We belong together. You should stop lying to yourself, Kate.'

## MARTIN

Martin had just finished advising old Mr Whittle on the benefits of rubber-backed runners when the phone rang. Adopting his best telephone manner, Martin picked up the receiver.

'Dad? Is it true?' Hayley's voice was agitated.

'Love? Whatever's the matter?' Martin said.

'How could you do that? To mum...to me! I can't believe it!'

'Hayley – slow down...I've no idea what you're talking about. You're scaring me now.'

Tripping over a garbled stream of words, Hayley told Martin what she'd seen and read that morning.

'Love – stop! However things look, I can tell you now, it is not the case. Give me ten minutes and I'll call you back.'

Martin turned the shop sign to Closed and marched down the high street, which was bathed in morning sunshine. The newsagent's was empty and after a grunt at Mr Patel, who as ever was on the phone, he bought a copy of the Daily Rise, folding it in half to conceal the mast-head. He couldn't remember ever reading it before, never mind paying for a copy.

Martin scoured the headlines until he got to page five. A bubble of acid came into his throat. God almighty – it couldn't be!

Under the headline 'Widowed WAG's Windfall' was a photograph of Lisa Dixon, posing in a red bikini, emerging from her Jacuzzi. A number of smaller, inset photographs were dotted further down the page – including one of Martin and Lisa embracing on the night of the Hunters' party. The caption read 'Lisa finds love again with mystery companion.'

A swooshing had begun in Martin's ears; he felt as though his chest might explode. Dear god – how could this have happened?

No wonder Hayley had been distraught. He scrutinised the photograph. His daughter had recognised him at once, in his best blue shirt, hair ruffled from dancing. Lisa was barefoot, standing on tiptoes as they kissed good night, creating an impression of intimacy.

He picked up the phone and rang Hayley.

'Now you just listen to your Dad,' he started, more calmly than he felt. 'I know what that photo looks like – it's horrible and I'm very sorry you had to see it. But it's not how it looks,' he began.

'Oh, please!' Hayley said, sounding older than her years. 'Dad, spare me the clichés and don't even bother to deny it. How long has it been going on?'

'Nothing is going on,' Martin was emphatic.

Patiently he explained how he'd gone to the party alone after Jan's meltdown; how he'd met a customer there, and they'd kept each other company as neither of them knew anyone else. Finally Martin explained how he'd walked Lisa home because he'd lent her his jacket.

'And that's it,' he finished.

'So why are you snogging on the door step then, Dad?' Hayley said.

'We aren't! It was a peck on the cheek.'

'Dad, do you think I was born yesterday? You're all over each other! And just look at the words... 'Lisa finds love with mystery man'! God knows what mum will do when she sees this!'

'You know what rubbish these rags print,' Martin said, as fresh horror dawned. 'Look, there's no point upsetting your mother, is there? She won't see this unless somebody points it out to her. Now promise me you won't say anything. Hayley, I swear to you – Dad's honour - there's no more to it than that.'

Hayley paused.

'Okay. 'Spose I'll have to trust you, won't I?' she said.

'That's my girl. Right – we'll say no more about it. I'll ring you in a day or two,' Martin said, hanging up.

Bombs were going off in his head. The article was a terrible piece, painting Lisa as an airheaded gold digger. And what did it mean about an inheritance? She'd said nothing about that.

Martin thought back to the giddiness of the Hunters' party – and how he'd felt weird ever since. Technically, he'd been honest with Hayley – certainly in the way she meant when he'd said nothing had happened. But something had happened. Martin had tasted something rich and syrupy – and he wanted more.

All day he felt restless and discombobulated - and at night, Lisa sashayed into his dreams. Twice in the last week alone, he'd locked the bathroom door, to touch himself, to release his frustration, while Jan snored in the next room. It was shameful, yes, but for the first time in years, he felt alive – energised by his own fantasies.

He'd taken to driving past Lisa's house most days, hoping to catch a glimpse of her – but without success.

Now they'd been pictured together, in one of the worst tabloid rags, snuggled up like the lovers he wished they were.

Lisa looked gorgeous in the photographs, voluptuous and youthful, her blonde hair shining in the sun. But the words were cruel...and lies, surely? That horrible reporter had made it sound as though she'd played Justin all along.

He pictured Lisa crying on his shoulder, devastated by the article.

'You're such a good friend, Martin. Thank god I can rely on you,' she'd say, as he mopped her tears and took her in his arms. Then they'd slide between cool white sheets in her French bed, and he'd peel off those teal silk panties and look into her eyes as he....

'Are you open mate?' A gruff voice shattered his reverie.

'Yes, yes - come in. What can I do for you?' Martin snapped back into work mode, pushing Lisa Dixon from his thoughts, at least for a moment or two.

⌘

## LISA

The snake had stitched her up and there wasn't a thing she could do about it. Andrew Anson's lies were out there for all to see.

Tanya had come to her house, the Daily Rise tucked into her fake Birkin bag.

'Lisa – you're not going to like this but I'm showing you as a friend. And just so you know, babe – I know it's all bollocks.'

'Lisa Dixon is a lonely, bitter, rich woman', the article began. 'Denied the family she craved, by the former striker, Justin Dixon, who died tragically earlier this year in an alcohol fuelled incident that some are calling suicide...'

'Oh my god, Tanya! He's twisted everything I said and made it sound horrible!' Lisa read the rest of the article in silence, before dumping the paper into the kitchen bin.

'What a total arsehole! Do you think I should sue?'

Tanya shook her head; 'My Grandma used to say, 'least said, soonest mended' and you carrying it on...well it just draws attention to it all.'

'But he's made me sound like a right money grabbing bitch, hasn't he?'

'You have to remember that this paper is in the toilet, babe. Nobody reads this rubbish – well not proper people anyway. Hey, and you look great in the photos...like a model, don't you think?'

'My boobs look good, I suppose,' Lisa admitted.

'Lisa, please don't let this get to you. The guy is a total loser and the best thing you can do is to rise above it. What I want to know is, who are you snogging on the doorstep, you devil, you!'

Lisa was indignant; 'I'm not - it was practicality an air kiss. Tan, don't you recognise him? Remember that funny little bloke at Claire's party? The one who trotted around after me all night? Well, he walked me home – and I don't know what possessed me, but I invited him in for a drink. Anyway, it was awkward, so he left after ten minutes and that was that.'

Tanya scoffed; 'You wanna be careful, hon. Blokes like that get the wrong idea. He was sweet, bless him, but you wouldn't...would you?'

'No, of course not. Anyway, he turned up here the next day. He said he was just passing.'

'Oh, that's creepy. Just stalking, more like,' Tanya said.

'Oh god, Tanya...what about Justin's family? They'll think I said those awful things – about Justin not letting me have kids and how I deserved the money for all the sacrifices I made,' Lisa said, her eyes filling with tears. 'I'll have to ring Sean and explain. What a mess. And what a hateful creep that guy turned out to be. I need a drink.'

Taking Tanya's car, they drove into Tunbridge Wells for some much-needed wine therapy, pitching up at The Gallery, which was buzzing with a cool after-work crowd.

The Maitre d' – a dead ringer for a young David Duchovny – showed them to a prime table near the window.

'They always put pretty people by the entrance,' Tanya said.

After ordering cosmopolitans and bar snacks, the women sat people watching.

Lisa's mobile lit up; Sean calling.

'Oh no! I can't. Not now – I'll ring him tomorrow.' Lisa bounced the call and dropped the phone as if scalded.

Two guys who'd been hovering sat down opposite them.

'You like dancing, hen?' said a gruff voice from a lived-in face, north of forty; 'You two can come wi'us. We're clubbing later.'

'I'll translate that, shall I?' his mate said with a grin: 'He means; would you two lovely ladies like a drink with us? I'm Paul and this is Angus.'

'Oh that's nice; thank you,' Tanya said.

But something about the way the men had joined them, presumptuous and swaggering, upset Lisa. She shot her friend a look.

'Not for me thanks, I have to go. You ready, Tanya?'

'What? We've only just got here - are you okay?'

But Lisa was already moving briskly towards the door and once in the car, she could no longer hold back the tears which had threatened all day.

'I'm sorry,' she sniffed, 'I know I'm being pathetic, but I just feel so alone. I did love Justin – but there's been no one since. And there never will be now, after the shit that's been written about me.'

'That's rubbish, babe,' Tanya said.

Then keeping her eyes on the road ahead, she put out her left hand for Lisa to hold.

'And FYI, Leese; you're not alone. You've got me.'

# CHAPTER 8:
## REGRETS

### KATE

Kate woke up with the smell of Ben still on her skin. After what had happened, there was nothing for it, other than to cut Ben off completely and start acting like the model wife Neil deserved. And that was the problem – she'd be acting. The question was; would Neil see through her?

Ben had been shocked and hurt when she'd dismissed him after their teenage fumblings on the study floor. What had he expected? That they'd cosy up on the sofa with a mug of Horlicks? Or that she'd pack a bag and go with him to the coast? What went on in Ben's mind had always been a mystery to her.

As for her own feral behaviour, it now seemed like a complete aberration. What on earth had possessed her to get sucked into a random bout of Ex-Sex? It was unforgiveable and an appalling cliché to boot.

What she needed to do was to hold it together and to think. It would be calming, Kate reasoned, to take Ludo to the woods for a long walk - it would help her to sort out her feelings.

'C'mon boy, let's go find some bunnies,' she said to Ludo, who seemed particularly skittish.

🍎

After a fortnight of heavy rain, the sun had made a welcome return; the combination had sent nature into overdrive and some of the woodland paths had all but grown over. After half an hour of walking aimlessly, deep in thought, Kate realised she was lost. Ludo, who would usually charge ahead and then loop back to her, was sticking close, picking up signals from his mistress.

It was ridiculous – she couldn't be lost; she'd walked here most weeks for the last ten months. Kate swivelled to find a pair of German Shepherds loping towards her. Heart in mouth, she froze, putting a protective arm in front of Ludo, who was instinctively backing away.

Where the hell was the owner? An unintelligible shout went up that stopped the dogs in their tracks.

'Ah, there you are; bloody stupid animals.' A man in country tweeds limped into view, leaning on a stick.

'Morning!' he barked, waving his cane at Kate. 'Better today... bloody rain.'

'Yes...much better.' Kate eyed the two dogs, even though they were now trotting to their master's heal and paying no attention to her or Ludo.

She called after him.

'Actually, I'm a bit lost, do you know which way goes to Eden Hill?'

'Damn estate! Well, if that's where you're going, follow me and you can peel off to the right.' The old man was cracking quite a pace despite the stick.

'Thank you,' Kate said, wondering if the old boy actually knew the way.

'Bloody developers. How much more do they want, hmm? I'll tell you. All of it! Inglethorpe Trust won't be happy until this has all been raised to the ground. Ripping up the countryside, acre by acre...and for what? To build bloody boxes – that's what. Do you live in a box?' he barked.

Kate hesitated, unsure how to answer.

'It's not personal, you understand m'dear. But I was born here, seventy six years ago, hmm? When I was a young man, I knew everybody, at least by sight. But the population's growing at an unseemly rate now...more than quadrupled in the last ten years alone. And what do we get? More car parks? No! Better rail services? We do not. A decent bank – or a bigger post office? Not a bit of it. Just more damn boxes!'

He was waving the cane again, and Kate was relieved to recognise a path that would lead her out of the woods, to the lane near Lisa's house.

'Well, this is me – thank you for showing me the way. Sorry you don't like Ede-' Kate began, but the old man was marching ahead, still muttering, the dogs loping at his side.

The encounter had at least taken her mind off Ben.

⌗

Desperate to hear a kind voice, Kate rang Alice.

'Hi darling. I'll be with you by about four o'clock – just in time for tea,' Kate said.

'Great. I'll get a cake or something – any excuse. Are you okay? You sound funny – a bit squeaky,' Alice said.

'Squeaky? Yes, I'm fine. I got a bit lost in the woods and some big dogs gave me a fright, that's all.' And last night I had sex with my ex-boyfriend, she wanted to wail.

'Ooh, that does sound scary,' Alice said. 'Okay love, be careful driving and we'll see you later. And Kate; stay as long as you want, tonight, tomorrow...it's rough being on your own so much.'

Her sister's concern brought tears to Kate's eyes. How on earth would she get through the next couple of days without spilling her guts – they'd told each other everything all their lives. Kate checked her mobile. Four unanswered calls from Ben; it was time to face the music.

He picked up on the second ring.

'Kate, thank god – I've been worried about you.'

'I'm sorry. Ben...last night...it should never have happened. I know I...instigated...things, but it won't happen again, I can assure you. It's best that we don't meet again. There's nothing more to say about it.'

'Well, I've got plenty to say. Kate, we belong together – last night was an unstoppable force...it didn't just happen, it was destiny,' Ben said.

He was being dramatic, which was Ben all over. When Ben wanted something, he wanted it now; sod the obstacles or consequences.

And yet, an element of doubt had wormed into Kate's psyche; what if Ben belonged in her future, despite their turbulent past?

🍎

The Victorian terrace, home to Alice, Pete and Natalie for the last ten years, glowed in the late afternoon sun. Ludo trotted along the path, watering a hydrangea as he went, his leather nose twitching at the prospect of new terrain to explore.

'You're too thin,' Alice said, hugging her older sister.

'I'm fine – and you look perfect to me. I've missed you, Al. Is Nat home?'

'She'll be back from school in ten minutes – she's desperate to see the dog. He's gorgeous, Kate. You must love him so much.'

'More than I could have imagined,' Kate said, watching Ludo snuffling around the chaotic pile of boots, shoes and crumpled carrier bags in Alice's hallway.

Seated at Alice's old pine table, drinking builders' tea and tucking into thickly buttered scones, Kate felt the tension begin to ebb away. Pinned to the walls were photos, drawings and scrawled lists. Pots of herbs and a broken mug for gluing jostled for space on the window ledge. Mismatched jars filled with tea, coffee, biscuits and baking ingredients lined the worktops. It was a comforting tableau, and a million miles from the sterile, show-home kitchens of Eden Hill.

The front door rattled open and banged shut.

'I'm home, mum,' called Natalie, adding her shoes to the pile before flat-footing it into the kitchen.

'Auntie! Hey...oh is this him? Arh, he's so cute. Here boy...I won't hurt you.' Ludo inched forward, bowing his head to Natalie's caresses while she tickled his silky ears.

'Way to a thirteen year old's heart,' Alice said. 'Don't go getting any ideas, Nat – he's just visiting.'

Resisting the urge to say 'haven't you grown', Kate surveyed her niece, who, with a mane of blonde hair that reached her waist and two small mounds evident beneath her school blouse, was fast becoming a young woman.

'Go and change please, Nat, and then perhaps you can walk Ludo if Auntie Kate says it's alright.'

When they were alone, Kate could see her sister studying her.

'What are you thinking?'

'I'm thinking,' Alice said, 'That something is going on. Something you're not telling me. Is everything okay...with you and Neil?'

'Yes!' Kate was keen to reassure her sister. 'I mean, to be honest, we are a bit distant at the moment, because he seems to be away all the time – but you know...other than that...' Kate's voice trailed off and she turned away. Alice was waiting for her to speak.

'Okay – you know Ben, who I used to go out with? Well, he contacted me recently and we met up for a drink,' Kate said.

'Katie, how could you even speak to him? He treated you like crap, and leopards don't change their spots.'

'I thought you'd say that, but actually, he's grown up a lot.'

'Well, so he should – how old is he now, sixty?' Alice said, warming to her theme.

'Fifty. Anyway, we met up, had a walk down memory lane, but I don't think we'll meet again – there's no point.'

Alice was frowning.

'Does Neil know you've seen him?'

'No,' Kate said, 'He doesn't need to – why worry him?'

'That's not good; you two shouldn't have secrets. But I guess if you aren't going to see him again...just promise me you won't.'

Kate had managed to speak about Ben without blowing her cover; she changed the subject before she cracked.

'How's Pete?'

'Something's off with him...whether it's work...or...oh, I don't know. He's never around and when he is, it's as though he can't hear me. I'm worried he might be ill,' Alice said.

'Why do you say that?' Kate said, alarmed.

'I don't know...he's so withdrawn. OK, too much information, but Pete has never cared about walking around stark bollock naked and now he's covering up and locking the bathroom door. And it scares me...what if he's found something?'

'What - you mean, like a lump?'

'Yes – oh I'm being silly,' Alice said, pouring out more tea. 'But I just want him to talk to me.'

'Then tell him you're worried. You two are solid; I can't imagine what he's bottling but it can't be that bad.'

Kate looked at her little sister and her heart swelled. China blue eyes gazed out beneath a thick blonde fringe; her frame was sturdier than Kate's, and even her hands - broad and square-nailed, spoke volumes of capability. Alice had always been so grounded and it was rare to find her pensive.

'Anyway, Pete's out tonight. He's taking a German client out to dinner – some big noise in engineering who's paying the company a fortune – so I thought we girls could go to the local Italian for dinner,' Alice said.

'Sounds lovely, but I'm not sure about leaving Ludo alone in a strange house.'

'Sorry, Katie, I wasn't thinking. Let's get a takeaway and cosy up at home instead,' Alice said.

## MARTIN

Three weeks had passed and not a living soul had mentioned seeing Martin in the paper. Either nobody recognised him (the photo was rather small and grainy), or – and Martin thought this the more likely scenario – the Daily Rise was a rag and nobody read it anyway.

To Martin's immense relief, Jan appeared not to have seen or heard anything about it, and Hayley had been good for her word, standing by her Dad as usual.

After Hayley's phone call, Martin had hidden the offending pages in his desk drawer at work. Lisa looked beautiful in a mussed-up and sleepy way, which alluded to them having spent a cosy evening indoors.

How he wished that were true.

The house was quiet without Jan bumping around. She'd been dispatched to her brother's on the south coast for a few days while Martin got to grips with the decorating. He'd cleared the living and dining rooms of furniture and knick-knacks on the Sunday, and bought dust sheets and emulsion ready for the painters to make a start on Monday morning while he was at the shop.

Martin stole another look at the colour chart. Potter's wheel; serene, elegant – and a million miles from the dusty peach walls that had been the backdrop to his life for the last eight years. The fitters were booked for the following week, to lay a mushroom-coloured carpet, in a thick, soft pile.

Jan had been bewildered.

'But why are you changing everything? I like things the way they are. It's wasteful ripping up a decent carpet. What's got into you, Mart?'

'Jan, we own a carpet shop, for goodness' sake. And anyway, I think it will do us both good to freshen things up a bit. Go for something a bit more trendy and stylish,' Martin said.

'Trendy? We've never had a trendy day in our lives...that's not us, is it?' Jan said.

'But why shouldn't it be us? I go into customers' homes all the time – especially on the estate – and you can guarantee none of them look like this...monstrosity.'

Jan had mumbled something about Martin getting pretentious in his old age and then picked up one of her soap magazines, noisily flipping the pages.

'Oh, charming,' he said. 'Well you won't be saying that when you get back from Russell's and this place looks like it belongs in one of your magazines.'

## KATE

Half insane with guilt, Kate had agonised over what to get Neil for his 48th birthday. After a massive trawl online, she'd booked a weekend in a hotel on the edge of the New Forest, blowing the budget on a room with its own sun-deck and hot tub. If she couldn't summon a little lovin' feeling in that environment, then they were really in trouble.

She'd dropped Ludo off at Alice's house on Friday lunchtime knowing he'd be indulged by Natalie, who'd bought him a bunch of new toys and a fleecy blanket with bone motifs on one side and 'I heart my dog' on the other.

'Don't worry about him, auntie; I'll take great care of him,' Natalie said earnestly.

Neil returned from New York, exhausted but buzzing. Kate felt sick, terrified her treachery would show in her face.

The pitch had gone well and Neil had hit it off with the senior client.

'This is it, Kate,' he said, without looking at her. 'If we get this account – and I'm pretty sure it's in the bag – it puts Harrington's in a whole new league. We'll be shooting global TV campaigns and I'll have to hire new people. There could be some big bonuses at the end of the year.'

'I'm happy for you, darling,' Kate said, feeling anything but.

Neil had promised to leave work at lunchtime but at three o'clock, he rang home.

'I'm sorry darling; I'm still at work. I'll be another hour or so but I should be home by six, latest.'

'Six o'clock? Neil, I had a big surprise lined up. Just get home as soon as you can – please, babe. It will be worth it, I promise.'

Neil showed up at seven, looking drained. Concealing her irritation, Kate ran to hug him.

'Happy birthday, husband,' she said, burying her face in his salty neck. 'You've just got time for a drink before I whisk you away.' Kate handed him an ice cold beer.

'Wow...okay...where are we going? What do I need to pack?' Neil said.

'It's all done. Our bags are in the car – the satnav is primed and I'm driving. Neil, this is my present to you. Trust me – you'll love it.'

But after twenty minutes of Neil braced in the crash position like a nervous air passenger, Kate pulled over.

'You're obviously very uncomfortable with my driving,' she said, getting out. They swapped seats and Kate steeled herself not to sulk.

Gazing out of the window as the rural landscape rushed by, it was hard to ignore the voice in her head; the one that had an answer for everything.

He always prioritises work over me. Ah, yes, but you cheated with Ben.

He's always late home, even on special occasions. Maybe - but you slept with Ben.

He hates my driving! So what? YOU HAD SEX WITH BEN.

On and on; a never ending dialogue that echoed in her head. Well this weekend, she'd silence the voice - by being the most loving, sensual and tender wife imaginable.

☙

'Katie, you bad girl! This place must have cost an arm and a leg; you shouldn't have – but I'm glad you did,' Neil said, as they pulled up at the opulent mansion and the valet parking swung into gear.

Their room was a blend of Georgian elegance and smart technology. Grinning like a school kid, Neil was loving his surprise, playing with the Bose sound system and the mood-lighting, and gleeful at the sight of their secluded Jacuzzi.

They ate light and early; several tiny but exquisite courses dreamt up by the Michelin Starred chef, Romeo Casilli.

'Why don't we crack open the mini-bar and get into the hot tub to unwind before bed,' Neil said, making comical eyebrows.

'Oh, I can do better than that,' Kate produced a bottle of their favourite Prosecco.

'Hey, good thinking, Batman - well done for sneaking that in.'

They slid into the warm, bubbling water – a soft glow coming from inside the tub. Kate looked at Neil's chiselled face, head tilted back, luxuriating in the steamy warmth. Moving closer, she ran a hand down his torso, willing herself to feel a stirring of desire, but none came.

'Mmm – that's lovely, don't stop,' Neil said, placing her hand over his groin.

Kate drained her glass.

'I'll just get us a top-up,' she said, stepping out of the tub and shivering in the cool night air.

'Why don't we take the next glass to bed?' suggested Neil, standing up to reveal exactly why he was keen to go inside.

Wrapped in thick white bath sheets, they lay on the king sized bed, hair frizzed in damp tendrils. Neil rolled onto her and for a moment, Kate fought the urge to push him away before relaxing into his embrace. But when she closed her eyes she saw Ben, his steely gaze holding hers, his tanned skin dark against her creamy limbs.

They made love slowly at first, as Kate struggled to feel any real connection, before finally letting go and using every trick she had to hasten Neil's orgasm. Sighing deeply as though she too had come, Kate extracted herself from Neil's arms.

'My god, Katie - that was amazing. Thank you for bringing us here – it's just what we needed.'

Within minutes, Neil was asleep while Kate lay awake, images of Ben flickering in her mind like Super 8 film.

After breakfasting on eggs benedict in the hotel's elegant atrium, they pulled on walking boots and set out for the forest.

'I think autumn will come early this year, don't you?' Kate said.

'Maybe it just feels that way because we don't want summer to end,' Neil said.

A sharp nip had crept into the air and the trees were beginning to yellow. The forest had taken on a musty scent as clusters of pungent mushrooms pushed through the earth.

Neil put out his arm, stopping Kate in her tracks, and pointed to a sturdy bird barely visible in the foliage.

'That,' he whispered, 'is a Green Woodpecker; isn't he a beauty?'

Kate looked at her husband. How did he know all this stuff?

That was the thing about Neil; he was what people called 'well-rounded.' He remembered the names of birds, plants and rivers, and dead footballers, obsolete sweets and vintage cars; his general knowledge was vast.

'I love you,' she said, giving his hand a squeeze.

Ć

Blessed with sightings of several ponies, dozens of deer (all of which reminded Kate of Ludo), and something dog-sized lurking in the undergrowth that Neil swore was a wild boar, they walked back to the hotel.

Kate rubbed her stomach.

'So much for the blow-out breakfast; I'm starving,' she said.

'What do you fancy? We can eat at the hotel if you like, but it feels a bit indulgent at lunchtime. Shall we get in the car and find a nice country pub?' Neil said.

He drove gently so as not to endanger any animals that might scurry into the road, while Kate gazed out of the car window, hunger rendering her silent. When her mobile thrummed in her pocket, she knew at once it was Ben. Glancing at Neil, who was wholly focussed on the job in hand, she read the message; missing you - call me. X

'From Alice; she hopes we're having a good time,' Kate said, deleting the text.

'Ask her how our boy is,' Neil said, grinning.

'That would sound like we're checking up on them and I know he's fine; Natalie can't leave him alone. I miss him – don't you?'

Her mobile buzzed again. Another message from Ben: where are you? There was no kiss this time, which hinted at either impatience or irritation.

She'd have to text him at the next opportunity and let him know she was with Neil. She'd been very clear about him not contacting her again; which bit didn't he understand?

Neil swung into the carpark of the Hare & Lettuce.

'This looks nice, don't you think, darling?' He said.

It was the last weekend of the month and the pub was heaving with visitors to the area, and locals keen to splash out after payday. The tourists were togged up warmly, and wearing walking boots while the locals were dressed in less hardy everyday clothing.

A woman in a bizarre-looking hairpiece looked Neil up and down, licking her red lips.

'You've still got it, stud-muffin,' Kate whispered. Engrossed in ordering drinks and menus, Neil hadn't a breeze what she was talking about.

Escaping to the Ladies' room, Kate took out her phone. She needed to respond to Ben in such a way that he'd stop texting her.

'Am in New Forest with Neil, so no privacy. Will call on return. Hope U R OK xx'

Ben's one word reply was instant; fuck.

Ć

When she returned, Neil had found a table and was chatting to an elderly couple. Their podgy, grey-muzzled terrier was sprawled on the stone floor, mindless of people stepping over him.

'And this is my wife, Kate,' Neil said, as she squeezed in opposite him. 'Hey, this couple know the hotel we're in; their son works there,' Neil said.

By now, Kate was psycho hungry and had no wish to be drawn into conversion with anybody, let alone a couple of pensioners who might insist on chatting all through lunch.

'Great,' she said. 'Neil, have you ordered?'

'Yes, scampi and chips twice and a side salad so we can pretend we're being healthy,' he said, adding quietly, 'Kate, that wasn't very friendly, was it? We're on holiday, relax.'

'Sorry, I'm just a bit light-headed,' she said, beginning to feel queasy.

The food arrived and Kate devoured every last scrap before trawling the sweet menu.

'What?' she said when Neil raised his eyebrows. 'We've had a long walk, and the fresh air has given me an appetite. I'll be back in the gym next week, don't panic.'

'Who's panicking?' Neil said, laughing.

# CHAPTER 9:
## DILEMMAS

### KATE

On Sunday evening, chilled and happy, Kate and Neil set off home. Kate rang Alice from the car.

'Hey, love. How's my boy doing? Look, would you mind having Ludo an extra night? I thought we'd pick him up tomorrow as it's a Bank Holiday.'

'Of course – it'll be a wrench giving him back. I think Natalie may go into a decline.'

'Aww, bless her. Thanks, Al - that's a big help. We'll see you about midday tomorrow if that suits?'

But the following day, Kate woke up feeling out of sorts, a wave of nausea causing her to sprint for the bathroom.

'Katie? What's the matter – are you throwing up in there?' Neil said.

Kate didn't answer, but continued to gag, resting her head on the cool white tiles.

'I'm okay,' she managed, when the retching stopped. What the hell had caused this?

Kate emerged to find Neil in the kitchen making tea and toast.

'Are you okay, darling,' he said, putting a protective arm around her. 'I guess last night's Thai takeaway is the culprit. I feel okay though.'

'You didn't have the prawns, did you? That must be it. Bloody hell - what a waste of a Bank Holiday. Neil, you'll have to drive over to Alice's and get Ludo in an hour or so... I don't think I can bear to sit in the car.'

But by mid-morning, Kate felt strong enough to make the journey to Hove, so armed with a couple of plastic bags in case of a relapse, they set off.

'I feel fine now,' she said, wondering what to have for lunch, and nibbling on a digestive biscuit.

'Well thankfully you seem to have ejected whatever upset you,' Neil said, manoeuvring into the fast lane.

&#9983;

When they arrived at Alice's house, Ludo greeted them wearing a red and white bandanna. 'You don't mind, do you, Auntie? It suits him. Hello Neil, how are you?' Natalie said.

'We're great, thanks, Nat, after our break in the country. You'd love it there – the ponies are adorable.' Neil said.

'In here,' called Alice. They followed the warm smell of vanilla in time to see Alice remove a golden sponge from the oven.

'Ooh, lovely. You're always baking, Al – you're such a domestic goddess.' Kate said.

'It's just because you're here. Builders' tea alright? How was it then? You both look incredibly well.'

'Well that's funny, seeing as I've got food poisoning! I'm not even sure I should have any of that gorgeous cake, might start me off again,' Kate said.

Neil disappeared in the direction of the cloakroom.

'Have you got something to tell me,' Alice hissed, once Neil and Natalie were out of earshot.

'Not that I can think of,' Kate said.

'So, you threw up this morning – and you're okay now,' Alice said, ramming the point.

'Ah, I see where you're going with this. No don't be daft; this is me you're talking to. Al, it's not that – I've got...you know... the gadget.'

'Well, they don't last forever. I'm just saying.'

Neil reappeared and they huddled around Alice's pine table, drinking from red mugs.

'Where's Pete?' Neil said.

Alice rolled her eyes; 'Sore subject; I can't believe he had to work today – on a bank holiday! It's not on. But all the big guns have gone in today – they're tendering for a hotel chain in the Middle East. Blah, bloody blah. I hardly care anymore – I'm getting used to him not being around,' she added.

'Yeah, Dad's rubbish,' Natalie said. 'Can we ice the cake now, please?'

But the rest of the conversation was lost on Kate; Alice had started a train of thought – one that could not be derailed.

Kate was relieved when Neil left for work at six thirty the following morning; it meant she could vomit in private and without justification.

There was no point in jumping to conclusions. She'd been fitted with a coil some years back, but the dates were a blur. It had been spring – that much she was sure of - because she'd arrived home from the hospital, sore and crabby, to find the flat filled with daffodils.

'Just cos,' Neil had said.

But what was the year?

Kate swotted up online, becoming clammy with panic when she read that the effectiveness of the device waned after five years. A trawl through her old desk diaries revealed that five and a half years had in fact passed. Surely the gynae clinic should have written to her – or perhaps they had - to her old address.

With her heart banging in her chest, Kate drove to the pharmacy. The sooner she knew, the sooner she could deal with things.

In the bathroom, hands shaking, Kate ripped open the pregnancy testing kit. Moments later, a delicate blue cross emerged.

No, no, no! There was no chance that she could become a mother. She could not allow it to happen.

And then the unspeakable truth dawned, which began as a whisper and quickly became a roar.

Whose baby was it?

♋

With Neil in London for the rest of the week and no work to distract her, Kate hunkered down into herself.

If she discounted the nausea during her first hours of waking, and a voracious appetite for carbs, she did not feel pregnant (whatever 'pregnant' felt like).

And yet, life smiled in her belly. A tiny person would grow from a seed, and unless she intervened, the tiny one would become big and real and present, in a matter of seven or eight months; a person who would resemble Neil – or Ben. It was unthinkable.

Kate called Ben, needing to hear his voice.

'Hello sexy,' he said, picking up right away. 'Knowing you were away with him has been torture. How are you? Where did you go?'

'I'm okay,' Kate said. Oh, and FYI – pregnant.

'Look, we have to talk. We can't just leave things as they are. I'm going out of my mind here. I want you so badly, I can't think of anything else. Kit, we can make things work...we just need to talk about stuff and come up with a plan. Babe, I've got so much to tell you.'

'Ben, nothing has changed.' Everything had changed.

'I'm married...to a good man, who loves me. We've got a home and a dog and...'

'And what? You don't belong there, Kate. Not in that place and not with that man. Jesus - have you forgotten what happened a few weeks ago?'

There was no danger of that now.

'Well...we can chalk that up to temporary insanity or too many cocktails. Either way, it was just wrong. Ben...I love my husband... oh, god this is awful.'

'Meet me tomorrow night – let's have a bite to eat and just talk. Please hear me out, Kate.'

'Okay, but not around here. Pick me up at seven.'

Shivering as she walked Ludo, Kate wondered whether it was due to the early September chill, or the fact that she felt queasy with apprehension about what lie ahead.

It was a mess. All the signs pointed to the baby being Ben's – but without knowing exactly how long she'd been pregnant, Kate couldn't be sure.

She and Neil had been through a drought, but two weeks before she'd seen Ben, they'd crashed into bed full of food and wine the day he'd announced his promotion and had taken her out to celebrate.

The tragic thing was that Neil would be overjoyed at the prospect of becoming a Dad, and unconcerned with dates and other extraneous details.

Ben, on the other hand, had never even imagined himself as a father.

Her sister had guessed, in that witchy, sixth sense way they sometimes had about each other, but Kate was relieved when Alice had let it drop. For now it had to be her secret and Kate couldn't remember ever feeling more alone.

ॐ

As they neared home, Ludo wagging his tale in anticipation of a biscuit, Kate found her neighbour Rachel deadheading in the front garden. Beside her, three year old Ellie was poking the ground with a pink plastic spade.

'Doggie,' she squealed, toddling towards them.

'Hi Rachel; how are you?' Kate said.

'Oh, fine – you know, same old, same old,' Rachel said, pushing hair out of her eyes.

'Doggie!' Ellie said again.

'Are you helping Mummy, Ellie? You're doing a good job,' Kate said.

Then, thwack, went the plastic spade, squarely on Ludo's muzzle. The dog yelped in pain as Ellie raised the spade, preparing to go again.

'Hey!' Kate roared, 'Stop that! You don't hit doggies!'

Rachel gasped; 'Kate, I'm so sorry.'

'Ellie, you get indoors right now – do you hear me? That was very naughty. Very bad indeed! She's off play-school with a tummy bug,' Rachel added randomly.

She's certainly sick, thought Kate, hurrying inside with the poor startled dog and slamming the front door. Reaching for a box of tissues, Kate allowed herself to cry until she felt a degree of relief.

Then she went upstairs, ran a deep bath and lay in the steamy water, scrutinising her body. Everything looked the same - even her smooth flat stomach.

For the first time, it occurred to Kate that she should see a doctor – get checked out and take advice, because whatever the fate of the tiny being inside her, it existed and had somehow got past enemy lines.

Blasting her hair with the dryer and dressing quickly, Kate phoned the surgery.

'May I book an appointment please? The earliest you've got, with Doctor Benson.'

'Doctor Benson's got nothing bookable for three weeks, but she has an open surgery tomorrow morning. Just come along and wait to be seen - you shouldn't have to wait more than an hour.'

It would have to do; she could spill her guts to Jane Benson without fear of being judged or lectured to.

The next day, flipping through a dog-eared copy of Your Baby in the peppermint-walled waiting room, Kate's mobile throbbed in her pocket: 'Can't wait to see you tonight. X', came the message from Ben.

What if Ben really was the father? She couldn't be with him... didn't want to be with him - Kate was clear on that. The whole sordid encounter had been a terrible mistake, one that could colour the rest of her life if she let it.

'Kate Farleigh, please – Room 2' said the receptionist from behind her screen.

Light streamed into a room sharpened by the smell of antiseptic, the sunshine creating a halo effect around Doctor Benson's fine blonde hair. She gestured for Kate to sit down.

'Hi, sorry to...' Kate began.

'Please – that's why I'm here. What's worrying you today?'

'I...I seem to have got myself pregnant. It was an accident...I have a coil...actually, it's all a total disaster.'

'Okay, one step at a time. Have you taken a test?' Doctor Benson was jotting notes.

'Yes and my period's a few days late. I really can't have this baby and...'

'Okay, let's get a sample and do another test, shall we? Then we'll know what we're working with. Just pop into the ladies with this, hand it in at the front desk and then wait a while, please. And Kate; please don't worry – we can sort it.'

Kate meekly obeyed, exhausted by it all. Fifteen minutes later, Doctor Benson confirmed that she was indeed in the early stages of pregnancy.

'I can't have this baby,' Kate said, beginning to hyperventilate.

'What does your husband feel about it?' Doctor Benson said.

'He...he doesn't know. I made a mistake – a stupid fling – and it may not be my husband's.'

'Ah.' Doctor Benson, set her pen down.

'Well that's between you and him – but the decision about whether to press on with the pregnancy rests entirely with you. Why don't you think about things for a few days and if you decide not to have the baby, I can help you to arrange a termination at a local clinic. The coil can be removed at the same time, and you'll get a full gynae MOT - make sure all is well.'

It sounded so clean and simple.

'Thank you, Doctor. I'll come back to you in a day or two.'

'Not at all. Don't bother trying to book; I've got another open surgery later in the week, just ring to check. Take care – bye-bye now.'

C

Kate made a cup of tea and put the television on; she hadn't the energy for housework. The doorbell rang and Ludo let out a sharp bark as he pranced towards the front door.

Rachel was standing there, arms crossed, face set; Ellie clung to her leg.

'Ellie's got something to say. Go on; tell Kate and Ludo, please.'

'Sorry doggie,' Ellie said, holding out a peace offering. 'Sorry for naughty spade.'

Kate laughed, 'Oh, so it was the spade was it? That's okay, Ellie – Ludo knows you're sorry. Is this a present for him? Look boy; what's this?'

Picking up its rubber scent, Ludo tore into the parcel with his teeth and ran towards the back door with his new ball.

'All friends again?' Rachel said.

'Of course. Do you fancy a coffee?'

'I won't, ta; we're off to the supermarket now...see what havoc we can create in there, eh trouble? Anyway, sorry again. See you later.'

If this baby were to come into the world, the first thing she would teach it would be kindness to animals, Kate thought, shutting the door.

♘

## BEN

When Ben thought about Spain and Gabriella it all seemed a world away. Seeing Kate again had made him realise just how stupid he'd been in throwing away the best thing he'd ever had. Now he had a real shot at getting her back and it was vital not to screw it up.

It was inconvenient that she was married – but it was obvious that there was no spark there, no throw-down. Kate had proved that by taking him back to her house and ripping his clothes off; he hadn't seen that coming! And all the guilt and shame that had come afterwards, was just shock – compounded by the fact that they'd been in the guy's own house, with curtain twitchers all around.

Tonight he'd try to convince Kate to leave Neil and start over again with him. It helped that he'd been sitting on a piece of mind-blowing news for the best part of a week; a real trump card that he'd thought was a wind-up at first.

☙

'Hi! This is Jodie from Electra Music; may I speak to Ben Wilde, please?' came a chirpy voice down the line.

'You got me,' Ben said, wondering why his record label could possibly be calling after a silence of several years.

'Are you free for a telephone meeting with Phil Merrick at say, 14.30 today?'

'As a bird. What's it about, Jodie?' Ben said.

'Mr Merrick will explain, and I'll confirm the call in an email. May I take your e-address, please, Mr Wilde?'

It had been a while since anybody had called him Mister. Whatever Merrick wanted, it must have been important - what with the PA calling ahead, and then backing it up in an email; what had happened to just picking up the phone for a natter?

☙

'Ben – how are you? Long time no speak,' Phil Merrick said. Ben couldn't remember ever meeting the guy; he'd dealt with Geoff somebody-or-other back in the day.

'I'll cut to the chase; I know you're busy,' Merrick said.

'Yeah, indeed,' Ben said, wondering how he'd fill the rest of the afternoon.

'What would you say if I told you that a major British retailer – best known for its lingerie and food – is talking to us about using Seagull for its Spring TV campaign? We're talking lifestyle; homes and gardens, fashion, swimwear - the works.'

'I'd say - you've got my attention.'

'There's more,' continued Merrick.

'They love the song, but want something less 90s, more current and relevant to today; which is why you'd be working with one of the hottest producers in Europe, Jo-Jo Dylan. Ben, you could find yourself with a major hit on your hands.'

A rash of phone calls and emails had followed, then a meeting at Electra's office in Soho. It had taken several days for the news to sink in. He'd texted Kate, keen to celebrate, but she'd been away with hubby – which had hurt – and had promised to contact him on her return. So he'd waited and waited, but when she'd called, she'd sounded odd, weary and flat.

He had to play it right tonight; show Kate that he was serious, committed – that he was re-launching his career and that he could be a grafter, too.

She'd be blown away when he told her about the TV campaign. It was all coming together now; studio time had been booked, and his Contract drafted – there had even been talk of an on-screen cameo, against a shimmering white background, with models dancing around him in swimwear. He'd chuckled at that part; it seemed particularly far-fetched, given his age and the fact that nobody would remember him.

'Ben, you've got a look they're after. The ad team thinks you'll hit the mark with their forty-plus female audience. You in a fabulous suit, amazing blown-out hair...it's all there, Ben. And anyway, 50 is the new 30 - haven't you heard?'

♻

'You look great,' Ben lied, attempting to embrace Kate, as she fumbled with her handbag and keys.

'I look like shit, which is pretty much how I feel. Can we go somewhere quiet, please? Kate said, with a weak smile.

'Whatever works for you, hon,' he said. 'Okay, you want low-key? I know just the place. Bit of a drive – about half an hour away - but the food's tasty and no one will bother us there.'

What had happened? Why the haunted look? Surely this wasn't about the last time they'd met – something else was going on here. Well, whatever had caused her to look so sad and angst-ridden, Ben would get it out of her.

He drove in the direction of Brighton for a while, coming to a stop outside a dimly lit Spanish restaurant, tucked into a small parade of shops. It was an unlikely setting, but as they passed through the shabby bar area and into a candlelit room at the back, they were greeted by the rustic smell of Andalusian food and the strains of Flamenco guitar.

'How on earth do you know this place?' Kate said.

'Oh, you know...been here once or twice,' Ben said.

♻

KATE

It was so obviously a lovers' haunt. A dozen or so tables were occupied, all by couples and despite the clichéd naff-ness of the place, with its candles jammed into wax-encrusted wine bottles, and its wedding cake walls, Kate had to admit it was cosy.

'I didn't think places like this still existed,' she said, scanning the menu.

They ordered a bottle of smoky Rioja and several types of tapas which they dove into as each terracotta bowl arrived.

Kate had spent all day getting things straight in her mind, quite sure that tonight she would cut Ben off, totally and for good. It would be the last time they'd meet and more importantly, she'd decided that Ben would never know about the baby; she corrected herself – the pregnancy - because the likelihood of Kate keeping the child was negligible, so why make a painful situation worse?

She'd have to tell Neil of course. The abortion would be grisly and it was too big a secret to keep from him. The thought of it dangling over her head like the sword of Damocles for the rest of her married life was too much to bear.

Neil would be upset, but she'd play-up the health risks - to her and the baby; both were significant.

Now, sitting here with Ben, Kate felt her resolve weakening. She looked across at him, shovelling in Potatas Bravas. There was something touching about him - big gormless kid that he was - living like a beach bum and still looking for the big break.

Well, hold that thought, Katie, girl! Life with Ben would be uncertain at best. He was talented, but he lacked focus and drive. Together, they'd be one step away from destitute. She could kiss goodbye to having a beautiful home and more significantly, to security for the rest of her life.

'Going for a slash,' Ben said, scraping his chair back.

A familiar laugh made Kate look up sharply. A few metres away her brother in law was sitting tight up to woman with tumbling brown curls and glossy red lips, who was clinging limpet-like to his arm, and hanging on his every utterance. Everything about the pair screamed intimacy.

Ben was heading back to the table, grinning, until he saw her expression.

'What's happened? You look like you've seen a ghost,' he said.

'Ben, we have to leave; now! I'll explain outside,' Kate said, gathering up her bag and phone, leaving Ben to sort the bill.

'I've just seen my brother in law cuddled up to another woman,' Kate said, once they were back in Ben's car.

'What? In there?' Ben said.

'Yes, it was definitely him. Some...female...was all over him like a rash. What the hell do I do now, Ben?' Kate felt sick. 'I hope to god he didn't see me. My poor sister!'

Ben started the engine.

'Let's find a little boozer and just chat,' he said.

Kate ignored him.

'Fifteen years, they've been married! I can't tell Alice - but if I don't, I'm colluding with him. Hey, and I have to admit, I am amazed. I didn't think Pete had it in him. That woman looked at least ten years younger.'

Ben was looking straight ahead, but she could tell he was thinking it through.

'Well, maybe it isn't what it looks like,' he said, after a pause. 'She might be a colleague or a client – or even a family member on his side – like, a niece or something.'

Kate shot him a look; 'Did you really just say that, Ben?'

She was hardly in a position to judge Pete, given that she was possibly pregnant with Ben's child.

'I need to think about this. Ben, please just take me home.'

'Okay, but one more drink...'cos, I've got news...something amazing to tell you – it will blow your mind,' Ben said, putting his foot down.

## BEN

Well that had put the kybosh on his big news. She'd already been weirded-out before they'd run into Pete, who was clearly playing away. He remembered Alice well enough; not a looker like her sister, but a decent woman, nonetheless.

It was none of his business – neither one of them meant anything to him. But Kate was freaked out by the whole thing; it didn't seem appropriate to go boasting about some big shot TV campaign now. On the other hand – maybe his news would be a bit of light relief, a welcome distraction. Who knew where women were concerned?

Spotting a well-lit pub, Ben turned in, tyres crunching on the gravel.

'Do you know this place?' Kate said.

'No. But it's a pub; how bad can it be?'

Kate didn't answer - just looked utterly miserable. Perhaps it was just her time of the month, but best not to mention that; in Ben's experience, nothing made women more furious than implying their hormones were to blame for any kind of upset.

---

'Go on, have a proper drink – it might cheer you up a bit,' Ben said, watching her sip Diet Coke.

'I can assure you, it won't.' Kate said.

She'd got the hump – miserable cow. He looked around, searching for inspiration. It was a Ma and Pa pub; conservatively dressed middle aged people were tucking into scampi & chips and shepherd's pie.

'Look at all these boring old gits,' Ben said; 'In their beige slacks and cardigans, with their Fords parked outside.'

'Ben, why do you have to be so rude and dismissive about everyone? They're just normal people – and sorry to burst your bubble, but some of these 'old gits' are younger than you! You should see a doctor about that Peter Pan complex of yours.'

'Oh, that's nice,' Ben said, 'that's charming, that is! Kate, what's got into you?' She didn't answer, just shook her head, eyes downcast.

'Can I do anything to help? Anything at all – just name it,'

'Ben. Please. Get off my case. Why do you think I feel like shit? The last time we met...you and me, rolling about on the carpet like savages. Nearly six years I've been married to Neil – and then you come along and wreck it all. It's broken now, Ben – things will never be the same.'

He felt sorry for her. Almost.

'It's not as though I attacked you. You wanted it every bit as much as me...regretting it is one thing, but don't be in denial, Kate - that's not fair.'

He was bored now; tired of the histrionics. All he'd wanted was a pat on the back – for her to share in his good news. He'd forgotten about her sullen streak – and how stubborn she could be. Maybe she did love her husband, and it had been a moment's madness. It was all looking too much like hard work now – and he had other priorities.

Kate sighed; 'So what did you want to tell me?' she said.

'I can hardly be arsed mentioning it now...'

'Oh, go on, Ben – please. What's happened?'

Ben explained about the phone call from Electra; the TV campaign – and the generous advance that went with it.

'I might even be in the ad,' he said. 'But that's not settled yet...

either way, this is massive for me, Kate - huge!'

'Seriously? Ben! That is big news,' Kate said. 'Congratulations! This could be it; the big break. Ooh, you're not just a pretty face, Ben Wilde.'

She was back in the room.

# CHAPTER 10:
## GETTING THINGS SORTED

KATE

Kate marvelled at her own powers of deception. She'd known she was pregnant for a week and still Neil was clueless. But that had to change. She called Doctor Benson and confirmed her decision.

'I'd like to go ahead with the termination, Doctor,' Kate said, 'I'm going to tell my husband this weekend – but really, it doesn't matter what he thinks because we are not having...no *I*...am not having this baby.'

'And that is absolutely your choice,' said Doctor Benson, 'But you know, you can take a little more time over this – things are at a very early stage. Why not confirm after you've talked things through at home.'

'I can assure you, I won't be changing my mind, but I'll give you another call on Monday to finalise things.'

Kate hung up, feeling sick at heart as well as in her stomach.

She'd played out the conversation with Neil in her head; it sounded thin and hollow. It was terrifying to the think that Neil might get a sixth sense about the possibility of the baby not being his – although common sense told her that it was pure paranoia to think such a thing. Why on earth would Neil even question who the father was? No, the problem would be getting him to accept her decision to end the pregnancy.

'Thank you darling; you know that lasagne is my all-time favourite. Are you okay, sweetheart? You look a bit tired.' Neil said.

Kate topped up his glass – then filled her own, thinking, sod it, I'm not having the baby so why avoid alcohol? And anyway, she needed the Dutch courage.

'Neil, I need to tell you something. I just want to... say it...and then we'll talk about it some more.'

'Okay,' Neil waited.

'I ... oh god.' Deep breath; 'I'm pregnant. Just a few weeks – but anyway, I am. And Neil, I'm not having this baby – I already know that.'

Kate watched as Neil's face registered disbelief, then joy, then confusion – emotions rolling over him like a Mexican wave.

'Oh god, Katie. How long have you known? Why the hell didn't you tell me?' He took a large glug of wine.

'Only a few days, but I've already seen Doctor Benson and I've told her I can't go through with it.'

'But...why...? Don't I get a say in this? Shouldn't this be a joint decision? I am the baby's Dad, after all.'

'Neil, please don't. You know I've never wanted children...and... have you any idea about the complications of having kids so late? The risks - to me...and the baby. Neil, the chances of it being...of... having some kind of special needs – are pretty steep. Please don't fight me on this. I'm clear about what I want.'

'So I see.' Neil drained his glass. 'So that's it? Honestly, I don't know why you bothered to tell me at all if it's a done deal.'

'Because you're my husband and I love you. And we don't have secrets, do we?'

Neil looked deflated; 'Shit Kate... look, I'll be okay. I just need time to adjust to the news. In the end, I'll support you whatever you do and I'll come with you for the procedure.'

At least he hadn't used the word abortion. Kate knelt before him and leant her head on his chest; even after a shock, Neil's heart beat strong and steady.

'My rock,' she murmured into his shirt. 'Thank you...that means so much.'

They put the television on as a distraction, but every other commercial seemed to be for baby products, or for family cars, with cute kids singing in the back seat.

'Let's take Ludo out,' Neil suggested.

They walked in silence at first, collars pulled up against the early autumn chill.

'Kate,' Neil said, 'What if we are making a mistake and this is fate. You know - our last shot at being parents...and it was meant to be.'

'It isn't fate, baby – it was an accident because my coil failed. Neil, we didn't plan this. There's too much that could go wrong and even if we had a healthy child, can you imagine all those sleepless nights at our age? And the buck stops with me, because you're in London all week. I just can't do it – I can't.' Kate's voice was shrill in the stillness.

'Shush, don't tell everybody,' Neil said, 'If you're absolutely sure – let's book it up and I'll take a couple of days off work.'

G

It had happened quickly, in a small clinic that looked for all the world like a smart Georgian townhouse, except for the tell-tale carpark and wheelchair ramp - and the smell of antiseptic and something unidentifiable that Kate would remember for the rest of her life.

Clutching Neil's hand, she'd been shown to a small room, with magnolia walls and a clean narrow bed. On it was a gown in a polythene wrapper. A wall mounted TV and a night stand were the only other objects in the room, its emptiness mirroring Kate's soul.

She'd barely had time to change into the gown (which Neil had tied because Kate's hands were shaking too much) when a smiling blonde nurse led Kate to theatre. It had all been explained to her beforehand at the rather business-like consultation.

She was to have an MVA; 'Or to give it its full name, a manual vacuum aspiration procedure. You're lucky; it's the gentlest method we use. Almost no pain, just some cramping and probably a bit of nausea, too,' the doctor explained.

Kate wasn't feeling very lucky.

But after an hour, she was back in the stark little room, with Neil sitting on the bed, holding her hand.

'It's over – how are you feeling, darling?' he said.

Kate opened her mouth to speak, but no words came. Tears coursed down her white face.

'Just awful,' she said. 'Like I've been turned inside out.'

'Oh Katie, you poor love. I'm so sorry. We'll be home soon and I am going to spoil you for the next 48 hours. Seriously, don't you worry about a thing.'

Overwhelmed by exhaustion, guilt and relief, Kate dozed on the sofa, under a cosy fleece, with Ludo curled up beside her. When she woke up, thirsty and disorientated, it was dark outside.

'Can you manage a little something to eat?' Neil asked.

'I'd love a cup of tea, please. Anyway, I'm not ill, darling – just tired and a bit sore.'

'But it's been an ordeal, too. You're bound to feel like crap for a while.' Neil's face was a mask of concern.

'What have I done to deserve you?' Kate said, pulling the blanket around her.

ⓒ

## MARTIN

Jan had returned from the coast in a reflective mood. No doubt her brother had been filling her head with nonsense all week. It wasn't so much that Martin and Russell clashed – these days it was more a case of them not acknowledging each other at all. There was no meeting of minds, no male camaraderie, and not a scrap of affection.

In the early days, keen to ingratiate himself, Martin had made considerable effort with his new brother-in-law, even though it was apparent from the off that he, and the real-ale drinking, railway-enthusiast Russell had little in common.

All the usual inroads for male-bonding, like football, golf and fishing, had been met with indifference. And Russell had a rather sneering and contemptuous way of letting Martin know exactly what he could do with his well-intentioned invitations.

'I don't do fishing,' he'd said, his six foot one bulk towering over Martin's compact frame. He had an unpleasant way of delivering such statements, unsmiling and whilst doing something else entirely, like polishing his wire spectacles on the hem of his shirt.

At first Martin had felt sorry for him - for his lack of success with women mainly, although Russell seemed disinterested in meeting anyone.

'He's got his trains, hasn't he?' Jan said, as though that explained everything – and to a point, it did. After all, how could any woman fall for a middle-aged man who played with a model railway most nights of the week - except for Friday evenings, which were rigidly reserved for drinking real-ale at the Phoenix Social Club on the sea-front?

So after being rebuffed several times, Martin had stopped making an effort - and had felt rather liberated for it. The consequence was that Jan made furtive phone calls to her brother either when Martin was at work, or in hushed tones sitting on the stairs while Martin was occupied elsewhere.

&#9731;

So after five days in Goring-by-Sea, Jan had returned with colour in her cheeks, a rounder belly (for which she'd blamed fish and chips eaten sitting on the sea-wall most days), and a distracted air that Martin couldn't quite place.

'Ta-da!' he said, throwing open the living room door.

Jan sniffed the air like a terrier. 'What paint did you use?' she said.

'Dulux. Does it matter? What do you think?' He waited.

'I suppose it looks fresher,' Jan said at last.

Fresher? If he'd wanted to be damned by faint praise, he'd have resurrected his parents for the day; that was just the kind of remark his mother would have made.

Ignoring Jan's lack of enthusiasm, Martin opened the back door.

'The garden's next. I'm looking into getting a hot tub.' he said, waiting for the information to percolate.

'A hot tub? Why on earth would we want a hot tub? And anyway, surely we can't afford one.'

'Jan, you've always left the money side to me – so don't start worrying about it now,' Martin said.

Why couldn't she be enthusiastic for once? He imagined the two of them, relaxing in a Jacuzzi, on the crazy-paving at the back.

But the picture was flawed. Jan's slack, putty-coloured limbs in a bathing costume, her lank hair frizzed by steam, wearing that perpetual look of disappointment; it didn't fit somehow.

'Most women would be excited,' Martin grumbled, 'A bit of luxury – Jan, you might show some appreciation.' He didn't care that he sounded peevish.

'I'm sorry, Martin, but it's a daft idea – I can't think why you're even considering it. And imagine what the neighbours will think. The Robson's are in their eighties – they don't want to look out of their bedroom window and see that! I don't know what's got into you – you've been weird for months.'

'I've been weird? I'll tell you what's weird – shall I?' He stopped abruptly. 'Anyway, stuff the neighbours. I couldn't care less.' He stomped into the kitchen, made tea and opened a packet of bourbons. Martin watched Jan blowing on her tea, tiny crumbs on the down of her top lip. When had they become so old? They'd both turned fifty-two in the last year, but Jan could be taken for someone considerably older.

Half-closing his eyes, Martin pictured Lisa.

Jan was looking at him, quizzically.

'What is it Mart? Please tell me. Is it...do you miss sex? I know it's been a long time, but...'

'A long time?' Martin said. 'Well, you could say that – if several years is a long time. But it depends, doesn't it? I mean, it's been so long, it just wouldn't be right now. And let's face it - we've both... let ourselves go a bit, haven't we?'

'You mean me, don't you? Do you think I like being like this? Martin, nobody wakes up one day and says to themselves 'ooh, I wish I had depression'. It's only the tablets that stop me doing myself in!' Jan shouted.

Well, let her shout; perhaps they needed to shake things up a bit, clear the air.

'Maybe you'd be better off without me,' Jan said, her back to him.

'Absolute rubbish! In sickness and in health, remember?' Martin sighed. 'I'm sorry, my love. You're right; I'm not myself at the moment...probably just tired after all that DIY, it's never been my thing.'

Martin put his arms around her; she smelt of fried food.

'I don't mind about the nookie,' Martin said, 'But I could do with a cuddle.'

He needed to get a grip. Jan was right; he had been acting weird, ever since Hayley had moved out. Something had come loose at that point, had unravelled, as he'd gazed into a future that promised emptiness and silence, drudgery and routine - an abyss that frightened him. Then he'd tasted something new and alive at the Hunters' party; he'd danced with a gorgeous woman, and drunk champagne; people had laughed at his jokes and confided in him. But none of that was real life. This was real life; the only life he'd ever known.

Jan was looking at the newly painted walls.

'It's a nice shade of grey,' she said, 'I'll get used to it.'

☾

## LISA

It was beginning to eat away at her; all that money, just sitting in the building society. Lisa had never given money a second thought, there had always been more than enough – Justin had seen to that. Now there seemed too much.

She confided in Tanya.

'Babe, you can never be too rich or too thin. What a funny thing to get stressed about! Wish I had that problem,' her friend said, examining the new manicure that Lisa has just paid for.

Lisa sighed.

'Sorry, I didn't mean it like that. I know I'm lucky and … what I'm trying to say is that it seems such a waste – me having half a million quid in the bank, just sitting there, when I could do something useful with it. The house is paid for, so is my car and I've got more clothes than I can ever wear. And you know what, Tanya? I always thought I'd go back to work - you know, train for something or open a little business. If Justin hadn't died, I'd have needed to earn my own living. It used to be a little goal for me, knowing that I'd have to do something in another six months or so – like a deadline.' Lisa said, stirring her cappuccino thoughtfully.

It was Saturday afternoon and the coffee bar was filled with locals, taking a break from the drudgery of shopping and tedious errands.

'Still doesn't sound like a problem to me,' Tanya said. 'That money'll give you security for life, babe. And anyway, there's nothing to stop you using some of it to start a business. There's loads you could do.'

'Like what?'

'You could open a little boutique... or a home interiors shop... or you could start some sort of service business, like cleaning or house sitting, or something.'

'Oh charming,' Lisa said, 'Is that how you see me?'

'No, you plonker – you don't clean, you manage a team that does. It was just a thought. But you know what else you should do, honey? You need to see a financial adviser – better safe than sorry.'

Lisa was about to ask Tanya how she might go about that, when Martin Bevan walked up to the counter and ordered a latte.

'And do you have the lemon muffins with the soft centre today?' he said, in his slightly nasal voice. The young barista shook his head and pointed out a number of alternatives.

'No thank you; it has to be the lemon I'm afraid. Why you keep taking them off, I'll never know.'

'It's him, from Claire's party,' Tanya said, nudging her friend 'I suppose we'd better say hello.'

Martin was walking towards them, carrying his takeaway cup.

'Greetings ladies,' he said, with a tight smile.

'Hiya, how are things?' Lisa said pleasantly.

'Oh, mustn't grumble,' Martin set his cup down as they rattled through the usual small talk topics of work and weather before he made his excuses and left.

'He gives me the creeps,' Lisa said with a shudder.

'I thought you liked him – you were dancing with him at Claire's. I thought he was quite sweet, funny too.'

'Well so did I when I had my champagne goggles on, but then he turned up at mine the next day – I told you, remember? And it was awkward... oh, and then when I did the interview with that tabloid tosser, he used that photo of us together, and it looked like something was going on, when it sooo wasn't. I don't know – he just makes me uncomfortable.'

'He's harmless. Do you want a cake?' Tanya returned with chocolate tiffin and two more coffees.

'How's your mum, Leese?' Tanya said.

'Alright as far as I know...we haven't spoken this week. You know Rita, she only rings me when she wants something – or to have a moan. At least she made an effort when Justin died - that's something I suppose.'

Tanya snorted; 'It was the least she could do.'

'Do you ever feel like you could just fade away into the

background and nobody would even notice?' Lisa said. 'I honestly think that if I died in a ditch tomorrow, nobody would realise for weeks, except Nellie of course.'

'That's a horrible thing to say – and it's not true,' said Tanya. 'I'd miss you like mad, you're my best friend.'

'I know, sweetie – thank you. But what have I got? No husband, no kids, my mum doesn't give a shit, my sister's in Portugal and I've lost touch with all my friends. I don't work – and now I don't even need to! I feel like I've become this... shadow person.'

'Lisa, if that's how you feel you need to do something about it. A part time job would be a start, not for the money, but to get you back out there. Hon, I don't think you realise how gorgeous you are and how much you've got to offer,' Tanya said.

☙

Bliss Recruitment appeared to be wedged firmly in the eighties with grey and red carpet tiles, strip lighting and pot plants sporting a visible layer of dust. The pungent smell of hair tint wafted up from the salon below.

Judging by the speed with which Beth, Simon and Dave respectively answered the surprisingly busy telephone lines, Lisa guessed they were on commission.

'Do you want to come over?' said a young man who'd answered the 'phone as 'Simon-Speaking'; he indicated the chair in front of him. Lisa sat nervously.

'So, you're looking for a local position,' he said, mine-sweeping her hastily scrawled application form.

'Yes. Well, preferably.'

'Right...so looking at this...Lisa – can I call you Lisa? You haven't worked for some time.' It felt like an inauspicious start; Lisa steeled herself to press on with the interview.

'It's been a long time since I had a formal position, but I've always kept very busy and I've continued to utilise my skills,' she said, sticking to the script that she and Tanya had devised.

'Okay, tell me about that,' said Simon, noting something on his pad.

'So, I was head receptionist at a spa and gym for nearly three years, which was where I met my husband. He was a footballer, you see, so I became his PA and...'

'Ah, the beautiful game,' Simon was wistful; 'Who'd he play for?'

'County; I was married to Justin Dixon. He was a striker but then he had an accident and...'

'Oh I know exactly who Justin Dixon is – was,' Simon corrected himself. 'He died recently, didn't he? Look, I'm so sorry. He was a superbly gifted player – the cruel hand of fate,' he said, shaking his head and drifting off for a moment.

'Thank you. It was a terrible shock as you can imagine. Well, anyway – I moved to this area recently and I'm keen to go back to work on a more formal footing, so to speak.'

'I see. Would you be happy with another front of house role? There's something just in that might be right for you.'

Lisa's eyes widened. 'Oh yes, definitely,' she said, encouraged.

Simon rattled his keyboard for a moment.

'Ah yes, this one might be perfect,' he read; 'A private clinic just outside Tunbridge Wells is looking for a receptionist, Monday to Friday, afternoons only – it's a job share with one other person. Well presented, well-spoken, required to greet all clients and guests, answer the telephone, keep the appointment software up to date, offer refreshments etc, etc. Think you can do that?' Simon gave Lisa the benefit of his flawless smile. 'Oh, and it says here that most of the procedures are cosmetic, and that many of the clients are celebrities. Discretion is a must, official checks blah blah blah.'

'Wow, sounds fabulous. Do you think you can get me an interview?'

'Let me play around with your CV, make it a little more... current, shall we say? Leave it with me, Lisa. I will certainly do my best.'

☕

After five days of radio silence, Lisa's mobile rang while she was still in her dressing gown, watching breakfast television with Nellie snuggled on her lap.

'Lisa? It's Simon from Bliss Recruitment. I managed to get you an interview at the clinic. It's all a bit of a rush though; can you do three o'clock this afternoon?'

'Er, yes – of course. Thank you so much!'

Then she'd panicked about what to wear and how to get there; what on earth had people done before SatNav? She rang Tanya from the car.

'Hello babe – it's me. You'll never guess what I'm doing...no, try again...I'm on my way to an interview! Receptionist for a private clinic... I'm so excited. And you know what, Tan? I'm going to get this!'

☕

# CHAPTER 11:
## DEGREES OF TRUTH

### Kate

After what Kate now referred to as 'the procedure', she had been weepy and listless for days. It wasn't regret exactly – after all, she'd been clear about not wanting children all her life and in that regard, nothing had changed.

But she could feel the lies beginning to calcify inside her. She'd deceived Neil, letting him grieve for a child that may not have been his. She'd been cold to Ben, shutting him out after leading him on – playing him like a fish on a line.

Almost as painful was that she hadn't told Alice about the abortion – or about the fact that she'd seen Peter smooching with another woman.

'You're bound to feel rubbish for a while,' Neil said, smoothing her hair; he seemed to be in a perpetual state of crooning, rubbing or stroking, which only made Kate feel worse.

'I don't deserve you,' she said.

♔

Even walking Ludo had become a chore. Summer had truly been extinguished. Browning leaves swirled on an unusually harsh wind for late September, and the rain beat cold on her face. Kate remembered the bleakness of the previous winter, and her feelings of utter desolation; remembering frightened her.

'Hello dear, penny for them?' said a kind voice.

Kate was startled. 'Moira. How are you?'

'Oh fine, thanks, Katie love,' her neighbour said, falling in step and absently patting the damp dog.

'I've just been up to the post office,' Moira said. 'Autumn's truly upon us now, isn't it? But we can't complain; we did have a glorious summer. Are you alright, love? You look terribly sad today.'

On hearing the softness in the older woman's voice, a flood-gate began to swing open.

'No, not really,' Kate said, blinking back the tears which never seemed far away.

'Why don't I keep you company to the Green and back, and then you and Ludo must come home with me and we'll have a cuppa. Clifford's gone to a museum with his pals, so nobody will bother us. Sometimes talking helps.' Moira said.

The two women walked to what locals referred to as the cricket green. As yet, no cricket team had materialised, instead it was a place where teenagers congregated to smoke and drink after dark and where the smaller children played ball games and made camps. Nobody was playing or hanging out today.

Cutting the route short, they headed in the direction of home.

'Come and tell me all about it,' insisted Moira.

'You're very kind,' Kate said, 'have you got an old towel for the boy?'

Ludo stood patiently in Moira's spotless hallway, while Kate rubbed him down and gave him a biscuit from her pocket.

'Come through, dear; white without?' Moira said, filling the kettle.

'Oh, Moira,' Kate said, 'I'm made a terrible mess of things. I don't know where to start.'

'Wherever you want to, Katie love. We all make mistakes - I'm not here to judge.'

Kate looked around Moira's kitchen; at the family photographs on the walls, the dresser stuffed with ceramic knick-knacks, of pinned-up postcards, the Hallmark plaque that said World's Best Grandma - and all the chickens. She surely could not burden this lovely woman, who, married for forty-odd years was loyalty personified, with her own sordid secrets. Could she?

'Moira – I recently had a termination...of a pregnancy, I mean.'

'Oh dear, Katie, love. How truly awful for you both. I'm so sorry – I had no idea you and Neil were trying for a family,' Moira said, looking cut up.

'We weren't – aren't. That's just it; the baby was an accident although if it was up to Neil, we'd have gone through with it. He'd always wanted to be a dad.' Kate was surprised by how much it hurt to say the words aloud.

'Anyway, the thing is...' she hesitated. Moira did not need the full unexpurgated horror story - she'd stick to the headlines, which were grim enough. Ben would have to remain her guilty secret; she wasn't in a confessional box, or on a shrink's couch, she was with her next door neighbour and the risks were immense.

'The thing is,' Kate continued, 'I haven't told my sister...and she's my best friend.'

'Are you worried she'll judge you for having the abortion?'

'No - well a bit. Alice is a wonderful mum and there's no doubt it would upset her. But there's something else, too.' Kate exhaled audibly.

'I'm listening,' Moira refilled Kate's cup with strong tea.

'Oh god – this is awful. Well, a couple of weeks ago I went for a drink with a friend, to some funny little bar in the middle of nowhere – can't even remember what it was called – but anyway... my sister's husband was there, snuggled up to another woman.'

Moira gasped.

'Yes, that is tricky. You don't want to be the bearer of bad news, but if you don't say anything...well, you know how that will end. But Kate, are you sure about what you saw? Could there have been an innocent explanation?'

Kate shook her head – that much at least she was sure of.

Ć

That evening, Kate rang Alice.

'Hello darling, it's me. How are you, Al? Yeah? Good. Look we need to talk and it's a long one, I'm afraid.'

'Okay, what's up? You've got me worried now.'

'Sorry, Al. Look, I'm fine - have you got fifteen minutes or so?'

'Of course. Anyway, I'm by myself. Pete's working late and Nat's on a sleepover, so chat away.'

Then taking Moira's advice, Kate gently told Alice about the abortion.

'Jesus, Kate. I wish you'd talked to me about it first,' Alice's tone was shocked and brittle.

'I...I just wanted it over with, I suppose.'

'But love, I'm your sister – I could have supported you... gone with you...'

'Or talked me out of it – and don't pretend you wouldn't have tried, Alice. Look I'm not proud of it...it was horrible - and upsetting for Neil, too.'

'Shit, Katie. How are you both? Do you think you need counselling?'

Kate scoffed; 'God, no! I don't want to go raking it all up again. It's over and that's the end of it. But I hate there being secrets between us and it would have come out sooner or later...so...'

Kate sighed. It was a relief to have told Alice about the baby, but there was so much left unsaid; about Ben and about Pete. When she'd confided in Moira about the mystery brunette, her reaction had been measured.

'I see your dilemma, dear,' Moira had said, 'But you can't go interfering in your sister's marriage – because that's how she'll see it - however well intentioned. And men are funny creatures; perhaps this woman is just a younger colleague, somebody who flatters him and in reality there's nothing much going on. By telling your sister, you risk creating a mountain out of a mole hill. If I were you, I'd try and ask him about it – but tread carefully, Katie love, you don't want to back him into a corner.'

'Alice,' Kate said, 'I'm sorry I didn't talk to you. I think I just went into shock about it. But I'm glad we've had the conversation now. You would tell me if you had anything bothering you, wouldn't you?'

'Such as?'

'Well, how are things at home...with Pete? Are you two okay?'

'Fine – if you dis-count the fact that he's never here,' Alice said.

'Well, why isn't he? You know I think the world of Pete, but there's more to life than work...and believe me, I have exactly the same conversation with Neil all the time.'

'Well at least I know he's not hiding anything now. I confronted him recently about creeping around and locking the bathroom door. And do you know what he said, Katie? He admitted he's embarrassed about having gained a few pounds...which surprised me, cos I never think of Pete as having a scrap of vanity.'

'Well, I hope for everyone's sake that's all it is,' Kate said, bringing the conversation to a close, before she could blurt out the real reason for Pete's furtive behaviour.

ど

The next day, before she could rationalise her way out of it, Kate rang Pete's mobile, something she'd never done, although they'd swapped numbers years earlier, in case of emergencies.

Pete sounded surprised, 'Everything okay?'

'Yes, fine. But I need to speak to you, privately if possible – can you talk?'

There was a pause. 'Not really – can I give you a call back in about ten minutes?'

There was an edge to his voice when Pete rang back.

'What's up, Kate?'

'Look Pete, I hate doing this, so I'm just going to come out and say it before I change my mind. I saw you out with a woman.'

Silence yawned.

'...in a Spanish restaurant, a few weeks ago,' Kate pressed on. 'Pete, who the hell was that?'

Again, a pause while presumably Pete was trying to figure out whether to concoct a story or simply deny everything.

'Peter; just talk to me.'

'Kate, please don't tell Alice – it was nothing. That was Melanie, someone I work with. She's going through a tough time...I was just trying to...to cheer her up. We're friends, that's all.'

'Oh, spare me!' Kate snapped. 'You looked like an item from where I was sitting! I was there, Pete...with a friend...I saw you cosied up together. How long have you been seeing her? Is it serious?'

'No! I mean, I'm not seeing her – it was a one-off and we haven't slept together. And we won't. Kate, please don't tell Alice, it would upset her so much – and needlessly when nothing has actually happened. Look, I promise you now, I won't even socialise with Mel again...it was the first, last and only time. Please, Kate.'

He'd sounded so desperate that Kate had agreed to tell no one; she'd made him swear to keep any contact strictly professional, and by then, Pete had been babbling with gratitude.

She'd hung up, wincing at the idea of judging someone else after what had happened with Ben.

## BEN

By three in the morning Ben had drained the mini-bar – he'd even eaten the nuts and chocolate and now he was buzzing, playing the day over and over in his head.

In the morning, he'd worked on the new mix of Seagull, with a twenty-eight year old shit-hot producer who'd made it sound fresh and current. Everyone in the studio had agreed that it wiped the floor with the original version – and he didn't know how to feel about that.

But it was very cool the way they'd treated him like a star; fawning around him, fetching whatever he wanted, and arranging a limo to ferry him around town. Ben hadn't expected to be put up in such a smart hotel either; bonus.

Then, as he was about to leave, Nicole, the studio manager, who'd been hovering at hand all day, had pressed her business card into his hand.

'Call me if you need anything,' she'd said, flashing him a huge smile that lit up beautiful, thickly fringed almond eyes.

'Right...er, thanks.' What had just happened? Had she hit on him, or did she mean in a professional capacity?

'Anything at all,' she'd added, sensing his confusion. He'd watched her glide away, long legs encased in skinny black jeans and boots with knitting-needle heels; she'd glanced back over her shoulder, tossing her long brunette pony-tail.

Bloody hell - he might just do that!

Things were going nowhere with Kate. Their last meeting had been awful - something had been terribly wrong, he'd never seen her so anxious and withdrawn. He'd sent texts, several emails and had tried calling her mobile more than once – and she'd blanked him. It was hard to believe she'd binned him off before things had even begun, but perhaps it was time to accept that she loved what's-his-face after all. Well how dumb would she feel when he was splashed all over the TV and the press?

In the afternoon, still on a post-studio high, Ben had met the director, Warren Burke who had an implausible accent and an elaborate comb-over. Warren and the casting director, Sandra-something, had gone over the story board to discuss Ben's role in the ad – which in truth, was nominal, no more than a walk-on, high-fiving a few of the girls as they jiggled past.

He'd almost choked when he saw the models they were using; of the five glamourzons that had been cast, he recognised four as true supermodels. How on earth was he going to get through the shoot without making a total idiot of himself, and getting a hard-on? He'd have to be on best behaviour. Ben laughed wryly – they were young enough to be his daughters, or even his granddaughters.

Things were starting to get very surreal indeed, but hey, he'd go with the flow. In two weeks he'd be filming, then it was out of his hands and into to the techie paws of the post-production geeks, and the next thing he'd know about it, would be when the campaign broke in the spring. Funny to think that one minute he'd be watching the telly like anyone else - the next, his own ugly mug would pop up. He chuckled in the darkness, despite the discomfort in his chest. No wonder he couldn't sleep; the nuts had given him indigestion.

Perhaps he'd ring Kate one last time in the morning; there was so much to say - and nobody else to tell.

## MARTIN

Fridays could go either way in the shop; dead some weeks, but on others it was a struggle to get everything done by the weekend. Today, Martin had completed two site visits by lunchtime, both on the estate. The first had felt like a fishing expedition, but the second, to a couple with a fleet of ostentatious cars in the drive and too many garden ornaments for comfort, had all but signed on the spot.

Lately business had been good. In fact, life had been good; well better, at any rate.

Jan seemed calmer – content almost, and he'd been encouraged by small changes, like the fact that she was bathing daily, and getting out more. She'd even come into the shop once – unheard of in recent years.

'You've just missed Jan,' Trina said, when Martin returned from a recce.

'Oh? What did she want?'

'Just saying hello, I think – she was on her way to Tesco's. She used the loo and then made tea in the back office, made me one, too – bless her.'

'Oh, that's nice,' Martin said, feeling a prickle of discomfort, although he couldn't think why.

That evening, Jan had been silent and watchful.

'Sorry I missed you today, my love. I was on a job over Sevenoaks way. Trina said you made her a cuppa.'

Jan had nodded - and then looked at him in the strangest way, before laying the table for dinner.

☾

Martin had made a concerted effort to forget about Lisa Dixon; he hadn't so much as driven past her house in the last few weeks. When he thought about her now – starting with the time he'd peeked into her underwear drawer – his skin crawled with shame. The woman was his mid-life crisis personified, he could see that now. How could he have thought for one minute that she'd fancied him? It was preposterous!

☾

'Ooh hello there – do you need any help, sir?' Trina sang loudly, in the way the young often address the old.

'Yes, thank you, Trina,' Martin said, shooting her a look.

'Still thinking about runners for your hallway, sir?' Martin said, smiling benignly at the old man. It was raining hard and Mr Whittle had brought leaves and other street debris in on his scuffed brown shoes.

'Would you like a cup of tea, Mr Whittle?' Martin said. 'Trina, love – put the kettle on and crack open those bourbons will you?'

'How's Mrs Whittle,' Martin asked, steering the old man to a seat.

'Not so good,' Mr Whittle said, blowing on his tea.

'Aww, you are lovely, boss. That was so kind of you,' Trina said, after Mr Whittle had gone. 'I reckon he just comes in for a chat and a warm.'

'You might be right there, Trina. If he comes in and I'm not about, make sure you look after him, will you?'

'Bless you,' Trina said, surprising Martin with a hug.

# PART TWO

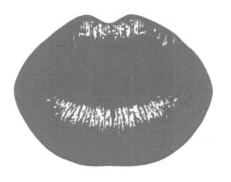

SEEKING EDEN

# CHAPTER 1:
## THE RETURN OF SPRING

### KATE

For the third time that evening, Kate was suffused with irritation and fascination in equal measure. For someone who didn't watch much television, she was certainly seeing a lot of Ben's smug face.

There he was - in a fashionable suit, his suspiciously dark mane smoothed and blown to perfection, moving rhythmically, as a collection of bikini-clad stick insects jerked past.

Nauseating as this spectacle was, Kate had to admit that the music was brilliant. Seagull had been speeded-up and remixed to a dance beat, and Ben's voice had acquired a new and smouldering depth; it came as no surprise when the new mix began to fly up the download charts.

But seeing the ad made Kate feel queasy; a stark (and regular) reminder of her biggest mistake.

'Do you know who that is?' she'd said, when she and Neil had watched the commercial together.

'Giselle?'

'Not her - the guy in the middle,' Kate said.

'Haven't a clue – should I?'

'That,' Kate had said, in as neutral a tone as she could muster 'Is my ex-boyfriend, Ben Wilde. The one that buggered off to Spain and never came back. I told you about him, remember? '

'Blimey,' Neil's eyes had glittered with intrigue. 'He's very good looking, isn't he?'

'Thinks he is,' Kate had muttered grudgingly.

'The ad's great. I'd kill for an account like that. And I love the music, it's so catchy...all the young people at work are singing it. You should send him an email; see what he's up to.'

Kate had been mortified; 'Why on earth would I do that?'

'I don't know - just a thought. Aren't you curious about him, about what's going on in his life?'

'No. Anyway, we can all see what's going on – and he's doing pretty well for himself it seems.' Kate said.

'Then you should be happy for him. You loved him once – don't be sour, Katie, that's not like you...unless of course, you're feeling wistful for the past. I can see the appeal of being a rock star's missus.'

It was a playful remark, but Kate had failed to see the funny side, wondering if on some unconscious level, Neil had been right – and that regret lurked somewhere deep in her psyche. Only last summer, Ben had made his feelings plain, telling Kate that he loved her – or as he'd put it during one last desperate pitch, was offering 'the whole shebang – marriage, the works, if that's what it takes.'

She'd sent him away, leaving no room for doubt. Raw from the abortion, consumed with guilt and shame, and desperate to regain equilibrium with Neil, Kate had cut Ben off entirely and after a while, the emails and texts had stopped coming.

Instead she'd thrown herself into a tough round of distraction tac-tics; contacting old clients in a bid to drum up more business – which had worked to a point - going to the gym most days, baking and cooking lavish meals, and enjoying a daily dog-walk with Lisa, which had become a favourite part of her routine.

It was comical to see Ludo and Nellie playing in the woods at the back of Lisa's house. What the little Chihuahua lacked in stature, she made up for in attitude, barking at Ludo to slow down and wait for her; he would dutifully obey, circling back to Nellie, going down on his front paws and nudging her with his pointy muzzle. The women were charmed by their 'fur-babies', as Lisa called them.

Springtime in Eden Hill was breath-taking; Kate found herself anticipating nature's bounty. She remembered that the cherry blossom trees lining the avenues began to pop in late March, and that in the woods, the lacy white flowers that covered the mossy floor appeared before the bluebells, through April and May. In the lanes, elderflower bushes quivered delicately, wafting their honeyed scent, while the cow parsley seemed to spurt up through the hedgerows overnight.

Not that the women's conversation was much geared to wild flowers. To Kate's surprise and delight, Lisa was funny. She had a way of telling even the most mundane story, with a roll of her eyes, or a throw-away, self-deprecating comment that made Kate laugh out loud. There was a sweetness about her, too – it was obvious that Lisa liked to make others feel good.

'Ooh, Katie, your hair looks fab today; have you used a new shampoo?' She'd say, or 'I can tell you've upped the squats and lunges; your butt looks amazing!'

'When we first met,' Kate said, while the dogs ran ahead, 'I thought you were absolutely gorgeous, but also very high maintenance! Well I was right about the first thing, but I'm so glad you're not one of those women that can't live without hair straighteners, or eyelash extensions – or something equally daft.'

'Oh, I probably was like that once. But then one day, you realise that it's all just superficial crap. Things happen that remind you what's important. It's been almost a year now, you know...' Lisa trailed off.

'Do you miss Justin?' Kate said.

'Not exactly; we hardly saw each other during the last couple of years of his life. You know what though, Katie? I have forgiven myself. And it's taken a long time, but I knew him better than anyone, and I'm certain that the way he died was an accident, and that I did my best for that man all through our marriage. You wouldn't believe what I put up with for all those years.'

'Must have been grim,' Kate shuddered at the thought of mopping up after a depressive drunk, year after year – even Ben had never put her through that.

'I was an idiot, too,' Lisa said, 'I can't believe I gave that horrible journalist an interview. I must have been in a right state to have done that. Beats me why he was so interested – it's like he was on a mission to dish the dirt; I do wonder sometimes where all that came from.'

'Don't think about it,' Kate said, 'It's in the past and it doesn't matter now. But what I can't understand is why you haven't met anyone else. You're smart, you're funny, you're kind – and look at you; er, hello-o?'

Lisa giggled; 'Bless you, Hon, you say the sweetest things. But I only seem to meet wide- boys and pillocks. There is someone I like though. Oh god, Katie - I'm such a cliché; it's one of the surgeons at work, Rupert Dale. And it's not just because he's drop-dead gorgeous – although that helps - it's because he's so clever. But, hey, I'm under no illusion – he'd never look at me.'

'Why on earth do you think that? That's ridiculous. Is he single?' Kate said, trailing her fingertips through the waist-high cow-parsley.

'The rumour is that he got divorced last year. They've got two teenagers at boarding school, so even if he did fancy me, it would be messy. Shame, I honestly can't remember the last time I even looked at anyone that way. Ha! That would be funny though...from footballer's wife to plastic surgeon's muse.'

'But why ever not, Lisa?'

'Because blokes like that aren't interested in women like me. We're from different worlds. Not like you and Neil. You're so great together – so perfectly in step. I'd kill for what you've got.'

For what I almost threw away, Kate thought, darkly.

'We're not perfect,' she said, after a pause, 'We're pretty good though – yeah, I'm very lucky.'

By the end of their walk, a mellow heat had settled on Eden Hill.

'Quick coffee?' Lisa said.

'Thank you, but I need to get back – I've got three blogs to write by close of play, so I'd better get on with it.' Kate said, hugging her friend goodbye.

'And Lisa,' she added, 'have a good afternoon at work – and just let your handsome surgeon see the real you.'

♙

## BEN

Scratching his balls, Ben watched Stacey's heart-shaped arse disappear into the hallway. It was one of her best features; another was that she didn't ask too many questions. When they were on, they were on – and when they were off... well, once he'd gone for three whole weeks without calling her, and she hadn't given him the cold shoulder.

Jesus, the room was a mess. Yesterday's jeans lay in a tangled heap on the floor, a pair of hot pink lacy knickers adorned the bedside lamp, and two wine glasses, misted with finger-prints stood on the nightstand. At least he hadn't smoked in bed; he'd finally given that up. Hearing the toilet flush, Ben sat up, trying to decide whether he was getting an erection or not.

It was already pleasantly warm. On a day like today, he missed the beach house, come to think of it - he missed a lot of things about last summer, not least, the peace, and the endless possibilities of what could lie ahead.

He'd moved back to London by default; it worked - and it didn't. There was no doubt it made getting around, seeing people, and booking studio time a breeze. But it didn't feel right –didn't nourish his soul or his creativity. It had been years since he'd lived within the chaotic, adrenalin-fuelled, throbbing vibe of the city. Some days, the stench of traffic fumes burned his sinuses and the fug left his hair greasy and his skin dull. And when did everyone get so competitive? He'd been shoved off the curb more than once and slammed into from behind, for having the temerity to pause and look in a shop window.

At the beach, he'd sung and played guitar and keyboards with abandon; the pensioners who lived nearby had never complained so he'd assumed they either couldn't hear or didn't care. Now, he scoped out new songs using headphones, tapping out mute melodies so as not to disturb the faceless neighbours in the Victorian conversion that had been home for the last six months.

Thank god he was only renting; it would do for now, but longer term – no way! Not that he could afford to buy a flat, even with the windfall from the TV campaign. He remembered when South-East London had been cheap as chips; the capital's poor relation – even that had changed. There were so many new developments – everyone squeezed in, cheek by jowl. He just wasn't feeling it; perhaps he was getting old.

'Is the kettle broken, Stace?' he called out.

'No - why?' Stacey replied – then after a second's pause, 'Cheeky sod. Come and make your own tea!'

He needed to get up anyway, tempting though it was to drag Stacey back under the sheets for a quickie before the day began.

❦

'Meester Ben,' said Helena, holding her duster aloft.

'Did you have party here tonight?'

'Did I have *a* party here, *last* night?' Ben corrected his Lithuanian cleaner. She was far too pretty to clean, but she was strong, too – going about her work with real gusto until the place shone.

'No, I did not,' said Ben, answering her question. 'I just had a friend over for the evening.' At least the incriminating frilly pants had departed with their owner, and he'd opened the windows to blow away the whiff of stale alcohol before Helena arrived.

'Right, my lovely - I've got a meeting with my manager in an hour, so I'll let you crack on. Leave my desk as it is, please - and use your key to lock up. Your money's by the kettle – and don't forget to make yourself a coffee. Ciao Bella.'

Helena beamed at him; was it his imagination, or was she wearing a skimpier top than usual?

❦

It had become obvious to Ben that Greg Lyons liked to eat. Meetings were rarely conducted in Greg's office, but over lunch - always in Soho, and usually in a restaurant where Greg knew the owner.

Today they were meeting at Brasserie Lagoon, where, under the shade of an umbrella, Ben spotted his manager already digging into bread and olives, and something utterly unrecognisable in a glass bowl.

'Hey, Ben. Sit – great to see you. You look well.' Greg signalled to the waitress, who reappeared with a bottle of red wine and a pitcher of iced water.

'How's tricks, Greg?' Ben said, somewhat distracted by the waitress's long tanned legs.

'Can't complain. Ben, I have one word for you; jingles.' Greg said triumphantly.

Ben wished he liked his manager better – and he trusted him about as much as a snake in a moustache.

'What about them? Not my bag.'

'But they could be. There's a lot of money to be made and...'

'And I'm working on the album, you know that, man.' Ben said, trying to keep the irritation out of his voice.

'Of course, but that's a slow burn. I'm talking about quick - and lucrative - hits. You of all people know the power of advertising; one commercial has totally relaunched your career - although god knows how an ugly git like you has become a sex symbol at your age.' Greg said, sniggering at his own joke.

Right on cue, two forty-something women at a nearby table had noticed Ben's arrival and were whispering behind their menus. Ben preened, sucking in his stomach and tossing his mane for effect. The women exploded with giggles, enjoying the floorshow.

'See?' said Greg, grinning.

Ben smirked, fighting the urge to go over and speak to the two women.

'Ben, think about it. You're not in an exclusive contract with the store – and we could package you as a score and jingle writer for film and commercials.'

'I don't think I want to be packaged as anything,' Ben said. Even when he was earning good bunce, someone else was always calling the shots. He'd wanted success so badly, to make a decent living out of writing and performing, but now it felt oddly empty. Just like the string of brief relationships he'd clocked up since moving to London; mindless sex with an array of good-looking women who massaged his ego, but left no trace on his soul. Well, it had to be that way. None of them were a patch on Kate, and she was spoken for; a fact that gave him a dull ache somewhere in his solar plexus whenever he thought about it.

Greg continued to babble on about opportunities, but Ben wasn't in the mood. Wine and sunshine - not to mention the aftermath of his night of debauchery with Stacey - had given him a headache. He longed for a nap, with the radio on low in the background, which wasn't very rock and roll. Ben excused himself, admitting he felt unwell, and wove his way through the thronging crowds before tubing it back to the flat.

The afternoon sun on the white stucco villa highlighted the cracks. One of Ben's neighbours had dumped a sack of rubbish beside the bins and foxes or cats had ripped it open, scattering the contents around the entrance. The stench was appalling.

'Fuck,' Ben said.

After banging the front door, he walked straight into a woman with an uncompromising bun and disappointment etched into the bones of her face. Despite the heat, she was dressed entirely in black, a gash of red lipstick the only colour in evidence.

'Excuse my French,' Ben said. 'That wasn't aimed at you, sorry. Some idiot has left rubbish out for the foxes...'

The woman swept past him without a word, her heels clacking down the steps.

'Oh, very neighbourly,' Ben muttered, plodding up to the first floor. What was it with people?

Inside, the smell of Helena's cleaning fluid was soothing and she'd thoughtfully left a high window open and the shutters closed. Mollified by the coolness, Ben gulped a pint of water then lay down on the grey sofa.

The beach house seemed like another planet. Lying very still, he could almost smell the sea, as the breath of the waves and the cry of gulls lulled him to sleep.

*Ben lit a cigarette, enjoying the sand sifting between his toes as he walked back up the beach in the direction of home. A skinny dog, almost camouflaged by the bleached hue of the dunes was bounding towards him. Ahead, a white-clad figure waited on his porch, hair haloed by the afternoon sun. Then the woman was walking towards him, slowly at first, then running, arms outstretched, as Ludo ran past them and into the waves. They were hugging and laughing, exchanging salty kisses.*

*'It's you, Ben – it's always been you,' Kate said, as he carried her into the shady bungalow, past the wild roses growing around the door.*

*Inside, without a word, Ben relieved Kate of her thin summer dress, delighted to find her soft round breasts unfettered – only a white lacy G-string remained. Pulling off his own shirt, he pushed her down onto the sofa. He wished the phone would stop ringing, it was very distracting. But it just kept ringing – and ringing.*

*'Why don't you get that?' Kate purred...*

'Ben? It's Greg – I've got some great news for you.'

'This better be good,' Ben said, irritated that his dream had been cut short by someone he'd seen only hours earlier.

'Oh, it's good. An ad agency in Covent Garden wants you to write the music for a soft drinks campaign. They loved the retail ad and they want more of the same,' Greg said.

'What, just like that? Well how does that work then?'

'There'll be formalities of course; the creative team wants to see you next week to thrash it out. How's your diary?'

After wrapping up the phone call, Ben made himself a strong coffee. It seemed a massive leap of faith that an advertising agency would want him to write the music for a whole campaign, purely on the strength of one track. What the hell; a meeting couldn't hurt. At this rate, he'd be able to buy his flat. Or get away from London entirely.

Ben closed his eyes momentarily, trying to recapture the dream, but like Kate's honeyed scent, it had gone.

&#x1F34E;

Harrington's, thought Ben, was awash with 90s clichés; from the shiny yellow-peril walls, to the glass-bricked entrance and the industrial-looking steel mezzanine above reception. Did all advertising agencies look the same? Certainly the handful he'd been in looked a lot like this one.

The receptionist, Annabel, asked him to wait. She had the look of a young Mia Farrow, an image which was mismatched by her cut glass vowels.

'May I offer you a drink, Mr Wilde? Coffee, water, coke?'

'No cake for me thanks, babe – I've just had lunch,' Ben said, knowing full well he'd been offered cola, but unable to resist a dig at her accent.

Mia/Annabel narrowed her eyes, not playing at all.

'Go on, then. I'll have water,' Ben said, nerves suddenly making his mouth dry.

After a few minutes spent flipping through *Campaign* magazine, an eager pair in their thirties came to meet him.

'Hi Ben! I'm Amy, this is Anthony; we're the creative team,' the woman effervesced, shaking his hand, 'It's a real pleasure to meet you; thanks so much for coming in.'

Ben was apprehensive – now it felt like a big deal.

He was taken into a semi-dark Board Room, chilly with air-con. Two other people were already seated.

'Ben, meet Hilary; she's the producer - and this is Davina, account director.' Anthony said.

'Hi,' Ben waved into the gloom, waiting for his eyes to adjust.

'We're waiting for one other person,' said Davina, who was all business, in a sharp suit and a sharper bob.

A tall, broad-shouldered guy with chiselled features entered the room.

'Hi. I'm Neil, the creative director.' Neil's handshake was firm, welcoming.

'Thanks for coming in, Ben. Have you travelled far to see us?'

'Brockley, South-East London.' Ben was surprised by the small talk.

'Ah. Know it well. So, let's talk about Helium. It's an energy drink – massive in the States, about to launch here. We won the account last year and have been laying the foundations ever since. We'll be shooting three ads, for the full product range, which will air in September - and we'd like to talk to you about the soundtrack. Seagull has just the vibe we're looking for.'

Neil paused and Ben noticed how everyone else was scribbling away; surely they knew all this stuff already.

'Amy and Anthony are the creative team; we can show you storyboards and so on...it's being cast at the moment. So as you can see, we are ready to rock. Currently, there is no one else in the frame – we wanted to speak to you first, Ben.' Neil was looking at him expectantly.

'Blimey. I'm flattered. Look, this is all new to me – I've been a songwriter for decades, but until the retail ad came up, I'd never done commercials.'

'I don't think that's relevant – you write great music, Ben – and it's what our client wants...hey, it's what we want. And anyway, we can't afford to use an existing hit; there are budgetary considerations of course.'

'Of course,' echoed Ben. 'I'm working on an album at the moment – there's one track in particular that might hit the spot.'

Delving into the man-bag he was forced to carry these days, Ben pulled out a CD.

'World exclusive,' he said, laying the disc on the board table.

# CHAPTER 2:
## COMMUNITY SPIRIT

KATE

Kate had been surreptitiously watching the woman for several minutes. Something about her - the dowdy but good quality clothing, the sensible shoes, and the way her white hands fluttered as she pocketed the shiny compact - told Kate that the woman was no common thief.

Apart from an elderly couple waiting for a prescription, Jebbit's Pharmacy was empty. Most people favoured the new Boots at the other end of the high street, but Kate liked the old fashioned and slightly dusty air of the place, with its smell of talc and cough-drops.

Satisfied that none of the white-coated assistants were paying any attention, Kate went up to the woman, who was now eyeing a tray of lipsticks.

'I wouldn't buy that one,' she whispered. 'I used it once and it gave me spots.'

Shocked, the woman returned the compact to its shelf.

'I was going to pay for it,' she hissed.

'Of course. It's just not very good - so I wouldn't waste your money. Are you alright? You look a bit pale,' Kate said, as the woman moved towards the door.

Outside, dust and debris swirled on the pavements - the last of the early summer blossom caught on the wind. Eyes pricking with irritation, Kate fumbled for her sunglasses and watched the woman go into the coffee shop.

Following her inside, Kate ordered a latte and two muffins. There were plenty of free tables but Kate walked over to where the woman was preparing to sit down.

'Mind if I join you?' she said, not waiting for an answer.

'Look, it's none of my business, but I saw what happened in the chemist's...and I couldn't care less, except that... you look like you could use an ear - and a cake - cake helps most things...well, I find that, anyway.'

'Why?'

'I think the sugar helps to-'

'No - why are you even talking to me?'

'Why not? We've all been there.' Kate stirred her coffee and bit into the muffin. It was dry and bland.

'I'm Kate. I live locally...up at Eden Hill.'

'Jan. I'm from here... Crabton, I mean. I wasn't going to take the makeup, you know. I hardly ever wear the stuff; it doesn't suit me. And anyway, I can buy what I like - my husband's very generous.'

It was an odd comment, defensive and unnecessary. By now, Kate was trying to figure out why on earth she had railroaded a complete stranger into having coffee with her.

'This cake's stale,' Jan said, 'Thanks anyway, though – it was very nice of you.'

'I just didn't...look, is there anything I can do?' Kate said.

Jan hesitated.

'I have to take tablets that make me a bit... vague sometimes,' she said, by way of explanation.

'Ah. Sorry to hear that...'

'Antidepressants,' Jan continued, 'They help in some ways, but... you know.'

'Oh, you poor thing. What does your husband do?' Kate said eager to change the subject.

'He's got a shop. Bevan's Flooring... it's been on this high street for donkey's years. It's a wonder it keeps going.'

'Oh, that's nice. I love old shops... I mean independent ones. Without them, market towns like this would be so bland.'

'That's what Martin always says. Most of his customers live near you, on the estate.' Jan said.

The Estate; how many years would it take for Kate not to feel stung by those two little words?

It dawned on her that Jan was only a few years her senior; she'd mistaken her for a much older woman at first.

'Have you got children?' Jan asked her.

'No. It's just me and my husband Neil.'

Kate thought back to the stark little room at the clinic, with its narrow bed and smell of antiseptic.

'We've got a daughter, Hayley - but she moved out last year. She's just like her father...a proper Daddy's girl, she is. She lives in Brighton now with her boyfriend. I expect she'll get married next year. Or maybe not...they do what they like these days, don't they?'

Jan sounded resigned, reminding Kate of herself during her first year at Eden Hill.

On impulse Kate wrote her mobile number on a napkin.

'In case you fancy a chat sometime,' she said, getting up. 'Or come to the woods with me and my dog Ludo.'

'Ludo?' Jan said, smiling for the first time.

&

'There was just something about her,' Kate told Lisa the next day.

'Yeah, it's called the menopause,' said her friend. 'I swear I'm having hot flushes already.'

'You're ten years too young!' Kate said, 'Me, on the other hand ...oh, don't get me started, I can't bear the thought. Ludo, come. Not too far boy.'

'Anyway, apart from rescuing shop-lifters,' Lisa said, 'How are you?'

'Oh, you know...same old, same old. Neil's working very hard. He's doing a big TV campaign for the launch of a soft drink...it's massive in America, so there's a decent budget. Hey, that reminds me; have you seen that ad for Benton's – you know with all the supermodels prancing around in bikinis?'

'Oh, I love the music,' Lisa said.

'Do you? That's my ex. The guy in the suit, singing... that's Ben Wilde – we were together for three years.' Kate said.

'No! Are you serious? He's gorgeous...he's got...you know... charisma, hasn't he? Why did you split up?'

'Because Ben was a selfish narcissist who refused to grow up,' Kate said, trying to keep the edge of bitterness out of her voice. 'He went to Spain for a few weeks – to sort his head out – and never came back.'

They talked in the rambling, whimsical shorthand they used – keeping an eye on the path ahead, making sure the dogs were safe, and exchanging pleasantries with other dog owners they met en-route.

It dawned on Kate how many people she knew these days; how she couldn't set foot outside the house without seeing a friendly face or hearing a kind word.

'Are you happy here?' she asked Lisa.

'Mostly...I'd like a gorgeous man in my life, but I'm okay. Content, I suppose – compared to this time last year. How about you, Katie?'

'Same really. But sometimes I look at the life I'm leading now - and I'm horrified by what I've become. I had such ambition, you know? In London I was so busy all the time, so dynamic – and well-connected. Work was everything...now it's all about the dog, the gym, the house – the small amount of work I do is kind of an inconvenience! Lisa, I'm a walking cliché...a suburban housewife.'

'But what's wrong with that? You're happily married – and you're...'

'Old?' Kate volunteered.

'No way! I was going to say, settled. You've got it all; wonderful husband, lovely home, cute puppy, enough work to retain your independence – it's all good.'

Well, put like that, thought Kate.

⚫

Back at the house, a sharp-suited man was saying goodbye to her neighbour. Kate recognised the estate agent at once – Jeremy Hunter was a familiar face in Eden Hill.

Kate hovered for a moment as he drove away.

'Hi Rachel, how are things?'

Rachel adopted her usual pose; hands on hips, chin jutting.

'Yeah, not bad – yourself?' she said.

'Ellie and Jordan alright?' Kate said.

'Oh yeah, they're fine, thanks. You might as well know – we're putting the house on the market. We're moving to the Midlands. Rob's firm is closing here. They've offered him another job – it's a promotion actually, but it's in Wolverhampton.'

'I'll be sorry to see you go,' Kate said. It was a white lie – there was no real affinity between the two women.

'At least we'll get a bigger house for our money, eh?' Rachel said. 'Right, must get on... I've got a mountain of laundry indoors. See you later.'

There was a sullenness about Rachel that bordered on aggression; it had put Kate off getting to know her better. Neighbours were one of life's lotteries, Kate decided, hoping she'd pull a winning ticket next time around.

♋

## LISA

A lock of long blonde hair fell to the tiled floor.

'No going back now,' said Chelsea, deftly wielding her scissors in time to the pulsating music.

Every chair in the salon was taken and several women were waiting in the magenta and gold reception area.

'Is it always this busy?' Lisa asked.

'Pretty much...well every Saturday anyway. Now what are we doing with the front? How about a long side-swept fringe?'

When Chelsea had finished cutting, blowing and straightening, Lisa studied her reflection in the gilt mirror.

The woman looking back at her was less WAG, more androgynist fashionista.

'I love it!' Lisa said, to the young stylist's evident relief.

'Thank god - I was a bit worried...taking so much off. You look years younger and so chic, too. Hope your man likes it.'

'Actually, I'm single – but I'm working on that,' Lisa said with a wink.

♋

Feeling light and energised Lisa bounced out on to Crabton High Street. Her sleek bob was more than a new 'do'; it was a fresh start that made her feel like a butterfly emerging from its chrysalis.

It had turned one o'clock; Tanya would be waiting for her in Crabton's smart new deli-style café.

'Sorry I'm a few minutes late, darling,' Lisa said 'It took ages.'

'Wow, Lisa!' Tanya shrieked. 'How fabulous do you look? Ooh, it makes me want to have the chop, too.'

'Thanks, hon – do I look okay?' Lisa said, fingering her sleek new do.

'Okay? You look bloody gorgeous.'

A gingham-covered table became free outside, so the two women moved into the sun. Lisa glowed, feeling box-fresh with her new hair, fabulous Gucci sunglasses and understated white shirt.

'All this,' Tanya said, circling her finger in the air, 'Is it about the hot doctor?'

Lisa was coy; 'Might be,' she said, toying with smoked salmon and walnut bread.

'I just fancied a change...all that long hair and nails – it's not who I am anymore. I don't need all that artifice.'

'Ooh, get you – that's a new word.' Tanya laughed. 'Bet you're wearing a sexy dress tonight though.'

'Of course,' Lisa said. 'I can't believe it's a whole year since their last party. Where has the time gone? Twelve months ago, I was in a complete daze. Justin had just passed away...looking back, I was in shock.'

'Yeah, it was a terrible time for you – horrible,' Tanya said. 'All those journos camped outside your house day and night – bloody vultures.'

'Don't remind me,' Lisa shuddered at the memory.

# CHAPTER 3:
## PARTY PEOPLE

LISA

The jury was divided on Claire and Jeremy Hunter, with as many locals ready to knock, as praise them. Lisa had little opinion on the couple; her own experience was limited to seeing them about town, and they were cordial enough.

So her invitation to Claire Hunter's birthday bash had surprised her. A year earlier, she'd been invited as a courtesy, after buying the property in Regent's Square. However closer inspection of the embossed invitation revealed that Claire's birthday was merely an excuse for some shameless promotion of the Hunters' property business, which was ten years old.

Lisa could not have cared less; any party was an excuse to meet new people in her view and given its corporate nature, she rallied a posse of Tanya, Kate and Neil.

'And if it's rubbish, we'll leave early and do something else,' Lisa said, pragmatically.

⚫

By early evening, a light rain had begun to fall, but the temperature was mild and Lisa wasn't going to let a shower put her off her stride.

Although the Hunters lived just a few streets away, the women's vertiginous heels necessitated going by car; after gushing over each other's outfits, they shared a taxi - Lisa and Tanya already giggly, pre-loaded with prosecco.

For a suburban house party it was shaping up to be a rather lavish affair. Flaming torches illuminated the entrance, and a velvet rope had been erected. The doorman, in a too-tight suit, with fake tan stains on his collar, studied their invitations carefully before allowing them across the threshold.

'Not a word,' Kate said, as they all tried not to giggle.

They were ushered through to the vast open plan kitchen and dining area, which, since the last party, had acquired an elegant orangery.

'This must have cost them an absolute bomb,' Lisa whispered, 'This extension alone will have set them back about sixty-grand.'

'And the rest,' Tanya said.

'Welcome, welcome – hello beautiful people,' Jeremy said, arms outstretched, miming air kisses all round.

'So lovely to meet you both,' he said, shaking Neil's hand and kissing Kate's.

'The ball and chain is in the marquee if you want to wish her a happy birthday. We've a full bar so please, order whatever you want.'

The 'marquee' was little more than a canvas canopy – nonetheless, it was doing an excellent job of defending the sixty or so guests from the rain. At one end, a DJ was on his feet, headphones clamped on, flipping through a crate of vinyl with one hand, and spinning decks with the other.

Tanya waved in his direction. 'I know him; he went to my school – haven't seen him for yonks,' she said, giving him a thumbs-up.

At the other end of the tent, linen covered tables were piled high with fruit and flowers and all manner of delicate finger-food covered by plastic film. Two serving staff hovered, waiting for the command.

'Oh, this is lovely,' Lisa said 'cheers, girls and boys – here's to a good night.'

♣

Spotting a number of familiar faces, Lisa was surprised by how many people she knew – at least by sight. She recognised several acquaintances from the gym, a handful of dog walkers, and her beautician, who was resplendent in a red dress. She even clocked a couple of young bearded hipsters from the previous year.

Claire, ever the gracious hostess, looked breath-taking in blue, bias-cut silk. She had the honeyed skin of the well-travelled, and the Pilates-honed physique prerequisite for most women over forty in Eden Hill.

And sitting with a woman she did not know, and who was looking decidedly anxious as she repeatedly smoothed down her black dress, was Martin Bevan.

'Look Tanya,' Lisa said. 'There's Martin; remember last year when he hung out with us? He was a great dancer actually, I'll give him that. Bless him – looks like he's met someone. There's hope for us all.'

Martin looked across then, and gave Lisa a small pinched smile.

'Let's go and say hello,' she said to Tanya, noting that Neil and Kate were engrossed with another couple.

'Hello, you!' Lisa said, as Martin rose to his feet, looking decidedly awkward.

'I like your new hair,' he said, 'It's a very flattering cut.' He made no attempt to introduce the woman beside him.

'Hi, I'm Lisa,' she said, addressing Martin's friend. Then, to Martin; 'Hey, I'm dead chuffed you've met a lovely lady. Divorce is so bloody awful – well done you!'

Martin could not have looked more uncomfortable if he'd been concealing a sack of eels in his trousers.

'You've got a good one there, love,' Lisa said, buoyed up by the champagne. 'I might borrow him for a dance later though...what a mover!'

⚭

## MARTIN

It was a mark of how far they'd come in the last year, thought Martin, that Jan was excited about the Hunters' party. Well, perhaps excited was too strong a word, but willing, certainly.

This year there would be no wardrobe meltdown at the eleventh hour; instead, Martin had taken Jan shopping to the cream of Tunbridge Wells' boutiques – and given her a bit of overdue princess treatment.

She'd picked out a plain black dress that was beautifully cut, cinching her in at the waist and showing off her legs. Then Martin had bought her some strappy sandals with four inch heels and in a moment of utter frivolity, he'd treated Jan to a faux-snakeskin bag, with bling on the clasp.

⚭

'Will I do?' Jan said, after taking over an hour to get ready.

Martin let out a low whistle.

'You certainly will, my love. You look stunning.' He took several photos on his mobile phone with the intention of showing Hayley the following day.

'Thank you for all the presents, Martin. I feel like a film star in this get-up.' Jan said.

◌

Couples' counselling had been a last resort, with Jan digging her heels in and flatly refusing to go at first.

'It's embarrassing,' she'd said. 'You needn't think I'm discussing our sex life with some smug git with a clip-board and a degree.'

'What sex life? That's half the trouble, isn't it?' Martin had been insistent, raising the subject repeatedly until Jan, bored and exhausted, had caved-in.

'That was awful, and a total waste of time,' Jan said, at the end of the first session. She'd been withdrawn for days afterwards.

'Love, I admit, it was hard – but give it a chance.'

They'd been assigned to Nigel, who had a wispy beard and quick hazel eyes that flicked from Jan to Martin and back again, as if he were watching a game of ping-pong, for a combination of one to one meetings and joint sessions.

Martin would have paid good money to hear what Jan had to say; but he could guess. Something along the lines of depression having robbed her of energy and self-worth for years, killing her sex drive, her sense of femininity, and crushing her confidence until she felt reduced to a husk – a non-person.

And all the while, Martin had taken charge of running things at home, as well as opening the shop for five and half days a week, playing badminton regularly – in fact, doing exactly what he'd done for years, making little concession to Jan's illness.

But inside he'd felt bereft – compounded by Hayley moving out; fretting too much about what he thought he'd lost, rather than what he still had. Worst of all, he'd developed a fixation with another woman – he could admit it now it was over – comparing Jan against Lisa Dixon; a former WAG - a spoilt, wealthy woman, who'd never needed to work, and whose life was entirely geared to her own vain and selfish pursuits.

He'd wasted months fantasising about them having a life together; sitting in his car outside Lisa's house, waiting to catch a glimpse of her, then trying to copy her style at home (all that grey paint and cream carpet! It had never looked right in their Edwardian semi). And as for his ludicrous ambitions to install a hot tub in their postage stamp of a garden which was overlooked by pensioners; the memory alone gave Martin palpitations.

But no real harm had been done – even after he'd been photographed with the object of his obsession in a national newspaper. It seemed to Martin that his midlife crisis had becalmed without consequence.

Nigel had proved surprisingly helpful - once they'd got past the beard, the beady eyes, and the irritating lisp. He'd helped to recalibrate their priorities, to live in the moment, to find beauty and tranquillity in small things. Some of the words he'd used sounded like bunkum and clap-trap to Martin – but the ideas seemed sensible enough.

After the fourth session, they'd gone for a walk together, just before dusk – not to get anywhere, but to be outside and to feel the wind on their faces. After ten minutes or so they'd heard the shrill warbling of a wren.

'Such a loud song for such a tiny bird,' Jan had said, following the sound upwards. And then they'd seen the little brown bird, its skinny legs braced firmly on a branch, face heavenward, with eyes like tiny beads of joy. They'd watched, spellbound, until a dog walker startled the wren and it flew away.

'Well I never,' Martin had said in wonder, 'That was a real privilege.'

But when he'd looked at Jan, there were tears in her eyes.

'I've been missing all this, haven't I? Martin, help me - I don't want to go on with this joyless existence.'

For a moment, Martin had misunderstood and panicked. Then to his utter amazement, she'd kissed him, pressing her lips to his so hard it forced his mouth open. And there and then, as the light was fading, they'd snogged like teenagers.

That night in bed, they'd snuggled for the first time in years, but when Martin had tentatively run his hand along Jan's thigh, she'd stopped him.

'One step at a time, Martin,' she'd said. It was a reasonable request – and a relief if he was being honest.

&#x15;

It was surprising, thought Martin, just how much better life had been since they'd been enjoying the occasional smooch. He didn't dare think about the next step. Making love; their flesh squashed together, grunting like animals, emitting all those sounds and smells – it seemed insurmountable. That was advanced stuff – it would take several more sessions with Nigel to get to that level.

His thoughts turned to Lisa; it would have been a different matter with her... but he was over all that now.

&#x15;

'Martin, did you hear me? Do you think I need a cardie?' Jan repeated.

'You need something, my love – it's raining a bit. How about your black jacket?'

They'd taken a cab. Martin was determined to have a drink or three, although probably not as many as he'd downed last year, running around with Lisa Dixon and her friends – he'd felt quite sick the next day.

♔

'Well I must say, they've pushed the boat out this year,' Martin said, eyeing the bouncer and the torches.

'It's like being on the red carpet,' Jan breathed.

'You look lovely enough,' Martin said, taking her arm.

♔

'Which one's Claire, then?' Jan asked, after they'd helped themselves to drinks inside the tent.

'That's her, in the blue dress,' Martin gave Claire a wave, 'Let's go and say hello.'

They hovered politely, until Claire had finished a conversation with a woman wearing more makeup than the average drag queen.

'What does she look like?' Martin whispered.

'Sshh, Martin! Don't be so rude,' Jan said, giggling. Her own make up, sparingly and inexpertly applied, had already begun to blur, but if anything it made her look fresh and pretty.

'We'll have a bit of a boogie later,' Martin said.

Jan shook her head; 'That's your department, not mine.'

'Hi! Thanks so much for coming,' Claire said, as the conversation with the drag queen tapered off.

'I'm Martin,' he said.

Claire laughed. 'Yes, I know. How could I forget you? You were king of the dance floor last year.' She was smiling at Jan, waiting to be introduced.

'Sorry ladies, where are my manners? Claire, this is my wife, Jan; Jan, it's Claire's birthday today.'

'Well not really, it was last week, but Jeremy wanted to make a big deal of our anniversary – the business's anniversary, I mean, not our...oh, you know,' Claire said, getting flustered.

'Well congratulations on both counts,' Martin said. 'And I must say, Claire, I do like your conservatory.'

Claire's smile faded; 'It's an orangery. Yes, we like it; it adds so much space to the kitchen.'

'Like they need that,' Jan muttered, as Claire was hijacked by another guest.

'Are you hungry, my love?' Martin said, realising they hadn't eaten a thing since noon.

'I feel too nervous to eat,' Jan said, running her hands over the skirt of her dress.

'Don't be, love. You look stunning and we've as much right to be here as anybody.'

'Why say it then? Why would you even mention it?' Jan looked put out.

'I don't know - probably because we don't know anybody. Now let's see what's on the buffet.'

The food was still covered in cling-film and nobody was eating anything. Martin helped himself to some wine, adding ice and soda to Jan's.

'You have to be careful – with your tablets,' he mouthed the last bit.

'Don't fuss, Martin; a couple of glasses is fine...they only say 'avoid alcohol' so that people don't go getting blotto and being sick.'

Martin spotted Lisa and Tanya. He'd clocked them earlier, but hadn't recognised Lisa, until those incredible blue-green eyes were turned on him, full-beam. The bouncy golden hair had been replaced by a silvery blonde bob; she looked leaner, too – which was accentuated by a simple emerald green sheath dress. She looked more beautiful than he remembered; sophisticated, elegant and prosperous. Martin felt his throat constrict, as Lisa smiled in his direction.

Then Tanya said something to her and giggling, they looked back at him. Oh god, they were coming over. Sweat prickled on Martin's top lip. Short of running from the party screaming 'fire', there was no escape.

'Are you alright, Martin?' Jan said, 'You look a bit flushed.'

'Hello, you!' Lisa said, before Martin could answer.

'I like your new hair,' he said, 'It's a very flattering cut.' It was the first thing that came into his head and his voice sounded odd above the squelching noise in his ears.

'Ah, thanks, Martin. I'm Lisa,' she said, addressing Jan directly.

'Hey, I'm dead chuffed you've met a lovely lady. Divorce is so bloody awful – good on you!' He could tell she'd meant it as an aside, but the words had come out loud and shrill.

Crikey. How would he survive the conversation, let alone the rest of the evening? He avoided Jan's eyes.

'You've got a good one there, love,' Lisa said, as though she and Jan were old pals; 'I might borrow him for a dance later though... what a mover!'

Lisa giggled and leant on Tanya for support. She seemed drunk - at least Martin would be able to factor that into his defence later.

'Back in a mo,' Jan said, walking carefully in her new shoes. Martin was torn between escorting Jan to the bathroom and trying to appear nonchalant in front of Lisa, who had begun to shimmy and sway in front of him as the DJ played another throbbing dance track.

ȼ

## KATE

'Someone's having fun,' Neil said.

Kate followed his gaze to Lisa, who was now dancing with a sandy-haired, slightly built man in his fifties, who looked decidedly reluctant.

'She's not the only one...there's a lot of booze here tonight; it could get very messy. In fact there's a lot of everything. Do you think the Hunters are loaded, or just showing off?' Kate said, taking in the amount of food and floral arrangements – as well as the fabulous house and garden.

Neil lowered his voice; 'I think that they are moderately wealthy, and that this party is some kind of tax write-off.'

'Cynic,' Kate said. 'Let's go and see if Lisa's okay - she does look a bit unsteady.'

'Katieeee! This is Martin,' Lisa said, 'We met here last year. He's a brilliant dancer, he can rumba and everything!'

Kate wondered what the 'and everything' could possibly refer to; he looked as though he could just about manage the Hokey-Cokey with a stiff wind behind him.

'Hi, I'm Neil. How do you fit in here, Martin?' Neil's voice was smooth as butter, and Martin grabbed the lifeline being offered.

'Nice to meet you, Neil. I'm a friend of Jeremy's...well, I say friend...we play badminton together regularly. Do you play, Neil?'

'Sadly, I haven't got a sporting bone in my body. The closest I get is watching Wimbledon and a bit of footie on the telly. But I work out a few times a week, to keep in trim...' Neil patted his flat midriff. Martin nodded, and they were off - speaking the universal male parlance of sport.

'You okay, darling?' Kate said; Lisa looked forlorn.

'No, I'm not! How come I'm always on my own? What's wrong with me, Katie? My god, even Martin has met someone.'

Kate shot her friend a warning look and steered her towards a couple of seats.

'The champagne's making you cross,' Kate said. 'Anyway, I'm starving; why don't we eat something? I'll get us a couple of soft drinks, too.'

'Okay,' Lisa was meek.

She really did look beautiful and very young, with her silky new hair and unlined golden skin. It was a good question.

'I think,' Kate said, returning with two Diet Cokes, 'The reason you are single, is because you are stuck in a rut of seeing the same people, week in, week out. I know you love your job – and I bet you're brilliant at it, too – soothing all those neurotic women, sticking needles in themselves, and going under the knife out of pure self-loathing and paranoia. But that's just it isn't it? It's all women. We go to the gym; it's all ladies, we walk the dogs...we meet more women. And, don't get me wrong, I love the company of women – but if you seriously want to meet someone, darling, you might have to be a bit more proactive.'

'I just want Doctor Rupert,' said Lisa in a small voice, wrinkling her nose at the Cola.

'But he's just got divorced, and you work together. Imagine if you two went out; okay, slept together, to be blunt - and it bombed... you'd end up leaving a job you love.'

'It would be worth the risk...and it's not like I need the money,' Lisa said, petulant now.

'No I know, but it's not about that, is it? It's about feeling useful and needed.' Kate paused and lowered her voice: 'Hey, you see that woman coming towards us in the black dress? I think that's my pharmacy shoplifter.'

'Hmm? Is it? Oh, I just talked to her, she's with him.' Lisa jerked her head towards Martin, who appeared to be having a very animated conversation with Neil.

'Simple souls, aren't they?' Kate was reminded that one of Neil's most endearing traits was his ability to get along with just about anyone.

The rain had stopped; groups of people – mostly women - were dancing with abandon, arms waving, and hair flying. Kate was relieved that Lisa had sobered up somewhat, and her good humour had returned.

She'd lost Neil to Martin, Jeremy and a couple of younger guys, one of whom Kate recognised from the gym; barks of laughter were erupting from the men.

It was the kind of party where everyone appeared to be having a fabulous time, and yet there was an air of fakery about it that Kate couldn't quite place. As though everybody were playing to the gallery, merely acting having a good time, and that at any moment, the Director would yell 'cut', the dancing would stop, and the scene would fade to black.

G

# CHAPTER 4:
## WEIRDER AND WEIRDER

**BEN**

Even in Harrington's air conditioned board room, Ben was struggling to keep his cool. More people were in the second meeting than in the first; so many hangers on! Surely all it took was the person who wrote the ad and the producer – but Uncle Tom Cobley and all had come to thrash out the details of the Contract; lawyers, a bunch of bag carriers...Ben didn't know or care what they all did, but he'd politely laid out everyone's business card on the black ash table.

And then it hit him like a truck and he'd almost physically recoiled.

*Neil Farleigh: Creative Director;* Kate Stone had married an ad-man by that name. So now he was in bed with Kate's husband, metaphorically speaking; a Class-A tosser and the main obstacle standing between him and the woman he loved.

Except that Neil wasn't; Ben actually liked the man, he was honest, unpretentious and seemed to genuinely get Ben's work. And as for being the main obstacle; enough time had passed for Ben to realise that he and Kate were planets apart, and no amount of nostalgia or wishful thinking would change that.

'Cheeky pint now the paper work's sorted, Ben?' Neil was on his feet, sliding long arms into a beautifully cut jacket. 'The Dog & Duck next door's not bad, and I could murder a beer.'

Neil's entourage melted away and then it was just the two of them; the tension was palpable.

'Actually, Ben, we've got something in common,' Neil took a long slug of the frosted amber liquid, 'or someone, I should say.'

Here we go...

Ben waited.

'My wife, Kate. You two were an item, back in the day.' Neil's words sounded overly casual. What exactly did he know? How did he know?

'Kate Stone? No way! Wow...how is she?'

'She's Kate Farleigh now, of course. Yeah, it's all good. She's well...happy enough. She ditched PR and she's a copywriter these days... blogging, corporate news letters, website pages, that sort of thing.'

Ben gulped his pint.

'Ah. So...er...is that a good thing or a bad thing, vis-à-vis working together?' Ben said, trying to sound neutral and not quite pulling it off.

'Hey, it's ancient history, so it makes no odds to me, Ben. Another drink?'

'My turn,' Ben said, getting up. Neil really was a decent bloke; no wonder Kate had clung on to him. The guy was a regular square jawed hero – handsome, successful and, much as it irked him, nice.

'So, how are things?' Neil said. 'When will the new album be released?'

'It should be out this autumn...we'll see. All this is a bit unexpected to be honest. I never thought I'd find myself being the menopausal woman's crumpet.'

Neil laughed; it was genuine, hearty.

'Yeah, right - it's not all twin-sets though, is it?' Neil said. 'Bet you had a blast working with all those super models for the Bentons Ad. Adrianna has to be my favourite model of all time.'

'It was a bit of a pinch-yourself moment.' Ben smirked, remembering the shoot.

'Are you married, Ben?' Neil said.

Ben shook his head. 'Not me. Can't see it happening. I've got a girlfriend, but she knows the score. We're just having fun. I live alone – and I like it that way.'

'Maybe the four of us could get together? Come down to ours for a barbeque or something – or we can meet in town if you'd prefer. Kate's always complaining we don't socialise enough.'

Weirder and weirder...

'Would Kate be cool with that? What does she think about me doing the music for Helium?'

'Nothing yet. I haven't mentioned it. I thought it would be nice surprise.'

It'll be a surprise alright...

They'd stayed a while longer, shooting the breeze like two old pals. It wouldn't be so bad to meet up as a foursome – stranger things had happened – and Ben was curious about seeing them together, like staring at a road accident when you knew you should look away.

'Right, I have to go. Ben, thanks for coming in today. I'm delighted about the campaign – let's get together soon - we'll sort some dates.' Neil said, shaking Ben's hand.

Ben set off home. Getting from Covent Garden to Brockley was an arse-ache anyway you looked at it, and on every leg of the journey he was crushed with sweaty commuters, tourists and chancers. He could tell a couple of people recognised him from the commercial – it was the hair of course; how many guys of his age could boast a shaggy mane of curls? He'd noted with some satisfaction that Neil's hair was thinning on top. Perhaps he wasn't quite perfect after all.

C

After opening all the windows in his stifling flat, Ben opened the fridge. There was nothing to eat except a pot of Stacey's soya yoghurt, and a cracked nub of cheese; some out of date milk and three bottles of Budweiser completed the inventory.

'Bud wins,' he mumbled, wondering what Neil would be having for dinner. Knowing Kate, it would be something colourful and nutritious, all cooked from scratch.

Feeling sorry for himself, he rang Stacey.

'Hello baby, what are you doing tonight?'

'Watching TV in my PJs.'

'Do you fancy going out for dinner?'

'Ben, it's nine o'clock. I've already eaten, and I'm kind of in for the night. Seriously, I've just painted my toenails and...'

'Okay Stace...another time. Good night, lovely.' He didn't need the details. It looked like takeaway was his best option.

It was still light and outside a welcome breeze was stirring up the dust and debris on the street. Ben walked a couple of blocks to the kebab shop where the familiar smell of basting meat and onions made him salivate.

'Alright, Mehmet?' he said, looking up at the menu board.

'Good evening, Ben. Your usual?'

Ben nodded; it was his third kebab that week.

C

## MARTIN

After the Hunters' party, cordial relations in the Bevan household had nose-dived. Overnight, things had slipped back into pre-counselling mode, with Jan bumping around the house, tight-lipped and sullen.

It wasn't Lisa's fault. She'd been gushy and indiscreet, but her words had been friendly and kind, if misplaced. And she'd flattered him, calling him a great dancer. It was a compliment that gave Martin no pleasure – seeing as the price had been Jan's withdrawal.

'Love, I wish you'd talk to me,' Martin tried the next day, after getting the silent treatment during a breakfast of cornflakes and weak tea.

Jan hadn't answered him.

By midday, he'd tried again; 'I know what you're upset about – and I can't say I blame you, but just let me explain things.'

'Explain?' Jan was peeling potatoes and carrots at the sink, having already seasoned a chicken; her back was impenetrable. Hayley was due for Sunday lunch at two o'clock – she'd been vague about whether she was bringing Simon or not.

'Jan, I don't want Hayley to sense an atmosphere – please, can we talk about things?'

Jan ignored him, banging a large saucepan on the counter before filling it from the tap.

'Martin, I have a roast to cook; instead of going on at me, make yourself useful!'

At a loss, Martin got the vacuum out and gave the carpets a perfunctory going-over.

Then he took out the rubbish, and cut the lawn.

By now, the smell of roast chicken had spread through the house, peaking his appetite.

'How long until lunch, love?' Martin asked.

'How long do you think?' Jan snapped, unhelpfully.

'Please yourself,' Martin muttered under his breath.

<br>

When he answered the door, Martin knew at once something was wrong. Hayley was alone, looking thin and dull-eyed.

'I think he's gone off me, daddy,' she said, her chin wobbling.

'Of course he hasn't! What's brought this on, love? Tell your dad all about it.'

But before Hayley could say another word, the escalating sounds of pots and pans in the kitchen signalled that Jan was serving up.

'Thank you for doing chicken, mum - you know it's my favourite,' Hayley said, when they were gathered around the table.

'And mine too,' Martin added. Jan glared at him.

'You've lost weight, Hayley,' Jan said. It came out as an accusation. 'How are things with you and him then?'

'He's got a name, mum. Simon's fine but things are bit...' Hayley swallowed hard before continuing. 'I've gone and ruined everything,' she said, 'It's all my fault!'

'Eh,' Martin said, 'it can't be that bad.'

So Hayley explained; how she had begun to drop hints about marriage and how Simon had admitted he wasn't ready.

'And then I said 'well perhaps you never will be', and that's when Simon admitted he wasn't sure if we even had a future. That was last weekend and we've hardly spoken since. It's as though he's just gone off me for no reason,' she sniffed.

'Well he's an idiot, that's all I can say!' Martin said.

Jan rolled her eyes; 'You're not helping Martin. Love, you've got to talk to each other...find out how he feels.'

'Ha! Pots and kettles!' Martin barked.

Hayley took no notice; 'Can I come home for bit? Dad, mum, would that be okay?'

'Love, there's nothing me and your mum would like more, but what about work?'

'I'm owed some holiday so I can take a couple of weeks off, and after that...well, either I'll have patched things up with Simon, or I'll have a long drive to Brighton every day, won't I?'

When they'd finished eating, Hayley went out to the car and produced a large holdall, stuffed to bursting point.

'Looks like she's stopping for a while,' Martin whispered as they were clearing away. 'He's not good enough for my daughter anyway, the pillock.'

'Oh, give it a rest, Martin.' Jan slammed the dishwasher shut and it started to whoosh and whir. 'You go slagging him off, and it's you that'll be out in the cold when they're back together in a week or two. That's young love, isn't it? Or can't you remember that far back?'

On Wednesday afternoon, Martin closed the shop at one o'clock and went home via the bakers.

'Little treat for us, my love,' he said, setting a box of chocolate éclairs on the kitchen counter. 'Shall I make a cuppa?'

'It'll take more than a few cakes,' Jan snapped.

'Where's Hayley?' Martin said, not rising to Jan's ill humour.

'She's gone into town shopping for a couple of hours. Which is why you and me need to talk.'

Finally.

'I'm listening, sweetheart.' Martin said before biting off half an éclair in one go.

'Don't you sweetheart me!' Jan unfolded a page from a newspaper and set it down in front of him. 'That's her isn't it?' she said.

Martin choked on his choux pastry.

'What's that?' he said, although he could see exactly what it was; Lisa, smiling and posing in a red bikini, and below it, a smaller photograph of him and Lisa embracing on her doorstep.

'She's cut her hair,' Jan said, 'But it's her alright. Is she your lover Martin?'

'Jan ... no. Where did you get this?'

'I found it in your desk drawer, months ago – I was looking for paracetamol – I recognised you at once...I bought you that shirt. Martin, don't bother denying it. I just want to know where I stand.'

'Where you stand?' Martin repeated. 'Where you always have – you're my wife I love you.'

Jan eyed him coldly.

'I knew if you ever saw that article you'd think there was something going on. But Jan, you have to believe me; there's nothing between me and that woman. Nothing! I can tell you the whole boring story if you like. But why now, if you've had that rubbish for months?'

'Because your girlfriend gave me all the proof I needed the other night. You were going to divorce me for her, weren't you, Martin?'

'Of course not! Jan, I can tell you exactly what happened, every last boring detail...'Martin explained about the Hunters' party, how they'd danced and chatted after he'd replaced Lisa's carpets weeks earlier, and how they'd both been grateful for a familiar face. And when it was time to leave, he'd lent Lisa Dixon his jacket.

'...And when we said goodnight, we had a peck on the cheek – and then, blow me down, there was a flash, and some idiot reporter had been hiding in the bushes...because Lisa's husband had just died. Do you see?'

'You've left a bit out, Martin...about you and her, cavorting in the hot tub,' Jan spat, 'No wonder you wanted one at home! Did you get a taste for it?'

Martin felt his face flush.

'Don't be ridiculous. For goodness sake Jan – what do you take me for? Love, you have to believe me. Hayley does.'

'Oh my godfathers! Why does that not surprise me? You and her, ganging up on me, keeping secrets.'

Jan stomped upstairs and came down carrying a bag. It was a cheap holdall that Martin hated, with flowers on the barrel and plastic handles.

'Russell's on his way,' Jan said, 'I rang him as soon as Hayley went out. You can explain to our daughter that I've gone because her father is a faithless bastard who's done the dirty.'

'You're going to your brother's? Love, that's ridiculous! Nothing went on. Jan, please, things have been so much better between us – since the counselling. You have to believe me – NOTHING HAPPENED.' Martin shouted.

A car horn sounded.

'Good-bye Martin – I'll be in touch. But you can take it from me - our marriage is over.'

Jan swept out. Martin had never seen her so determined.

♉

'She's done what? Christ on a bike, dad. How could you let her go?' Hayley dropped her boutique bags in the hallway.

'I couldn't stop her. She'd made up her mind...your mum thinks I've got a girlfriend.'

Once he'd ached for Lisa – now it seemed unthinkable. The trouble she'd caused was untold! No wonder her husband had topped himself – she'd probably driven the poor man to it.

'Dad, look me in the eye and tell me that you've never...you know...with that Lisa woman.'

Martin tried to speak but the words dried in his mouth.

'Dad; we'll sort this,' Hayley said. 'First, a cup of tea while we decide what we're going to say - and then I'll ring mum.'

'She won't even be there yet. Hayley, you do believe me, don't you?'

'Yes. For a start, women like her aren't interested in boring old gits like you, dad.'

'Oh, thanks very much...well...anyway....we've got to convince your mother now.'

He could cope with Hayley in his corner.

♋

## LISA

Lisa nervously checked her watch; it was almost noon.

'I wonder, Lisa, will you meet me in Café Nico at one o'clock, please – and don't mention it to anyone; people can be rather silly about these things unfortunately,' the consultant surgeon had said on the telephone.

Now Lisa's stomach was fluttering like a sparrow learning to fly. After months of subtle flirting, she was finally going on a lunch-date with Rupert Dale; it was all she could do to stop herself skipping from room to room.

Looking around the restaurant, Lisa spotted him immediately, his sober suit and swept back silver hair at odds with the young, casually dressed café crowd.

'Hello Mr Dale,' she said, sitting opposite him.

'Rupert, please,' he said, looking over wire-framed glasses and smiling. 'Now what are you going to eat? They do a wonderful artichoke salad here and I've asked for a couple of spritzers. Is that alright?'

'Perfect on both counts,' Lisa said.

'You're probably wondering why I wanted to meet you here,' Rupert said.

'Well...yes.' Lisa's mouth was dry with anticipation.

'I'll get to the point. We're making changes at the practice and my partners and I have been hearing very good things about you, Lisa - not only from clients, but from members of staff, too. It seems you're well liked, and much admired.' He paused for a reaction.

'Ah...well, thank you. That's... good to know,' Lisa said, waiting for the punchline.

'So, we'd like to offer you a different role – and to move you off reception and into something a little more challenging. How would you like to act as PA to Jonathan and me? We'd pay you rather more of course, and we'd need to boot up your hours... catering to the needs of two consultants can be pretty demanding.'

'Thank you...I...I don't know what to say.' She really didn't. Above all Lisa felt foolish and embarrassed for believing she'd been invited on a date. She'd never had a grown up and responsible job in her life; the prospect was terrifying.

'Can I think about it and let you know tomorrow? Of course, I'm grateful and very flattered...I just didn't see it coming, that's all.'

'Of course, take a few days if you need to. But Jonathan and I would both be delighted if you felt you could put up with us.'

At that moment, Lisa knew that there was no chance of Rupert Dale ever seeing her as a love interest. She could cut her hair, ditch the makeup, read books, get into art and classical music, even take elocution lessons, but they were simply from different worlds.

Lisa smiled bravely; 'I don't need to think about it,' she said, 'it's a great opportunity – thank you so much...when do I start?'

☉SEEKING EDEN

'Well congratulations! That's fantastic news,' Kate said during their morning walk the following day.

'Scary though. This is a proper job, Katie, with two important people relying on me.'

'And you'll rise to the challenge brilliantly, I know you will.'

'I guess I'm a late bloomer,' Lisa said, linking arms with her friend, 'I never saw myself as a career woman...I'm not sure I do now, but I'll give it a go, Katie. It means we won't get our lovely long walk every day though...my hours will change a bit.'

It had rained during the night; the air was muggy and steam rose up from the sun-warmed woodland floor. Nellie and Ludo trotted to heel. It should have been a moment of contentment.

'I'm lonely, Katie,' Lisa almost whispered – she hadn't meant to say it.

'Ah, darling. Is that how you feel? Look, this new job could open up all sorts of new situations for you.'

'Why will it? I want a man, Katie, a soul-mate. I feel such an idiot, because I thought Doctor Rupert was asking me out... anyway, he's much too old for me, I know that now. But I feel as though this is my comeuppance for Justin.'

'Whoa - hold it right there, missy!' Kate said, stopping in her tracks. 'I don't want to hear that kind of talk. For years you were more carer than wife to Justin. You put your own life on hold - and finally the drinking killed him. You are not to blame. Why are we here again?'

'But there's been no-one since and I...I just think...maybe that ship has sailed.'

'Lisa, stop it. You're not destined to be alone. For god's sake, woman! You get hit on all the time.'

'Yes, but by losers... not by anyone I'm attracted to - anyway, it's more than that. I think the money has brought me bad luck.'

Kate shook her head emphatically.

'Justin left me half a million pounds, Katie, and I feel so guilty – as though it's bad karma, you know? I mean, of course, it's great to have security, but everything I have is paid for - and I actually have a decent job now, with an income...sometimes it's tempting to just give it away!'

'But Lisa, Justin wanted you to have it. By all means, give some away to charity or whatever, but don't feel guilty – from what you've told me, you bloody-well earned it!'

Lisa sighed; lately the feeling was always there, nibbling away at the back of her mind, like a maggot in a peach.

'It's a karma thing, Katie. I have to do something...think of all the people it could benefit. Will you help me?'

'Me?'

'Yes - you and Neil have business connections in PR and marketing...'

'Well, if you're serious, let's have dinner at mine tomorrow night and see if we can put our thinking heads on. Sure, I'll help you – if it's important to you.'

'It is,' Lisa said.

# CHAPTER 5:
## THE WRONG CALL

KATE

Neil seemed preoccupied with something, but when Kate challenged him, he blamed the Helium campaign.

'Darling, are you sure that's all it is? I feel like you're not telling me something.'

'I'm just knackered and there are some logistical problems to overcome before we shoot the campaign in two weeks. It doesn't help that we're on a tight deadline, the first media burst is due to break mid-September.'

'Oh, yes. That is tight. Is there anything I can do to help?'

'As it happens, there is. You can come and support me after the shoot. We're having a wrap-party when it's all in the can.' Neil said, absently rubbing two days' stubble.

'You make it sound like a movie. You don't usually...'

'Because it's a launch, the UK client is making a big deal of it, so the team at Harrington's, plus the cast and crew are having a bit of a hoedown afterwards. Please come, Kate. I know it's not your bag these days.'

'Of course I will - for you, my love, anything. Can I bring Lisa? You'll be in Boss mode, working the room – so I'll be standing there like a lemon, otherwise. Anyway, she's a bit down at the moment - a change of scene will do her good.'

'Then, absolutely – I'll email you the details, baby.'

Ć

The weekend had been commitment free and mellow. On Sunday morning, after a long trek with Ludo across sun-baked fields, they'd showered together and then read the Sunday papers wrapped in terry-cloth robes, listening to opera.

'Puccini always makes me sad, but in a good way. Do you know what I mean?' Kate said.

'I do - those soaring arias sound achingly sad, even though I haven't a clue what they're about.'

They'd read a while longer, until Neil announced he was taking Kate out for lunch.

'Get dressed. Let's go to Kane's.'

'Wow, that's smart,' Kate said, 'but surely we won't get in; it'll be packed today, no?'

They rang ahead and were lucky enough fill a cancellation on the terrace.

'Have I told you recently how gorgeous you are, and how much I love you, Kate Farleigh?' Neil said, as they sat sipping Bellinis and nibbling olives.

'I don't think you've mentioned it for a while,' Kate said, batting mascaraed eyelashes and arching her back.

'You look knock-out in that dress baby, topaz suits you.'

'Now that's why you're the creative director of a London advertising agency; most men would have described this dress as blue.'

She was flirting with him now, and it felt good. Inexplicably, she thought of Ben; an involuntary shudder rippled through her.

'Are you cold, darling, do you want to move inside?' Neil was attentive as ever.

'No, just a shiver. How's the lamb?'

'Delicious. Katie, are you happy here now?'

'What a question – yes, mainly...I don't know. I mean, I don't think about it anymore. It's miles better now that I've got a few pals. But it still upsets me when I think how our old friends cut us off overnight. We live an hour from London, not in Land's End... but then I think how we used to talk about people who lived out of town – and now we're card-carrying members.'

'I couldn't go back, could you?' Neil said.

'Baby, you never really left - you've got your own room at Jonno's flat during the week.'

'Well, one day, I will...and then, oh I dunno... maybe we should travel for a bit.'

ै

They left the restaurant, holding hands, suffused with contentment. But when they arrived home, a familiar hatchback was parked outside. Whey-faced, Alice and Natalie spilled out.

Alarmed, Kate and Neil ushered them inside.

'Nat, Ludo is desperate for a walk, would you take him please, poppet?' said Kate, handing her his lead.

No sooner had Natalie closed the front door behind her, Alice began to howl.

'Pete's gone, Katie – I...I just needed to see you.'

'Oh, Alice – what's happened? Neil, get Alice a glass of wine will you love, and then perhaps you can watch some footie upstairs?'

It was not-very-subtle code for 'give us some space'; Neil got it at once, pouring a large glass of wine for each of them, before taking the stairs two at a time.

'Pete's left us. He's got a girlfriend, Kate...and he...he says...' Alice burst into wracking sobs.

'Jesus, Al, just tell me, please!' Kate said, alarmed.

'Okay. I need to say this before Natalie gets back; she heard us yelling and knows we've split up. But I don't want her to know that Pete's mistress,' (Alice spat the word) 'Is five months pregnant! My bastard, faithless husband is planning to marry a thirty year old with a baby on the way. Shit, Kate - there's no way back from this, is there? What am I going to do? I wish Mum was here.'

Kate held her sister, letting her rant and cry, until Ludo bounded into the room, signalling Natalie's return.

'Darling, I'm so, so sorry. Okay, first things first. You should stay here for a few days, let the dust settle.' Kate said.

'Is that okay? We brought a few things,' Alice said.

'Can Ludo sleep on my bed, Auntie?' Natalie said, stroking his silky ears.

'Of course, darling. How about I put you in charge of him for a few days, eh?'

Feeling overdressed, Kate ran upstairs to change, and debriefed Neil in hushed tones.

'Pete? No! Oh, god. That's awful. Is Alice sure about this...it's not just some fling that's got out of hand, is it?'

Kate gave Neil a withering look.

That night, Kate hardly slept. Sickened by her own (albeit minor) role in Pete's duplicity, it pained her to see Alice so totally undone. Giving her brother-in-law the benefit of the doubt – and keeping her discovery to herself – had been the wrong call. At the time it

     ☺SEEKING EDEN

had seemed like prudence, now it felt like treachery.

Not that exposing Pete's affair would have changed the outcome. He'd used words like 'thunderbolt' and 'destiny', heaping on the agony and the drama - the pig - as if that somehow excused his betrayal.

She looked at Neil's silhouette in the dimness; his strong profile, his fluffed-up hair, and her heart swelled. He'd been so kind, bringing everyone hot chocolate and cookies before bed. He was good with Natalie, had a natural way with her. Come to think of it, Neil had a way with everyone.

♌

Monday morning dawned bright and clear. After saying good-bye to Neil at six thirty, puffy-eyed from lack of sleep, Kate made tea and went into the garden, Ludo at her heels. The dew had intensified the scent of petunias and geraniums, which were now leggy in their pots, their petals spilled like confetti on the lawn. Weeds had begun to sprout abundantly in the borders and Kate marvelled at the way everything grew and grew, without intervention.

'Life will find a way, eh boy?' she whispered to Ludo who, with great concentration, was bird watching.

'Good morning, love,' Kate said, feeling Alice's hand on her shoulder. 'Did you manage to sleep at all?'

'A bit, thanks. I've left Natalie in bed – she's growing so fast, she needs all the rest she can get, bless her,' Alice said.

'You're amazing, you know that?' Kate was awed by Alice's capacity to put another's needs ahead of her own, especially after such emotional carnage had taken place.

They drank tea, ate toast, put Radio 4 on; nobody mentioned the 'P' word, until Kate said: 'Al, we can talk about it – or not, it's up to you. Will you contact Peter today? There's a lot to discuss, surely?'

'What's to say?' Alice said, her mouth set. 'He's got another family now – Natalie and I don't figure in his plans.'

'But there's loads to talk about...the house, for one thing. Where will everybody live?'

Alice let out a bark of bitter laughter.

'I'm not going anywhere – Natalie and I are staying put in Hove. The money Mum and Dad left us is tied up in that house, and if he thinks I'm moving out, he can go fuck himself.'

'And you tell me not to swear!' Natalie was standing in the kitchen doorway, rubbing the sleep from her eyes.

'Sorry, Natalie – swearing's horrid. I'm just upset. Want some breakfast?' Alice said.

Somehow they muddled through the day – Kate watchful, Alice tense and shrill.

'Are Mum and Dad getting divorced?' Natalie said when Alice went for a soak at Kate's insistence.

'Yes, they might be. But whatever happens, you've still got a Mum and a Dad – and they'll both love you just the same.'

'I heard them arguing; he's got a girlfriend, you know, Auntie. Gross! I mean, Dad's practically bald. I bet she's horrid.'

'Yeah, I bet she is too,' Kate said.

Ǵ

## MARTIN

It had taken three unanswered calls and several ignored texts to motivate Martin into the car and onto the M23. Now his windscreen wipers were barely keeping pace with the sudden downpour that had slowed the traffic to a crawl.

The SatNat was predicting an ETA of 13.30 - which was annoying because Jan and Russell would have already eaten, and he'd like to have taken her out for lunch.

She'd be cooking for Russell now, big idle lump that he was; he could pack it away, too, thought Martin, absently patting his own flat stomach.

But supposing they were out? If that was the case, Martin would wait outside, at least then he was guaranteed a conversation with Jan, even if it took place on the door step.

Getting past Russell's unpleasant and considerable bulk would be a challenge – if the phone calls were anything to judge by.

'My sister's got nothing to say to you, Martin. Now stop ringing this house or I'll change the number and report you to the exchange for harassment,' Russell had said, before putting the phone down.

'This is hopeless Hayley,' he'd said, despair setting in. 'How can I convince your Mum that it's all a mistake, if I can't even speak to her?'

'You'll just have to go down there, Dad. She'll have to talk to you when she sees how upset you are.'

He couldn't fault his daughter's logic, but now the outcome seemed less certain. Jan had always had a stubborn streak, and there was no moving her when she'd made her mind up about something.

The traffic was beginning to flow more freely now and as the rain stopped, Martin was relieved to pull off the motorway and go cross-country for the last leg. With a knot in his stomach the size of a cricket ball, he pulled up outside Russell's house. It was an ugly property, with small windows and no front garden to speak of, just a concrete car port that housed a row of dustbins. Even the front door was an indiscernible colour caught somewhere between beige and brown.

Martin rang the bell.

'What?' Russell said, as though they'd been in the middle of a particularly tiresome argument.

'I'd like to speak to my wife, please, Russell. Is she here?'

'I doubt she'll want to see you,' Russell smirked, drawing himself up to full height.

'Well then, I'd like to hear that from her.' Martin was resolute. 'Are you going to let me in, or can you please ask Jan to come to the door?'

'Er, no...and no - I can't.'

'Russell; may I remind you that Jan and I are still married.'

'You should have thought of that before you went off with your fancy piece, shouldn't you, Martin?' Russell was enjoying himself now.

'Oh, mind out, will you, Russ? Let me speak to him.' Jan pushed past her brother.

'Martin, what do you want?'

'Love, do you need to ask? Please, can we talk? Can I take you out for lunch?'

'We've eaten.'

'Well, coffee then.' He tried not to get exasperated. 'Jan, you can't just call time on twenty-odd years of marriage and refuse to talk to me. What about Hayley?'

'That's not fair, Martin...leave her out of it.'

Martin glared at a neighbour, who had come outside and was baldly eavesdropping.

'Do you mind?' he said, eyeing the old man.

'For god's sake, Martin – stop making a spectacle of yourself. Go back to the car; I'll put some shoes on and come for a coffee with you.'

From the car, he watched Jan walk down the path; wearing beige slacks, and a bobbly cream cardigan, she reminded Martin of a rice pudding.

'You look well,' he lied.

'Oh, don't bother, Martin. I know I look awful and honestly, I couldn't care less.'

'Where can we...?'

'There's a café just up on the right. They do a nice chocolate cake in there.'

It was a soulless tea-room, with grubby lace curtains, and a counter that would have been called retro had it been in better nick.

The smell of eggy-fried food made it impossible for Martin to contemplate eating anything - let alone chocolate cake.

Christ, he was about to try and save his marriage in this stinking hovel, with the cacophony of chairs scraping, coffee machines whooshing, and microwaves pinging in the background. 'How is she?' Jan said.

'Hayley's fine - misses her Mum of course and she hasn't patched it up with Simon yet, but they're speaking on the phone most days. She'll be back at work next week.'

'I meant her - your girlfriend.'

Martin gaped.

'Unbelievable!' he said, 'I'm not even going to dignify that with a response. Jan, please love; you've got to hear me out...'

'I haven't got to do anything,' Jan said.

Martin sighed.

'Jan, you're my wife and I love you - as much today as when we said our vows, which I meant then, and I've stuck to them. All this silliness has got to stop.' Martin paused, half expecting Jan to protest; she didn't.

'The thing is, love, I am guilty, but not in the way you think. I'm guilty of being an idiot, for taking you for granted and for getting daft ideas. I swear on Hayley's life that nothing happened with Lisa, or with any other woman. All that rubbish in the paper? They were out to get her; it was a bit of scandal that might have helped to sell a few copies. Jan, I admit...' Martin hesitated, knowing he was taking a gamble.

'I admit that she turned my head a bit when I first met her.'

Jan pursed her lips; 'She's pretty I suppose, if you like that sort of thing.'

'Actually, that's not it. She just seemed so...oh I don't know... alive. Hayley had just moved out and...I felt...so old. You and I had stopped talking...and I couldn't see things changing. Next thing I knew, I was drinking champagne, having a dance, and pretending I was one of them.'

Jan's gaze was steady.

'Love, you've got to believe me.'

A gaggle of elderly walkers in bright cagoules burst noisily and chaotically through the door, and after much bellowed conversation about who was having what, Martin grabbed Jan's hand.

'Come on. I can't hear myself think.'

They sat in the car with the windows down, facing the grey opaque sea. A few people were on the beach, despite the wind and spotting rain.

'Hayley had a red mac like that, do you remember?' Jan said, watching a sparrow-legged little girl digging in the sand while her parents stood by stamping their feet in the wet.

'It had a hat to match...' Martin said, feeling a lump come into his throat.

'Jan, please come home. What's the point in staying here in this dump? Your brother will take every opportunity to poison you against me – the longer you stay here, the less chance we've got of saving our marriage.'

'I just need to think,' Jan said, still looking at the sea. 'Even if you haven't had an affair with that woman – and I've only got your word for it – what's left for us, eh?'

'Everything! How can you be so defeatist? I thought things had been much better...since all that work with the counsellor. We can book up a few more sessions if you like.'

'But that's the point, isn't it? We aren't any happier, we've just made more effort - don't you see?' Jan said. 'You've done your duty, Martin - looked after me and Hayley all these years, but perhaps we don't belong together now. You go home, love. I'll speak to you in a day or two. I just need a break.' Jan opened the car door. 'I'll walk back. Give Hayley a kiss from me and be careful driving.'

Tears rolled down Martin's cheeks as he watched Jan's beige shape recede into the distance.

♻

## KATE

During eight years of marriage, Kate could not remember feeling more angry.

'I just think you should have told me! God, Neil, how would you like it if I fixed up an evening out with one of your ex'es? I'll tell you, shall I? You'd be fucking mortified!'

Neil was sheepish; 'Okay, well I'm sorry I made the wrong call. You haven't seen the guy in almost two decades - surely it's all water under the bridge now. Kate, honestly, I thought you'd be fine about it.'

'Well I'm not! We didn't part of good terms – and I...oh, look forget it, Neil. I just can't believe you kept this from me.'

'Kate, I'm sorry. Look, you don't need to come – it's no big deal either way.'

'But it looks like a big deal if I stay away, doesn't it? And anyway, Lisa is looking forward to a night out. I just don't want to go dredging up the past...and it's creepy - thinking of you two palling-up.' Kate carried on stacking the dishwasher, unable to meet Neil's eyes.

She needed to calm down, before emotions overwhelmed her and something incriminating slipped out.

Neil was contrite; 'I should have told you, Katie. Things just escalated. I mean, at the first meeting, I was just checking him out...I was curious to be honest, but then Ben played the most perfect track for the campaign and after that, there was no one else in the frame. Anyway – I like him. He's good fun.'

'That's because he's a fifty-odd year old child!' Kate said.

'That's harsh.'

'Don't even get me started,' Kate said. 'Lisa and I will come as planned, but seriously, if he starts winding me up, I am out of there.'

Neil raised his eyebrows: 'Why would he do that? You are funny sometimes, Katie.'

Ben Wilde and his colossal ego were the least of Kate's problems. Alice and Natalie had gone home to Hove, but the signs were not good.

'Mum's having a lie down at the moment and says she'll ring you back, Auntie,' Natalie said, when Kate telephoned for the second time that day.

'Okay. Nat – how are you both?'

'We're fine...well I am, but Mum's very tired so she's sleeping a lot.'

It was three in the afternoon; for Alice to leave Natalie to her own devices in the middle of the day was unheard of, except for when she'd been ill with flu – and even then her sister had always managed to soldier on.

'Give her my love, won't you, Natalie? Oh, and tell your Mum if she doesn't call me back, I will drive over there tomorrow.' It was a threat of sorts but Kate hoped it would galvanise Alice into picking up the phone.

It worked: 'Please don't worry about me, Katie,' Alice sighed, 'I'm just tired. I'll be fine in a week or two.'

'Alice, you can cut all the stoical crap with me – you need help. I think you should go to the doctors' and get some counselling. You also need a bloody good solicitor.'

'Do I? Why?' Alice said wearily.

The conversation ran on a loop, until Alice became tearful, and Kate was losing her patience.

'Al, I'm concerned about you – not for the long term, because I know you'll get your life back on track and you'll be happier than before, you'll see – but for now. Natalie will be back at school in a fortnight and I don't want you spending too much time alone.'

'Please, stop fussing. Oh god, Katie – I haven't even asked about you...I've been so wrapped up in my own stuff,' Alice said.

'Oh, don't worry about me. I'm cross with Neil because there's a work-do in London tonight and my ex is going to be there.'

'What? Why?'

'Because my husband has used a sound-track written and performed by Ben-bloody-Wilde for a new ad campaign. It's going to be massive...Ben could make a lot of money.'

'Well that's just weird...it'll be freaky having your husband and your ex in the same room tonight.'

'I couldn't agree more, Al. But if I don't go, it will look like I'm making a statement – as if I can't face Ben. At least I'm going with a friend. Actually, I need to get ready and get out of here. Look, keep your pecker up, sis, and call me day or night. I mean it…I can be with you in an hour or two, so please, don't suffer in silence. Gotta run – love you.'

Kate hung up. In an hour, Lisa was due to drive them both to Crabton station. From there, they'd take the train to Charing Cross, then take a taxi for the last leg of the journey.

She'd earmarked jeans and a frilled top, but it felt all wrong – safe and frumpy - so after a hot shower, Kate trawled the depths of her wardrobe, coming up with a sleek black dress that she hadn't worn since leaving London. She was gratified to find it still fit her perfectly. Ramping up the eyeliner as an afterthought, Kate spritzed on perfume and was ready to go with five minutes to spare.

'Ooh, look at you – you look bloody gorgeous, Katie.' Lisa was generous as always, as they sped towards the station at Lisa's default speed of sixty miles an hour.

'You look amazing, too.' Kate said, eyeing Lisa's short clinging dress and killer heels.

'Do you think there'll be any fit, single men there tonight?' Lisa said.

'There may well be…I don't know Neil's colleagues. I meet them once a year at Christmas – if that. Tell you who will be there; my ex-boyfriend, Ben - the one who did the store commercial? Not that I recommend him, you understand!'

'Oh, I don't know,' Lisa said, changing down and hunting for a parking space. 'I think he's quite sexy, in an aging rock star/done it all and bought the T-shirt kind of way.'

'He'd agree with your there.' Kate said, laughing nervously.

# CHAPTER 6:
## WRAP

KATE

They'd chatted and giggled on the London train, but once they'd arrived, Kate felt distinctly apprehensive.

The Click Club was faux-glam in a trite nightclub palette of black and gold, with rococo gilt mirrors that fought with the Art Deco themed bar. Standing several inches taller than the huddle of agency people around him, Kate spotted Neil easily before her eyes were drawn to Ben.

He's been rocking that look for twenty years, Kate thought wryly, taking in Ben's unruly mane and his slouchy black suit, beneath which she could see a Rolling Stones T-shirt. Beside him, a waif-like blonde in a tight red dress was hanging on his every word; she looked almost young enough to be Ben's daughter.

'What are we drinking? Hey - there's Neil,' Lisa said.

Then to Kate's immense relief, he was at her side, kissing her and hugging Lisa, before sweeping them towards the bar, where he steamed through a roll call of names and job titles that she knew she would never remember.

Kate smiled graciously; she was the boss's wife now, and with that came considerable scrutiny. She saw the way Neil's female colleagues looked her up and down; she noticed too the lascivious way in which most men in the room were looking at Lisa, although her friend seemed blissfully unaware.

'It means a lot that you made it tonight, thank you. I'm so lucky,' Neil said.

Over Neil's shoulder, she could see Ben mugging it up with one of the creatives.

'I'm the lucky one,' Kate said.

⌖

## BEN

Ben had never been to a wrap party before. It sounded terribly glamorous, as though he'd starred in a movie, rather than written the music for a couple of ads.

Excited at the prospect of a big night out, Stacey had upped the ante and was looking hot.

'Well, don't you scrub up a treat?' Ben said, letting out a low whistle.

'Of course,' she said, affecting hauteur. 'I have got legs, you know.'

'I can see that,' Ben said, wishing he could tear off her short red dress and inspect them more closely.

Harrington's had sent a car for them, which was a result, and given the shoes Stacey was wearing, necessary too.

'Can you take us to The Click, please mate? It's in Ely Mews, just off Wardour Street,' Ben instructed the driver.

It was still light when they arrived at the venue, but after passing through a discreet black doorway, they were plunged into a semi-dark mirrored basement with a sweeping Deco-style bar. A crowd had already gathered and the room was filled with the sound of clinking glasses, animated conversation and cool blue note jazz.

Ben spotted Neil Farleigh and a couple of the suits he'd met at Harrington's. He could pick out the Helium client a mile off; a balding guy in his fifties surrounded by a clutch of pretty young women who appeared to be listening intently and laughing at his jokes.

'Let's get a drink, Stace,' he said, steering her to the bar and ordering two vodka martinis.

'Ben - so glad you could make it tonight,' said a familiar voice to his left.

'I wouldn't have missed it. Neil, this is Stacey. Stace, this is Neil, he's the big cheese in these parts.'

'I don't know about that!' Neil said. 'Well Ben, congratulations. The rushes look great. We're going to enter your soundtrack for 'best use of music' at the Creative Circle Awards next year, so fingers crossed.'

'Yeah? That's fabulous, cheers!' Ben clinked Neil's glass with his own.

Further introductions were made, small talk about who did what, and other projects they'd worked on. It was competitive banter; Ben barely registered the details, happy enough to soak up the atmosphere and the free booze.

They were joined by the ad's director and its two stars, Caitlin and Huck; Ben was about to introduce Stacey when his words froze in his mouth.

Kate had entered the room in a dress so tight, it looked as though it had been laminated onto her; better still, she'd arrived with a pneumatic blonde who was similarly dressed. They made a striking pair.

'Excuse me,' Neil said, moving towards the two women. Ben watched as he kissed Kate before giving Lisa a quick hello-hug, and inviting them into the group.

He'd pick his moment to speak to Kate – let the woman get a drink down her neck before wading in. Who knew what kind of reception he'd get; she'd blanked all communication for the last nine months.

Kate had seen him; she'd looked over, and looked away. Smiling, Ben waved. Perhaps it would be better to bite the bullet, diffuse any awkwardness early on so that they could all relax.

Neil was shepherding Kate and her hot girlfriend around the agency team to a chorus of hellos and handshakes. Ben could read the tension in Kate's body language from across the room; she should know that the last thing he'd do would be to make trouble for her in a situation like this.

'Pretty, aren't they?' Stacey said, following Ben's gaze.

'Not as pretty as you, princess. Actually, this'll make you laugh... the taller, darker one is my ex, Kate. She's Neil's missus now – small world, eh?' Ben drained his glass.

'So how many other women in this room have you slept with, Ben Wilde?'

Ben spluttered on his martini before realising that Stacey was teasing him.

'Lucky I'm not the jealous type,' she said, smiling. 'I'll get us a couple more drinks, shall I, babe?'

With Stacey at the bar and Neil now in earnest conversation with the director, Ben found Kate.

'How are you, Ben?' Kate said.

'Can't complain...I've got plenty of work on – thanks to your old man, of course – funny how things turn out, eh?'

'I had no idea,' Kate said after checking Neil was out of earshot. 'About what?'

'That you were working together - that you were behind the music for this campaign. All the musicians and writers he could have used and Neil picked you. He told me last night; you can imagine how delighted I was.'

'That's between you and him. I'm just enjoying the cash...no skin off my nose who I work for.'

'Is that your girlfriend? Shouldn't she be doing her homework?' Kate said.

'Oy! She's thirty-six - not exactly jail-bate. What can I say? We're just having a good time.' Ben smirked.

'So you're not serious about each other then?' Kate said, looking over at Stacey who was coming towards them carefully carrying two cocktails.

'Would you be jealous if we were?' No one could blame him for enjoying Kate's discomfort; he'd laid it all on the line for her a year ago and she'd binned him off.

He changed the subject; 'Who's your mate? She's stunning.'

'I told you about her - that's Lisa Dixon. She was married to the footballer who died last year.'

'Oh yeah, I remember. Is she single?'

'Oh, grow up, Ben.' Kate turned her back and began a conversation with one of the creatives. My, she was touchy tonight.

'Thanks, Stace, you having a nice time, babe?' Ben said, taking a martini from her.

'Yeah, lovely. I'm starving though...forgot to have lunch today,' Stacey said with a shrug.

'No wonder you're such a skinny kid. Take it easy with the cocktails then, hon – I don't want to carry you out of here.'

'Ha-ha! You're so funny,' Stacey said wrinkling her nose at him.

She was very pretty, good fun, and easy going. Bendy as a pipe cleaner, she could hold his attention all night long - and still put a smile on his face in the morning. And yet, something didn't gel. Perhaps Stacey's lack of feistiness was part of the problem; with

Ben calling all the shots, all the time, she was simply no challenge.

Suddenly Ben was aware of a perfume so sensual he was compelled to turn and see who the wearer could be. He watched Lisa Dixon sashay past him - and felt the judder somewhere in his gut. Now there was a woman who looked like his idea of a challenge.

'Back in a mo, Stace,' Ben said, before following Lisa in the direction of the cloak rooms.

'Do you always hang around ladies' loos?' Lisa said emerging minutes later with freshly glossed lips.

'It's not something I make a habit of,' Ben said, 'but for you, I'll make an exception. I'm Ben, I...'

'I know who you are,' Lisa said, flashing her headlamp eyes.

'I'm flattered.' Ben said.

'Well you're practically a celebrity.' Her voice was breathy and light, but without being squeaky and irritating like so many women he met.

'As are you, Mrs Dixon,' Ben said, raising his glass.

'We both know that's not true – and even if it was, it's certainly not for the right reasons. Anyway, I've put that scene behind me. I'm just a regular career girl now.'

'Good for you,' Ben said. 'Look can I take your number and give you a call?'

'Impressive – straight to the point. What about your girlfriend?'

'Stacey's more of a mate; we're not actually together,' Ben said, glancing in her direction.

Taking Ben's mobile phone, Lisa tapped in her number.

'There. Now you've got it. I have to find Kate; have a fun evening, Ben.'

Ben stared after her – he was vibrating all over.

They'd shared a taxi home, but he'd dropped Stacey off first. It had surprised her, but she didn't protest.

'No cuddles tonight then?' she said, pouting prettily. It was endearing the way she referred to fucking as cuddling.

'I'm knackered babe; I'll give you a bell tomorrow.' Ben said, before giving her a kiss goodnight.

Then he'd gone home, crawled into bed in his underpants, and had passed out straight away, waking to the sun tickling his eyelids; he could never remember to pull the damn blind.

A racket was coming from the hallway – a bumping, banging and scraping that went on and on, while Ben dressed and made coffee. Curious, he feigned checking for mail.

Wearing the same look of disdain as when Ben had seen her in the hallway before, the bun-lady-in-black was directing two removals men.

'Morning - you moving out?' he said.

'You can see I am,' the woman said in clipped tones.

'All the best then,' Ben said, before closing his own front door.

Sipping frothy coffee made with his new pod-machine, Ben mused that there were only two types of women in the world; ladies he could charm, like the birds from the trees, and women who thought he was a complete wanker. The thought made him laugh out loud. Bun-lady was clearly in the latter camp, but the fact that Lisa had given him her number last night put her firmly in the former category, so the signs were good.

He imagined un-wrapping her from the tight ruched dress she'd been wearing. He already knew what lay beneath; she was slim - not athletic slim like Kate - but curvy slim with large high breasts, a small waist and just the merest hint of a rounded belly.

Ben knew her legs would be toned and shapely from all those gym sessions, and that she'd be the colour of golden syrup, thanks to the occasional sunbed and a variety of lotions and creams.

She'd probably need coaxing in bed (unlike Stacey, who could be savage and visceral) but once he'd warmed her up, he'd make her scream.

He'd give Lisa a call in a day or two – if he could bear to wait that long.

# CHAPTER 7:
## ALL LOVED UP

KATE

High on sugar, three little spooks jostled at the door, out-creeping each other in their lurid nylon costumes and masks.

'Trick or treat!' they yelled in unison.

'Treat!' Kate said, holding out a tray of home-baked spooky-iced biscuits she'd copied from a TV show that morning.

'Haven't you got any proper sweets?' said a tiny ghost who could have been either boy or girl.

'These are proper...have one, they're delicious.'

'Are they gluten free?' said the tallest of the trio.

'What? Er, no...I'm afraid they aren't.'

For god's sake! She hadn't expected to negotiate with a bunch of pre-schoolers about the quality or allergen risks of her Halloween snacks.

In another hour, Neil would be home for their mid-week meal together, at which point, they'd hide out in the back of the house and stop answering the door; a relief no doubt, to poor Ludo, who was exhausted from running up and down the hallway to guard against ghouls and evil spirits every ten minutes or so.

Arriving right on schedule, Neil looked tired.

'Hello, sweetheart – what smells so good?' He said, draping his jacket over the stair banisters. Sighing, Kate hung it in the hall closet.

'Well not my Halloween biscuits, apparently. Next year, I'll just get a bag of chocolate mini-bars like everyone else. I've made shepherd's pie. You look shattered darling; are you okay?' Kate said, removing a piping hot dish from the oven.

'I had to fire someone today. It was horrible – she took it pretty badly.'

'Oh how awful. Anyone I know?'

'You've met her once or twice...Davina, she's an account director...she's been there a while and didn't see it coming.'

'Oh, what went wrong?' Kate could picture Davina – a vision of perfection and control; it was hard to imagine her losing composure.

'She was officious. Clients didn't warm to her, and the team were scared of her - but the real problem was that she'd been leaking stuff to the press.'

'Oh no! That's bad.'

'Oh yes; her boyfriend works at Campaign and she'd been very indiscreet...anyway, she's gone...decent pay out, good references... it happens.' Neil said, piling his plate.

After making short work of the pie, Neil patted his full stomach and reached for the Malbec. 'I needed that, thank you. More wine, darling?'

Kate nodded.

'Anyway...enough about work,' Neil said, 'I'll be back there in twelve hours. How was your day, sweetheart?'

'What, apart from an endless stream of kids at the door since dusk? Fine. I met our new neighbours. Nick and Charlie; they seem nice.'

'Oh great. What's Charlie like? Do you think she'll be a new friend for you?' Neil said, swirling wine around his glass.

'Charlie's a man...' Kate said.

'Nick then, Nicola?' He took a sip.

'Also a man.' Kate waited for the penny to drop.

'Arh - a gay couple. Well that's nice...isn't it?'

'It is,' Kate said. 'It means things are opening up around here, becoming more diverse. They're younger than us – and guess what? They've got a dog, too. A Yorkshire terrier called Sparrow... he yaps a bit, but he's very sweet. Maybe we can walk together sometimes.'

'Kate, for god's sake, patch things up with Lisa. I know you miss her. You were such good friends - how can you let a bloke come between you? It's not as if she stole Ben from you.'

'Of course not. It was never about that, it's just uncomfortable seeing them so loved up. I mean, I wanted Lisa to meet someone... and to be happy but not with him! I know Ben too well – leopards don't change their spots, as my sister always says.'

'Surely you don't have to see Ben if you don't want to, you can just do girls' stuff, like before. Honestly Katie, it seems like you're cutting off your nose to spite your face.'

Neil had a point. But it was complicated. Seeing Lisa and Ben together was just plain weird; they were so smitten, like fumbling teenagers, unable to keep their hands off each other –although Kate suspected a degree of play-acting on Ben's part for her benefit.

'You're right,' Kate said, 'I'll fix up lunch with Lisa – just the two of us...I need to get over myself, don't I?'

'That's the spirit,' Neil said. 'You and Ben were a lifetime ago – there's no point in hanging on to the past.'

A pang of guilt swept over Kate; hot and unpleasant. She'd got away with their sordid interval insomuch as Neil was clueless, but the collateral damage to Kate's soul was undeniable. She busied herself with clearing the table, unable to look at her husband.

The next morning, keen to build bridges before she changed

her mind, Kate sent Lisa a text inviting her for coffee or for a walk with the dogs. But as the hours ticked by and no reply was forthcoming, Kate felt crushed and foolish. She thought back to their last conversation during which she'd been snippy and bad-tempered. Lisa had been visibly hurt when Kate had accused her of 'breaking the girl code' and they'd scarcely spoken since.

At four o'clock, feeling sad and lethargic, Kate forced herself out of the house with Ludo, mindful of the fading light. The thought of another long winter ahead made her feel old.

And then, rounding a corner, she was face to face with Lisa; wearing a fur hat, wool coat and long boots, she looked like a beautiful Russian doll. Nellie waddled beside her.

'Katie! How are you?' Lisa said, smiling.

Kate hesitated: 'I'm fine. I was thinking about you...which is why I sent that text...'

'What text? Today? I left my phone at Tanya's last night. I'm just popping round to get it now – thought I'd take Nellie and kill two birds with one stone - I hate this weather, so depressing. Have you got time to walk with me?'

Kate smiled. 'Yes. Silly really, but I thought you were blanking me,' she said.

'Absolutely not. Kate, I know it's a bit weird with Ben and everything, but I miss talking to you. And how are you doing, boy?' Lisa scratched Ludo's ears as he nuzzled her hand.

'So, how's your new job?' Kate said, settling on neutral territory.

'Great, thanks. Some days it's crazy busy, but everyone is so friendly and it gives me a real sense of purpose, you know? I'm off for a couple of days, so if you're free for lunch tomorrow...'

'I'd love that. How are things going with Ben?'

'I feel...' Lisa groped for the right words; 'I feel as if I've known him forever, and that we were meant to be.'

'Wow.' Kate swallowed hard. 'Look, I won't pretend it doesn't freak me out a bit, but I'm happy for you and...'

'Which is why he's moving in with me.' Lisa's eyes were shining.

'Oh! Really? But...you've only just...Lisa, are you sure?'

'Yes! I know we only met a few weeks ago, but we're just perfect together – and we make each other happy. Why wait, Katie? We're not kids. It just feels right.'

'So you love him?' Kate pressed on, lancing the boil.

'I do - and I fancy him like you would not believe. Oh my god! Now I know what all the fuss is about. Ooh, sorry Katie; too much information?'

Kate grimaced; 'A bit. Look, I'm afraid I can't do lunch tomorrow, I've just remembered I've got a...thing...but soon, eh? I...I need to get back, actually. Let's go for a walk next week, shall we?'

'Oh, okay. Katie, have I...?'

'Take care, bye-ee.' Kate waved over her shoulder and hurried in the direction of home.

Jealousy was an ugly emotion and she had no right to feel it; she loved Neil, they were solid, and when Ben had made a play for her that summer, she'd sent him packing. So why was it so painful to think of him with Lisa?

Almost as galling as their whirlwind courtship, was the hypocrisy of the man! He'd wasted no time in berating Kate for selling out - unleashing his subversive commentary like a broken record at every opportunity. Now he seemed ready to embrace a lifestyle he claimed to abhor.

Arriving home to a dark and chilly house, Kate turned up the heating and went around lighting the lamps. Clifford and Moira walked past in matching anoraks - seeing her silhouette in the window, they waved.

'That's me and Daddy in twenty years,' Kate said to Ludo, who cocked his head at the mention of Neil.

Kate paced, made tea, ate yoghurt standing by the fridge; she could not settle.

She rang Alice.

'How are you doing, Al? Kate realised almost a week had passed since she had checked on her sister.

'I'm okay, love - no thanks to my ex-husband.' Alice said.

'Oh god...what's he done now?'

'He's trying to rush things...he wants to start divorce proceedings and he says we'll have to sell the house so that we can both take our equity out and start again.'

'Jesus, the man's such a pig. But Al – let me ask you something; do you want him back?' Kate said, playing devil's advocate.

'After what he's done? Even if I could forgive him...which is simply not possible...I could never trust him again. I can't believe you could even ask me that!'

'Then give him his divorce and get yourself a damn good solicitor. I know it's only been a couple of months and it's still raw and shocking, but if you know that you can never forgive him – make the break. Alice, in a couple of months, he'll have a new baby and...'

'Are you saying I should give his new family a leg up? I thought you of all people were behind me.'

'Alice, I am totally behind you, one hundred percent. I despise Pete for what he's done. All I'm saying is...maybe a clean break would be a good thing. Make sure you get what you're entitled to – which will be at least half the house – and certainly maintenance for Natalie. Then he can go to hell.'

'But Kate, this is our home. Why should we move? Lord knows what broom-cupboard we'll be reduced to by the time we've split everything down the middle.'

'Alice, you can go back to work – you've got a brilliant brain and I bet the house is worth much more than you think. Come and live near me! The schools here are excellent – well so I read, anyway – and love, we'd have each other.'

'I don't think I've got the energy to go through a move. And you know what? I feel so angry when I think of them...Pete with his young dolly and their perfect new baby – honestly, there are days when I feel I could shoot the lot of them.' Fury was building in Alice's voice.

'One word, Al; Karma,' Kate said, 'She won't stay with him; why would an attractive thirty year old want to make a life with Pete? He's overweight, balding and can be as dull as ditch-water sometimes.'

'How do you know she's attractive?' Alice said.

'I don't,' Kate lied, 'but we have to assume that she isn't a complete moose, otherwise it wouldn't have happened in the first place. Alice, she'll dump him sooner or later, you'll see.'

'Maybe, but that's no consolation to me, is it? Kate, I'm a mess. I can't sleep, my appetite's shot and my head's all over the place. I think Natalie is looking after me these days. She's such a good girl...but honestly, I don't think she'll forgive Pete in a hurry. He might be gaining a new baby, but he could lose a teenage daughter, Nat's furious.' Alice said, with a degree of satisfaction.

Kate had called Alice wanting to talk about Ben and Lisa, but now it felt all wrong – her own issues were trifling compared to her sister's. Instead, they spent several more minutes slating Pete before saying good-bye.

The conversation had done nothing to mollify her. If stodgy, salt of the earth, dull Pete could play away, how could any man be trusted? Perhaps even Neil was capable of cheating. But as soon as the thought had formed in her mind, Kate felt ashamed. After all that had happened with Ben, how dare she question Neil's integrity?

That night, clutching a mug of hot chocolate, Kate went to bed early and watched reruns of Sex and the City with Ludo sprawled beside her. Feeling cocooned, she fell into a deep sleep, until her alarm and the sound of rain rattling against her window roused her at seven.

🍎

## BEN

Lisa had caught Ben off guard. He'd wanted to mothball the whole love and romance thing but something about her had got under his skin.

True, she was beautiful and smoking hot, too...with those incredible eyes – and that body; Jesus! The first time he'd taken her to bed, she'd taken his breath away.

But it was more than that; there was a sweetness about her, too. He'd dated (or maybe 'slept-with' would be a more accurate term) dozens of gorgeous women, but in Ben's experience, beauty often came with an unwelcome side-order of vanity, petulance and stupidity and he was delighted to learn that Lisa possessed none of those qualities.

So in stark contrast to his usual bad-boy routine, Ben found himself raising his game and wanting to spoil Lisa; to buy her gifts, cook for her, massage her feet, take her shopping – he hardly recognised himself - it was unnerving.

That she was a mate of Kate's was unfortunate, but it wasn't like he'd planned it – any more than he'd planned on working with Kate's husband, Neil. Anyway, he reasoned, life was full of coincidences; it was how you dealt with them that mattered, and at this juncture, Ben intended to grab every opportunity that came his way, whatever the route.

Now it seemed likely that he and Kate would become neighbours – who could have seen that coming?

The conversation had arisen gently, organically. Ben had spent the weekend at Lisa's house - all very chilled and civilised. On the Saturday night, they'd cooked spaghetti together and drunk a bottle of Shiraz. Then despite the November chill, they'd taken a dip in the hot tub, under a velvet sky studded with stars. They'd kissed, long and deep - and then Ben had tried to relieve Lisa of her bikini top. Lisa was having none of it, saying it was indecent and that somebody might be watching.

Ben couldn't have cared less if a ticket-buying, popcorn-munching audience had cheered them on and scored them out of ten, but as Lisa could be surprisingly shy, they'd gone inside and had mind-blowing sex in her beautiful French bed, before drifting into blissed-out sleep.

On Sunday morning, they'd taken her rat-dog (who was a sweetie once you got to know her) for a walk in the woods, and even in a waxed jacket and wellingtons, Lisa managed to keep him in a priapic state.

Later they'd gone to a local pub for Sunday lunch, where they'd run into friends of Lisa's and she'd introduced him as 'my boyfriend, Ben'. It had given him the warm-fuzzies for the rest of the day.

'Did you mean that earlier?' Ben asked while they were curled up on her sofa, 'About me being your boyfriend?'

She'd looked worried; 'Of course...what, you think it's too soon? I'm sorry, I didn't mean to embarrass you - it just felt natural.'

'Yeah...well, to me, too.'

And then it has just come out...the L word and without further ado, Ben had spilled his guts, telling Lisa that he'd fallen in love with her, and hated them being apart.

With Lisa due at the clinic the following morning, he'd meant to go home - but then they'd smooched for a bit, and gone to bed. This time, it was more than gratuitous sex, and they'd clung to each other, limpet-like, soul bearing until the small hours. Ben ached with tenderness – what had she done to him?

'I hate saying good-bye to you, baby,' he'd said the next morning, drinking coffee while Lisa buzzed about, getting ready for work.

'Well let's not keep doing it then,' she said, applying lipstick from a gold tube.

He was confused.

'Come and live here,' she added.

'Seriously? Do you think that would work? I mean...I'm not very domesticated, just ask my cleaner.'

It was a lame joke – he was stalling for time, but she'd laughed anyway.

'Ben, I've said it now. Move in, or don't. It's all fine with me. I love being with you – you make me happy.'

But being Ben, he'd panicked. Things were moving too fast. So he'd done what he always did when he needed a lift. He'd gone on the pull - this time to a Moroccan-themed nightclub in South London. There he'd downed several mojitos whilst perving at the young women gyrating on the dance floor. Half of them looked as though they'd left the house in their underwear - and when exactly had teeth whitening and breast implants become the norm? It was all a far cry from his day.

Ben's thoughts were interrupted by a raven-haired woman standing so close he could see the powder on her heavily made-up skin.

'I know you, don't I?' she said.

'Not that I know of.'

'I've definitely seen you around...no, wait. I know who you are; you're on TV, aren't you?'

'Guilty as charged,' Ben said, preparing to run with his usual patter, 'You might have seen me in...'

'Oh no, don't tell me...I'm thinking frilly shirts, loud suits... got it! You're that interior designer...the makeover guy. You look different in real life – older, if you don't mind me saying,' she had a look of triumph now.

Ben did mind; he minded a lot - about this woman, who clearly had personal space issues, mistaking him for some TV decorator prat; he minded about the incessant throb of the euro-trash dance music that was beginning to give him a headache - but more than anything he minded that he'd gone out with the intention of picking up a woman.

Without acknowledging the woman any further, he walked out onto the street and leant against a wall, his head spinning.

What the hell...? He was in love with a warm, kind and funny woman – who, to any straight man, was the stuff of fantasy, and yet here he was, in a club on the pull. Sometimes he grossed even himself out. He hailed a passing taxi.

Once inside his miserable flat, Ben rang Lisa.

'Hey, baby girl.'

'Ben? What time is it?' her voice was fuzzy with sleep.

'Late – I'm sorry. But I had to tell you that I've missed you...so much... and I love you, sweetheart. I know I don't deserve you... Christ, Leese – I am the luckiest man alive... and if the offer still stands, I think we should live together.'

'Okay - that's nice,' Lisa yawned. 'But can we talk about this tomorrow, hon?'

'Yeah…I'm coming home, baby. But right now, I have to throw up.'

Ć

The irony of moving to Eden Hill had not escaped him, but Ben had never been happier to eat his own words. He'd given Kate a hard time about settling down (and selling out) in 'Stepford' as he'd so rudely called it. But after years of living in Spain like a bum, then hiding out at the beach with just a few pensioners and dog walkers for company, living in London had been a massive shock to the system and he was over it. In fact, he was so over London that he resented even being there to work.

But Ben wasn't daft; he knew how things looked. Lisa was a wealthy woman. Big house, tasty motor, designer clothes; all a hangover from her WAG days. But he'd been aghast when she'd told him about the inheritance. Half a million quid was more than he could hope to earn at his age. Thank god she'd told him about her stash after they'd decided to live together – god forbid she'd think he was hustling her; he'd love that girl if she was pot-less.

But Lisa had made it abundantly clear that she couldn't care less about their fiscal imbalance.

'It's just money, baby. Please don't let it come between us. We're so lucky to have found each other – nothing else matters.'

'But you know what people will think…that I'm a freeloading git, taking advantage.' Ben said.

Lisa was philosophical; 'Ben, sod what people think. Since Justin died, I've been accused of all sorts and in the end, we have to do what we think is right.'

Ć

After giving notice at his flat, he'd cleaned up his act, much to the surprise of Helena.

'Meester Ben – why you do my job? Where is all towels on floor and cups in sink?' Helena said with mock irritation, wagging her finger.

'Sweetheart, thank you for looking after me, but I'm moving out in a couple of weeks, so here's a month's money.' He handed Helena an envelope.

'Thank you so much! But I clean at new house, no?'

'I'm leaving London - getting the hell out of dodge. Too far for you, babe. Tell you what, I'll recommend you to all the neighbours before I go - how's that?'

ꙅ

December 1st dawned cold and clear; it was what Lisa called a sunglasses and fur-coat day.

The removals van arrived early and by nine o'clock Ben's meagre possessions were loaded. On another day, he might have felt sad, pathetic even, that he amounted to a mobile recording studio and a few sticks of furniture. On the other hand, he was debt-free – and thanks to an advance from the record label, he was doing okay for readies. The new album would be released in February – just in time for Valentine's Day. The PRs talked a good game, pitching him as a housewives' dreamboat. It made him squirm a bit, but they were the experts.

And it was true that the album was full of love songs; songs that had taken on a new depth and significance since he'd fallen for Lisa.

Carrying out one last check in the echoing flat, Ben rescued a photograph from the kitchen pin board; a selfie with Kate and

Ludo, taken at the beach. Like the memory itself, the photo had faded, giving it a dreamlike quality. Thinking back, the whole messy episode had been a pipe dream.

Looking back made no sense. Looking forward was a much better option, and in a couple of hours he'd be moving into an elegant home, in a smart gated development, with a total goddess of a woman who loved him. And this time it was no pipe dream.

# CHAPTER 8:
## A MELTDOWN AND A THAW

### MARTIN

Christmas came early in Eden Hill. By the first week in December at least one house in every street was bedecked with fairy lights; it was fast gaining a reputation as 'nappy valley' and pester-power had a lot to answer for.

Any evidence of festive spirit only depressed Martin as he contemplated Christmas alone. It was incredible the speed with which his life had derailed. Jan showed no sign of returning, preferring (absurdly, in his view) to stay with her brother at his bleak seaside bunker. Hayley and Simon had patched things up (to a degree, there was still no evidence of a ring on her finger) and they'd mooted going to Tenerife for the holidays.

Martin shook his head; *focus*. Melancholy was slowing him down and he was already running late for his meeting at the Farleigh house.

Parking directly outside, he walked up the path and rang the bell. A dog barked. Perhaps he should get a pet - at least a dog wouldn't up and leave on a whim.

'Hello. Please - come in,' said a willowy woman, pleasantly. 'Would you like some tea Mr Bevan? I'm just about to make some.'

He followed Mrs Farleigh into the kitchen. A skinny dog trotted between them, eyeing Martin with suspicion.

'That's very kind indeed – white with one, please. This is a lovely house, Mrs Farleigh,' he said, wondering what she'd paid for it.

'Thank you...well, it works for us,' the woman said.

She looked familiar; 'Have we met before?' Martin said.

Mrs Farleigh dropped tea bags into cups: 'Yes, at a party in August, at Jeremy Hunter's place.'

It was a painful night to recall. One drunken, clumsy remark by Lisa Dixon had caused him untold grief. It seemed light years ago.

'Yes, a friend of mine recommended you,' she added, handing him a steaming cup of tea; 'perhaps you know her...Lisa Dixon?'

She continued to chat away as he followed her upstairs, through the master bedroom and into an opulent bathroom.

'It's a shame, because it's all so new - but we've gone off these tiles – and we like the wood effect in your showroom; much warmer looking.'

She left him to measure up. It was a straight forward enough job – any of his fitters would be able to crack it in a day or two.

Martin was about to leave when he heard himself asking after Lisa.

'Oh, fine I think.'

There was a tightness in Mrs Farleigh's voice and in Martin's experience 'fine' was often a euphemism for something quite the opposite.

'Well I'm glad she is, after all the trouble she's caused!' he almost shouted.

And then whoosh! Months of dignified silence came to an abrupt end, as Martin let rip a tide of misery - about his harmless flirtation with Lisa, the tabloid newspaper photograph, and finally how his wife of over twenty years had left him, believing he was having an affair.

'And it's so unfair!' Martin finished, his words hanging in the air like smoke.

Mrs Farleigh looked on, saucer-eyed. She reminded him of a deer, just like that dog of hers.Martin sighed heavily; 'I'm so sorry – I've been under a lot of strain recently, but there was no need for that. Please forgive me...I would never normally... I'll let you get on with your day, Mrs Farleigh. Thank you for your time.'

Martin moved towards the front door but to his astonishment, the woman placed a hand on his arm.

'Call me Kate...please. Look, I can tell you're very upset and after what you've just told me, I'm not surprised. But can I say something? Lisa has not one unkind bone in her body and if she had any idea of the problems you're having, she'd be mortified. Lisa's only crime is that men are dazzled by her. She can't help that...believe it or not, it isn't something she seeks. But there must be something we can do.'

We? She sounded so sincere that Martin wanted to hug her – which would have been even more inappropriate.

'Look, I... I'm sorry you had to hear all that; you must think me an absolute nutcase. I'll be happy to help you find another supplier...' Martin muttered, shame-faced.

'What? No, no ... don't be daft. Book it up - sooner the better. Don't worry Mr-'

'Martin – just Martin,' he said.

Her smile was warm; 'Look, please don't worry, Martin – I'm used to people telling me things. I think I've got one of those faces.'

In the car, he waited until he was out of view of Kate's house, then with balled-up fists he banged the dashboard several times, letting unintelligible sounds of rage escape. People were walking past, peering in but he didn't care.

I'm going mad...it's actually happening, he thought, driving home slowly.

That night, unable to face badminton with Jeremy Hunter and his smug cronies, Martin rang Jan's mobile – his call went straight to voicemail.

'Jan; it's me, darling...just calling to say that I love you, very much. And that I miss you. This house seems so empty without you in it, my love.' He hung up. What was the point?

For the second time that week, Martin ate from the chippy and went to bed at ten o'clock. Bloated and sleepless, he lay replaying the day's events, getting stuck on his meltdown at Kate Farleigh's house.

Oh, the shame of it.

✪

## LISA

On Saturday afternoon, Ben had taken Lisa to a reindeer farm. It was for kids, but she'd been ridiculously excited, rubbing the animals' fuzzy noses and feeding them carrot sticks from her pockets.

Ben had feigned cynicism, but she saw through it; he was even more of a big-kid than she was.

The next day, they'd gone in search of a Christmas tree and after ten minutes in the car, they'd pulled into a layby off the A20, where a twenty stone man dressed as an elf was selling a selection of beautiful pines ranging from deepest bottle green to a dusty blue.

Picking a six-footer, it was a miracle they managed to get the tree home without being stopped by the Police as it skewered the length of Ben's car, its spiny tip bent out of the passenger window. Lisa howled with laughter all the way home, imagining the spectacle.

Then they'd put on Christmas Carols and decorated the scented pine, drinking mulled wine and eating nuts and Twiglets.

'Pinch me,' Lisa said puckering up for a kiss.

'Are you happy, baby?' Ben said, with that languid sexy smile of his that reliably turned her spine to jelly.

'More than I thought possible,' Lisa said, pushing niggling superstition to the back of her mind; the last time she'd been this happy, Justin had been found dead and things had spiralled into nightmare territory for months afterwards.

The thought of losing Ben caused Lisa physical pain but she was torturing herself needlessly. Ben was robust; straight-backed, strong armed and looking younger every day, thriving under Lisa's TLC.

'Hon, do you mind me popping out for a couple of hours this evening? I don't know what Kate wants to talk about but she was kind of serious.' Lisa said, finishing up the mulled wine.

'Of course not. That's the thing about Kate; she is serious – so bloody dutiful. I should know...' Ben shook his curls.

'Sometimes it still weirds me out...I mean, all those years living in Spain, and then I come back and fall in love with my ex's mate – you couldn't make it up, could you?'

 �־

Luigi's was the kind of restaurant frequented by women of a certain age. The menu was safe and predictable but no less delicious for it, and Lisa had been anticipating a steaming plateful of Cannelloni al Forno all day.

Ben had dropped her off at seven o'clock sharp, only to find Kate already sitting in the window, brooding over a glass of Rioja.

'Lovely to see you, Lisa. My goodness, you look well,' Kate said, rising to hug her friend.

'Thank you – you too,' Lisa said, although it wasn't strictly true.

'Katie, is everything okay? I can tell you're worried about something. Is it to do with Ben?' Lisa braced herself for some unwelcome revelation; it had all been going so well.

'Okay. Look, this is going to sound odd, so just bear with me, and then we can put our heads together,' Kate said, taking a sip of wine before telling Lisa in some detail about Martin Bevan's emotional outburst.

Lisa listened with growing irritation; why was Kate even telling her this and what the hell did it have to do with either of them?

'I'll never be free of this, will I?' Lisa said, folding her arms.

'What do you mean?'

'Katie, nothing happened! We had a dance and he walked me home - end of. Maybe Martin thought he was on a promise, but I didn't fancy him – he's just not my type. It wasn't my fault we got papped.'

'Well, okay – I believe you, but that guy's marriage is over because of something that didn't even happen! We have to help him, Lisa...he's in a bad way.'

'Oh, Katie, you're such a pushover sometimes. Why is any of this your problem? And why should it be mine?'

Kate pursed her lips and studied her glass.

'I don't want to fall out with you, Katie...especially with the Ben factor and everything. But seriously...what can I do?' Lisa said, doing her best to be conciliatory.

'You can tell Martin's wife what you've just told me. She'd recognise the truth – you're very straight talking.'

'How? Where is she?' Lisa was horrified.

'I don't know...I said I'd give Martin a call at the shop and sort something out.' Kate said.

'Oh well, that's something to look forward to!' Lisa said texting Ben to pick her up.

ⓒ

Kate had driven to the restaurant, so they were spared being an awkward trio in Ben's car. 'What was all that about?' Ben asked, driving through the deserted lanes between Crabton and Eden Hill.

Lisa hadn't bothered trying to conceal her annoyance. They were living together now and things wouldn't always be fluffy.

'What happened?' Ben pressed her.

'Oh, it's a long one. I just want to get my PJs on and make a cup of tea,' Lisa said, falling silent until they were home.

Snuggled into blue gingham pyjamas, mug of tea in hand, Lisa explained Martin-Gate to an incredulous Ben.

'Bloody hell! You femme fatale you!' Ben smirked.

'Oh, I'm glad you think it's so bloody hilarious,' Lisa snapped.

'I'm sorry, Leese. Just trying to lighten up. Anyway, what's it got to do with Kate?'

Lisa pouted; 'That's what I said.'

'She needn't be so bloody sanctimonious – since when was Kate appointed marriage guidance councillor of this parish, eh? She's got her own issues! The woman's a hypocrite. She should get her own marriage straight before she starts interfering in other people's.'

'How can you say that? Kate and Neil are lovely together, one of the happiest couples I know,' Lisa said.

Ben snorted; 'Yep, you just keep thinking that, babe.' He opened the back door, where Nellie was whining to go out.

'Has she said something to you?' She could tell by Ben's tone that he had a real beef.

'It isn't what she's said...it's what she's done. Look, I've already said too much. Forget it. Shall I make more tea?'

Nellie barked to be let in and then sat demurely for a 'good-girl' biscuit, after which Ben put the kettle on. Lisa loved the way he was already so at home; the way he cared for Nellie, unprompted, and that he even replaced milk, bread and orange juice...not to mention toilet rolls in the bathrooms; unheard of male traits, at least in Lisa's limited experience.

She returned to the matter in hand: 'Ben, you can't say all that about a close friend of mine, and then clam up. I won't tell her. Go on, what happened.'

Ben winced; 'We almost did - two summers ago. Me and Kate had a bit of a... thing – and at the time I wanted us to get back together. I mean, thank god we didn't, but it was a distinct possibility for a while. Anyway, we lost contact until the night I met you at the wrap party in London. And the rest, as they say, is history.'

'Oh my god. No wonder she had a problem with you and me! Did you sleep with her?' Lisa's gaze was unflinching.

Ben grimaced.

'Shit, Ben – you did, didn't you? I should have known... it was all going too well. We're going to bed,' Lisa announced, snatching Nellie up and leaving Ben in no doubt who the we pertained to.

'Lisa...babe – why are you so upset? We didn't even know each other then.'

'Because she's a married woman, Ben. How could you do that? You can sleep in the spare room tonight.'

Lisa firmly shut the bedroom door and climbed between the sheets. The bed was cold and she snuggled Nellie to her like a little hot water bottle; Nellie sighed with contentment.

It was possible she'd over reacted – Ben would certainly think so. But nothing altered the fact that he'd pursued someone who was married, for his own selfish reasons. What had he hoped to achieve?

Equally shocking was that Kate was capable of cheating on Neil – and of being furtive and disingenuous with her friends. As for Lisa embroiling herself in someone else's marital mishaps; it was out of the question now; Kate could stick it!

A soft tap on the bedroom door prompted a yap from Nellie.

'Quiet, Nellie. Leave me alone, Ben. I can't even look at you right now.' Lisa called through the closed door.

Ignoring her, Ben entered the room and perched on the bed.

'Baby, I'm sorry. I'm not that person anymore...loving you has changed everything. I'd never do something like that now. It was wrong...I totally get that. Please don't shut me out, Leese. Let's not ruin what we've got for a moment of madness that happened before we even knew each other.'

Ben opened his arms but Lisa sat rigidly against the pillows.

'I don't know who disgusts me more, you or her!' Lisa said.

Ben looked hurt.

'I'm sorry, alright? I was a mess at the time and I was just being...' Ben searched for the right words.

'A twat? Oh, get in,' Lisa said, holding the duvet open.

Without a second's hesitation, Ben stripped off and slid into bed beside her, his default soppy grin returning to his handsome face.

She'd make him suffer for a day or two, but not too much; punishing Ben for crimes committed eighteen months earlier seemed pointless.

'Come here, gorgeous,' Ben said, enveloping her in his warm caramel smell; 'The whole Kate scene was a terrible mistake, but you could say that she brought us together, so...you know... sometimes things happen for a reason.'

'That's no excuse for shabby behaviour,' Lisa said, giving in and snuggling against him, 'Ben?'

But a change in Ben's breathing signalled that he was already asleep.

&#x1F34E;

## MARTIN

Overjoyed to hear Jan's voice on the telephone, Martin wasted no time in driving to the coast to fetch her, leaving Trina in charge of the shop.

'Don't read anything into it, mind. This isn't about just carrying on like before,' Jan had said over the fuzz of her mobile connection; 'It's about Hayley knowing where her mum and dad are at Christmas. Do you understand, Martin?'

'Of course, my love. One step at a time – I'll be with you by tea-time.' Martin had hung up, and all but sprinted home.

It was dusk by the time Martin arrived at Russell's place.

'Happy Christmas, Russell,' Martin said, extending his hand.

Russel ignored the gesture: 'I don't approve of this, by the way,' he said, before stepping aside to allow Jan to squeeze past.

Martin smiled serenely as he and Jan walked to the car.

'Oh, love - I'm so relieved to see you,' he said, 'Let's go home.'

But after a few miles, the silence became oppressive.

'Do you mind if I put the radio on?' Martin said.

''Course not. Does Hayley know I'll be at home for a spell?' Jan asked.

'I haven't told her yet, so it will be a lovely surprise. They're not going away now, so we can have a good family Christmas, just like the old days.'

Half an hour from home, the traffic came to a halt.

'There must have been an accident,' Martin said, tapping the wheel rhythmically.

'Don't, Martin. Please.'

Martin stopped tapping.

'What's Russell going to do this year?' Martin could not have cared less but he was desperate to get a conversation flowing – about anything.

'Same as every year; turkey dinner with his pals at the social club, followed by snoring in front of the telly like everyone else,' Jan said.

'I bet he was gutted you wanted to come home,' Martin said, unable to keep the glee from his voice.

'Not really. Martin, we're not teenagers, having a few ciders because it's Christmas – we're both too old for all that. And so are you and me. Like I said, this is for Hayley's benefit...nothing more than that.'

Up ahead was the unmistakeable eyeball-searing glare of blue lights.

'Must have just happened,' Martin said, 'The Police are still clearing the debris. Makes you think, doesn't it? Somebody's Christmas has already been ruined.'

As they crawled past the twisted cage of metal debris, Martin caught site of a child's teddy bear smiling benignly from the wreckage.

'Arh, I hope the little one's okay,' Jan's voice was soft.

'These days, what with air bags and so on, people often come out with just a few scratches,' Martin said kindly.

With Martin carrying her bags, Jan went inside, sniffing the air like a terrier. It annoyed him, the way she did that, but it was just her habit, the same way she always sniffed milk before pouring it into a tea cup.

'Tea or coffee?' Martin said, rubbing his hands together briskly. He'd left the heating off and the house was chilly.

'You've kept everything nice,' Jan said.

'Well, it's just been me, and I don't have time to mess things up, do I?'

'Suppose not. How's Trina getting on?'

Martin couldn't remember Jan ever asking about his young employee before.

'She's fine...looking forward to some time off, of course. Now Jan, we've got lots to do tomorrow...'cos now you're home, Christmas is full steam ahead.'

'Full steam ahead?' Jan repeated.

'Just you leave everything to me, my lovely.' Martin said, with a wink.

☙

The next day Martin opened the shop early and was pacing eagerly by the time Trina arrived. He handed her a mug of Nescafé and announced she was in charge.

'Again?' Trina said, raising heavily pencilled eyebrows. 'What have you got planned today then, boss?'

'Jan's home and I've got family business to sort...of the festive variety,' he added, shrugging on his coat. 'Just call my mobile if you need me. Thanks, Trina – you're a good girl.'

Trina beamed; 'Yes, I know. Martin...I'm glad she's back.'

Once in the car, using the hands-free gadget Hayley had bought him, Martin rang one of the fitters.

'Darren? How are things? Good.... how are you fixed for the next hour or two? I need you to follow me with the van for a bit. Can you meet me at Enwright's Garden Centre on the Old Hawk Road in twenty minutes? I'll see you right for a few quid – don't you worry about that.'

☾

So Martin had torn around the aisles of Enwright's Christmas Village, picking out a robust six-foot spruce pine, and filling his trolley with lights, baubles and festive ornaments, before loading everything into Darren's van.

'Thanks, Darren – you're a pal. Right, next stop Sainsbury's, so we can stock up on booze. Jan will be so surprised. It'll be like Father Christmas came early,' Martin said, rubbing his hands with excitement.

'I hope so, Mart. You can never tell with women - they're a complete mystery to me,' Darren said.

☾

By noon, Martin and Darren were dragging the huge tree through the back door of the house, leaving a trail of pine needles and muddy marks on the kitchen floor.

'Oh, Martin - look at the mess you've made!' Jan wailed.

'It'll clean; don't stress. Arh, smell that; the very essence of Christmas!'

'Where's this going, Mart?' Darren bumped through the door a second time, carrying a case of wine and bringing in more mud.

'Oh, for god's sake!' Jan said, clasping a hand to her forehead. At least she was dressed, Martin noted, always a good sign.

When they were alone, he opened the mixed case of drinks and carefully slid out a bottle of the palest blush wine.

'You'll enjoy a nice drop of rosé with your turkey,' Martin said.

'Oh, will I now?' Jan said, trying not to smile.

♻

That afternoon, Jan and Martin gently liberated dozens of new baubles from their tissue paper, placing each one carefully on the tree. Then Martin added two strings of white lights and placed a glittering star on the top.

'You didn't need to spend all this, Martin. There's nothing wrong with last year's decorations.'

'Nothing but the best this year, my love. You and I are going to make this a Christmas to remember.'

For the first time in a long while, Martin felt truly hopeful. He'd sent Hayley a text explaining that Jan was home for Christmas, and inviting her and Simon for dinner 'at 15.00 sharp'.

He got a 'woo-hoo', a heart and a smiley face by return. He was beginning to see the appeal of this texting lark.

♻

After spending the night in Hayley's old room, Martin woke Jan at eight o'clock with a pretty tray.

'It won't work you know, Martin. I can't be bribed with coffee and croissants. Ooh, they are lovely though,' Jan said, relishing every crumb.

'Can't a man spoil his wife for a change?' He said, tucking into pan au chocolate, perched on the edge of the bed.

Martin's strategy was simply to woo Jan with love and kindness, until her doubts were assuaged and she remembered why she'd married him in the first place.

Kissing her on the cheek before she could object, Martin said goodbye and set out for the shop.

'Morning, Trina. I'll be in the back using the computer,' Martin said. Then feeling modern and tech savvy, he went online and bought Jan a beautiful winter coat he'd seen in a magazine. It was charcoal grey, made from wool and cashmere, and cost Martin at least three times more than anything else in her wardrobe. Then from the same store, he ordered a bottle of Chanel No. 5; it had been the first present he'd ever bought her. If that didn't stir up some warm and fuzzy feelings, nothing would.

Gift sorted, Trina helped Martin to order Christmas food online and arrange a delivery from Sainsbury's.

'Bless you, Trina. I don't want Jan trudging round the shops two days before Christmas – although I'm rather hoping we can cook the turkey together...I wouldn't know where to start.'

She'd giggled when she caught him watching an internet tutorial later that day.

'Jamie Oliver is always a good starting point for blokes,' Trina said.

On their last day of trading, Mr Whittle shuffled in carrying a package wrapped in red-spriggy paper.

'Just a little something,' he said, tapping the package with a bony index finger. 'You've been very kind to me, Mr Bevan...and you, young lady. Who knows, I might even buy a carpet next year.' His laughter was a bronchitic rattle.

'Merry Christmas Mr Whittle – that's very kind, eh Trina? I'm glad you popped in, Mr W; you've saved me a delivery.'

Trina disappeared into the back office and returned with a hamper; in it were two bottles of velvet stout, a bottle of sherry, tins of pate and ham, water biscuits, and a large bar of chocolate. Trina had attached a glittering red bow.

Tears sprang to the old man's eyes.

'Is this all for me? Well...thank you very much. How kind of you – I'll take this to the hospital to share with Margaret...see if they'll allow her a little tipple.'

'I'm sure they will,' Martin said, his voice catching. He looked at his watch.

'I'm due to meet my wife for coffee in a while. Let me escort you home, those bottles are heavy.'

Outside the temperature had fallen.

'Looks like snow, Mr Whittle,' Martin said, glancing up at the white chiffon sky.

# CHAPTER 9:
## HOME TO ROOST

LISA

It was a relief not to have Ben under her feet all day. Much as she loved his company, the thought of a few hours alone, followed by coffee with Tanya seemed like an absolute treat. And anyway, Ben needed the odd blast in London with his muso mates; it was a win/win.

Lisa had expected the gym to be dead but it was rammed with people who'd already broken up for the holidays. Spurred on by the thought of imminent indulgence, Lisa ripped through a punishing workout, and then drove into Crabton to meet Tanya.

'Well how gorgeous do you look?' Tanya kissed her friend on each cheek before adding 'Loved up, or what!'

After a brief debate about which cake had the fewest calories, the women ordered Americanos and low-fat muffins, and spread themselves out at a corner table.

'So, how's it going with Ben?' Tanya said.

'Honestly, it's fantastic, Tanya. I can't believe how good things are between us. We laugh so much together...about the daftest things...and I fancy him like you would not believe.'

Lisa lowered her voice: 'You know how normally it's like, an effort? With Ben, I can't wait to go to bed at night – he's got the libido of a thirty year old. Seriously, it's like a dream. Well, most of the time. He's not perfect – we've already had a couple of arguments.'

'Well, thank god for that. Who wants perfection? Way too much pressure! I'm pleased for you, hon. You deserve it...after everything. I just hope I'm next.'

'Darling, it will happen. Look at me and Ben; it came out of nowhere.' Lisa said.

'So how are things with Kate?' Tanya asked, taking tiny sips of the strong coffee. Lisa made a face; 'Not brilliant. There's some stuff I found out...and we need to clear the air, but I can't face it yet. Shall we have another? My turn,' she said, getting up.

Hearing a familiar voice, Lisa turned to see Martin and Jan Bevan scouting for a table.

After finding a couple of window seats, Martin headed for the counter.

'Hi Martin,' Lisa said.

He looked startled as a fawn.

Lisa tried again; 'How are you? Can I have a word?'

'I'm in enough trouble because of you already,' Martin said from the corner of his mouth.

'Yes, I know, and I'm so sorry – that's what I want to talk about. Just give me a minute...please.'

And while Martin was caught up with the business of ordering coffee and cake, Lisa sat down beside Jan.

'I'm Lisa,' she said.

'I know exactly who you are,' Jan's pale eyes fixed on Lisa's.

'No, that's the point. You don't...you think something happened between me and your husband. Well I can tell you now, on my Nellie's life, nothing happened – you've got the wrong end of the stick.'

'The camera never lies,' Jan said. 'So don't-'

'Well actually, sometimes it does. You're talking about that scandal-rag, aren't you? That photo was completely out of context, and nearly everything that was written in that article was a downright lie. Your husband was just being a gentleman. He walked me home that night because I was on my own, and he lent me his jacket because I was cold. And yes, I thought he was single, but that was just me getting confused.'

It was a white lie, but now Lisa was on a roll. 'Anyway, I didn't fancy him then - and I don't fancy him now. So you should cut the poor man some slack, and be thankful that you've got a good husband. Right, that's all I'm saying. Happy Christmas to you both.'

Lisa looked up to see Martin hovering beside them, his mouth opening and closing wordlessly.

Lisa grabbed her coat and bag; 'Let's go, Tanya. I'll fill you in outside - but right now I need a stiff drink,' she said to her bewildered friend.

The two women hurried into the street where snow was falling from a white sky.

'Bugger. I knew I shouldn't have worn these heels today,' Tanya said, as they bolted for the pub across the road.

ⓒ

## KATE
Getting her sister to agree to Christmas in Eden Hill had required vast amounts of tact and diplomacy - and all because of Alice's fierce pride.

'I don't need Pete for me and Natalie to have a good Christmas and I'd be in the way at yours,' Alice said with an air of martyrdom.

'Alice, please. I can't bear the thought of another Christmas with just me and Neil - it'll be so boring. You and I can put on a fabulous dinner – and I'd like to spoil my niece for a change; don't deny me that.'

'But what about Neil?' Alice said.

'What about him? He wants you to come as much as I do, please Alice – it makes total sense. And with the baby due any day, I just want to be there to support you when-'

'Kate, stop. I can't talk about that. Look, we'll come...for Christmas – happy now?'

Kate chewed her lip; mentioning Pete's baby had been a step too far and the subject had been swiftly shut down, but at least Alice had agreed to spend the holiday together.

Gift shopping for fifteen year old Natalie had been a joy. Buying teenage vampire novels, lacy bras, sparkly belts and nail polish had been a welcome distraction from Pete-gate and on Christmas Day, Natalie had squealed with excitement to find the large stash of be-bowed gifts beneath the tree.

'You can't compensate for her father being a shit by buying all this stuff – so just stop spoiling her, Katie,' Alice said, not looking up from the mound of parsnips she was peeling.

'I know...I wasn't trying to. Do you think that's enough Brussel sprouts for four?' Kate said, shoving Ludo away for the umpteenth time.

Neil appeared in the doorway: 'Poor dog, the smell of turkey must be driving him crazy,' he said, looking cute but ridiculous in a Christmas jumper bearing an appliqued reindeer's face.

A gust of girlish laughter erupted from the sitting room.

'We're watching Home Alone,' Neil said, by way of explanation, 'but let me know if we can help with anything.' He disappeared before Kate could even reply. Kate and Alice looked at each other and laughed. It was warm and comforting in the steamy kitchen.

'Remember when Mum had the 'flu and we made Christmas

dinner together? We were only in our teens...and Dad kept marching up and down, shouting 'everything's under control.' My god, it's amazing we didn't all have food poisoning that year...' Alice trailed off.

'Yeah...I miss them, too,' Kate said.

More giggles and guffaws echoed from the next room.

'Bless Neil,' Alice said 'He's so good with Nat – he'd have made a great dad.'

'Al, please don't go there today...look, can we just cheer up a bit? It's Christmas day and honestly, I just feel lucky to have you and Natalie here this year.' Kate moved to baste the turkey, which was developing a deep golden hue.

'And we're glad to be here, but I can't stop thinking about what's about to happen. In the next few days, Natalie is going to have a baby brother...what am I supposed to do with that?'

'Oh, sweetheart...' Kate handed Alice a tissue.

'No! I will not cry about this today.' Alice blotted her face. 'Is it wine o'clock yet?'

Kate nodded vigorously, 'Hell, yes.'

The champagne cork flew out with a loud pop, drawing Neil and Natalie into the kitchen.

'To a family Christmas,' Kate said, hastily filling four glasses.

'To family,' they chorused.

'Ooh, my first champagne,' Natalie said, her eyes pinging wide open.

'Well sip it slowly, madam, or it will be your last!' warned Alice.

🍎

Kate's best white linen peeked beneath garlands of ivy, tied bundles of cinnamon sticks, and silver-sprayed twigs. The table was groaning with festive fare, sparkling glassware and church candles in several sizes.

'Wow – it looks like a fairy tale in here,' Natalie breathed.

Neil and Alice murmured awestruck admiration.

'Katie, I think you may have tapped into your inner craft goddess. The table looks stunning,' Neil said.

Crackers were pulled, wine and champagne guzzled and several pounds of crispy roast potatoes, parsnips and carrots devoured. The huge organic turkey was succulent and even the greens disappeared, yet the mood remained low-key and subdued.

'I wonder what Dad's doing today?' Natalie said, voicing what everyone else was thinking.

'Well, whatever it is, he won't be having a Christmas dinner as good as ours, nor will he be in such great company,' Neil said, helping himself to another spud.

'Amen to that,' Alice said.

&#63743;

After making a large dent in the Harrods Christmas pudding that Neil had snaffled from work, Kate suggested a walk.

'Who else needs some fresh air before we tackle the washing up?' she said.

'No thanks...I'll make a start on these,' Alice began clearing the table.

So Kate, Neil, Natalie and a stir-crazy Ludo set out, swaddled against the cold – even Ludo in his new fleecy coat – feet sloshing through the last of the snow.

'Thank you, darling,' Neil said, kissing Kate on a flushed cheek. 'That was the most delicious and perfect Christmas dinner ever.'

'Yes, it was lovely – thanks so much, Auntie. Hey, who's that waving?'

Out of the gloom, Kate spotted Clifford and Moira coming towards them.

'Happy Christmas,' they chimed in unison, before explaining they were on their way to feed a neighbour's cat.

'You are good, Moira,' Kate said, meaning it. 'Tell you what - on your way back, why don't you pop in and have a glass of wine with us...oh, this is my niece, Natalie...'

'Hi!' Natalie beamed.

'Natalie is here for the holidays with my sister, Alice. Anyway, the more the merrier so please come in for a drink, won't you?'

'Oh yes, we'll certainly do that,' Clifford said, before they walked on arm in arm.

'Dad's got a cat now,' Natalie said. 'He's called Diesel.'

Kate's eyebrows shot up; 'How do you know that?'

'He messages me all the time. He wants me to meet his girlfriend. Auntie – you do know she's pregnant, don't you?'

'Jesus, Natalie. Does your Mum know about this?' Kate was horrified - who knew what Pete had been filling her head with. Alice would blow a gasket.

'I haven't told Mum because anything to do with Dad just upsets her...and then she starts boo-hooing for Britain and I don't know what to say.' Natalie said.

'Well...do you want to see your Dad and meet... everyone?' Kate said, vaguely.

'I'd like to see the baby when it comes – babies are so cute. But not if Alice is going to have a meltdown about it...so, you know... whatever.'

'Hey Nat, since when did you start calling your Mum Alice and using words like whatever?' Kate said as they arrived back at the house.

♔

Christmas passed by in a blur of excess; too much rich food, too much alcohol, too many gifts; just too, too much, period – Kate thought, feeling her jeans pinch around her middle.

Baby Jacob Jones (Jones being his mother's name) was born on December 27th. As predicted, the news arrived by text, and Alice's response was one of great stoicism.

'Well – that's that, isn't it? None of this is the baby's fault. Poor little chap hasn't a breeze what he's been born into – or that his father is such a shit. I guess we've all got to move forward now. If Natalie wants to see her baby brother, I won't stop her. New Year's a good time for a fresh start and as long as Pete continues to pay up, I'll just crack on with my own life. Perhaps it's time to think about moving, too.'

'That's the spirit,' Kate said, proud of her sister's renewed fortitude.

Then, out of the blue, Neil suggested having a New Year's Eve party.

'What, here?' Kate said, 'It's a bit short notice, isn't it?' She thought of Ben and Lisa. If her sister could handle her husband of twenty years having a new baby, then surely she could deal with her ex-boyfriend and best mate living together. Inviting them round on New Year's Eve would send a clear message that she was cool with the whole thing and she and Lisa could get back on track.

Kate reached for her mobile; 'Okay; let's find out who is free.'

♔

Party food and copious amounts of wine were hastily bought, but Kate vetoed fireworks on the basis of Ludo's wellbeing. It was bad enough that the sky would be alight with whiz-bangs, let alone that he should see and hear them exploding in his own back yard.

On New Year's Eve, Kate and Alice rose early, then tore around the sales in Tunbridge Wells, looking for party dresses, egging each other on. The net result was that they each bought far more racy outfits than they were used to.

'Bloody hell, Alice! Your body looks amazing in that – you should show it off more,' Kate said, admiring her sister's silhouette in a burgundy lycra dress and high heels.

'Yeah, well – the divorce diet works wonders...I look alright, don't I?' Alice sounded surprised; 'Ha! Shame there are no single men coming tonight!'

Kate had opted for a midnight blue dress with a chiffon panel at the midriff. It was blatantly sexy and Kate knew it.

'Neil's in for a treat,' Alice said, helping Kate zip up.

'It's not for him...it's for me. I can't host a party where my ex-boyfriend and my best mate are going to be all loved up without some new armour, can I? I just want to feel good about myself, you know?'

'As long as that's all it is. Katie, be careful. You know my feelings about Ben; he's bad news...always has been.'

Kate blew a raspberry; it sounded like a ripping fart.

'Well that was grown up,' Alice said primly. They both began to giggle, becoming hysterical, until a sales woman stuck her head through the curtains and asked if they needed help, by which time, they were falling about, spluttering nonsensically.

'How old are we?' Kate said, wiping her eyes.

⚬

Back at the house, Neil and Natalie had done a sterling job of tidying everything away and vacuuming up pine needles from the now-listing and balding tree.

They'd agreed it should be a low-key affair, not least because the guests were to be a small and disparate band, consisting of Ben and Lisa, a few neighbours, and Tanya and her mysterious new beau.

So with candles alight, rooms spritzed and glasses polished, they waited for people to arrive.

Neil let out a low whistle; 'Don't we all scrub up well. Natalie, you look about twenty years old,' he said, taking in her makeup and tousled mane.

Natalie tossed her hair and smiled.

'Thank you, Neil,' she said. 'Does that mean I can drink tonight?'

'Don't push it Nat,' Alice said, 'you can have one – and then it's Coke or juice. Got that?'

♻

Moira and Clifford were first to arrive on the stroke of eight.

'I hope we're not early,' Moira said, handing Kate a box of milk chocolates. 'We won't stay long; we haven't seen the New Year in for years, have we Clifford?'

Clifford's jowls wobbled; 'No dear, but you never know...I'm in the mood to party,' he gave Kate a conspiratorial wink.

Next through the door were Nick and Charlie, waving bottles of beer and champagne.

'Well, how fabulous do you look?' Charlie said to Kate, indicating she should give him a twirl.

'And you smell divine darling,' Nick said, inhaling Kate's perfume.

When the doorbell rang again, it was Tanya, raven hair maxed-out into big waves, and wearing a tight black jumpsuit. Gripping her hand and wearing the expression of a seal about to enter shark-infested waters was a tall, dark haired man-boy.

'Everyone, this is Jason,' Tanya said, beaming with obvious pride.

'Hi,' Jason said, raising a hand but not looking at anyone.

'What's the weather like up there?' Charlie said, lifting his gaze towards Jason's handsome face. Jason smiled benignly.

'Bet he's never heard that one before,' Nick sniggered.

'He's a bit shy, bless him, aren't you, Jason? Here, have a glass of bubbly babe, that'll make you feel better,' Tanya said.

'Is he old enough to drink?' Nick said in a stage whisper.

Drinks were poured and introductions swapped, as everyone created a context for their presence. With each new guest a surge of energy whooshed through the house – which peaked with the tardy arrival of Ben and Lisa.

'Sorry we're so late,' Lisa said exchanging glances with Ben, who smiled sheepishly.

'Women,' Ben said. 'Why do they always take so long to get ready?'

'Ooh, take that back, Ben Wilde; I was ready two hours ago, until you...' Lisa stopped speaking abruptly, and the room fell silent as people processed the real reason why they were late. Blushing prettily, Lisa grabbed a glass of white wine as though it were a lifeline.

'Hello, Kit. Looking lovely as usual,' Ben said, pecking Kate on the cheek and handing over two rather smart-looking bottles of wine.

'Wow! Look at you, Katie. I love that dress,' Lisa purred. 'Thank you so much for asking us. We nearly got the train up to London...

but I'm glad we didn't, this is much nicer.' She began gamely introducing herself to Kate's neighbours.

Kate bristled inwardly. Together, Ben and Lisa shone – each reflecting the other's beauty. Dripping charisma, they rendered everyone else in the room invisible, like birds of paradise moving among a flock of pigeons.

Kate's gut twisted with something dark and rancid, and the harder she tried to push it down, the more it bubbled up, filling her chest and throat with bile.

She had to get a grip of herself. Lisa had been a good friend to her... and Ben? Ben was just Ben - and not her problem.

Kate watched the men in the room gravitate to each other, forming an unconscious them and us zone. But all eyes were on Lisa.

'Are you a model?' Natalie asked her.

'Oh, god no! I'm too short and much too old.' Lisa's laughter tinkled musically.

'Goat's cheese tartlet, anyone?' Kate said.

'Mmm, delicious. Did you make these, Katie?' Lisa said.

Kate's smile froze; 'No, of course not...life's too short for making pastry. Did you and Ben have a good Christmas?'

'Dreamy,' Lisa sighed, leaving no room for doubt as to why they'd enjoyed it so much.

Ben looked over indulgently, moving away from the male pride to stand beside his mate.

'You wouldn't think that a woman this gorgeous would be able to cook as well, would you?' Ben said to anyone who was listening; 'But Lisa did a knockout Turkey-roast. I thought to myself - Ben, you've hit the jackpot this time.'

Playing to the gallery, Kate laughed along with everyone else.

'Do I know you from television?' Charlie said, his eyes sweeping over Ben appreciatively.

'Maybe; I've done a couple of ads but I'm a musician really.'

'And he's very talented,' Lisa crooned, playing with a lock of Ben's hair.

Give me strength! Kate thought, nauseated. They were so lost in their love bubble – it was as if there was no one else in the room. It was either that, or they were on a mission to wind her up.

If Lisa was aware of Kate's chagrin, she did not show it; instead she began chatting to Tanya, tempting Jason out of his shell, asking him about his work and how long they'd known each other.

Hovering by the warmth of the oven with Alice, Kate busied herself replenishing snacks, her face flushed and set.

'Don't rise to it,' Alice said, 'He's just trying to make you jealous.'

'Why would he even bother? Ben's happy, that's all. And you know what? I'm happy for him. Lisa's a great girl and-'

'And drop dead gorgeous - which doesn't help much. Kate, Ben broke your heart...it's okay to feel-'

'And Neil mended it. Honestly, I'm fine...those two have got nothing I want. Ben and Lisa deserve each other.'

'Now why doesn't that sound very nice?' Lisa said softly.

'Lisa! I didn't know you were standing there. I...I just meant that... you've got a lot in common and seem so happy.' Kate was flustered.

'I don't think you meant that at all. Look, can we talk about this... things are a bit awkward between us and I'd like to work it out. You're my friend Katie, which means a lot to me.'

'Kate, thank you for a lovely evening, but we're going now, love.' Moira said, coming to her rescue.

'But it's only ten-thirty – aren't you going to see in the New Year?'

'No darling; you young people enjoy yourselves – Clifford's ulcer's playing up a bit and it's past our bedtime. Happy New Year, Katie. Thanks again, good-night.'

Clifford mouthed 'happy new year' from the doorway and they were gone.

The moment had passed; Kate turned to see Lisa talking to Nick and Charlie - even gay men seemed to be dazzled by her, she thought, attempting a conversation with Tanya and Jason, which she soon gave up on. With her head beginning to throb, Kate escaped into the darkened study and leant heavily on the desk. Within a moment, someone else entered the room.

'Why are you so pissed-off?' It was Ben's voice.

'What? I'm not - I've just got a headache.'

'You don't like it do you, Kit? Me and Lisa...getting it on...happy.'

'Don't flatter yourself, Ben.'

Ben laughed softly and touched Kate's hot cheek.

'Just think, the last time we were in this room together...'

'Don't you dare! That was a mistake...one I've regretted ever since. I was in a bad place...it wasn't even about you...'

'What was it about then?' Neil's voice cut through the gloom like a laser through stone.

'Go on, Kate...what do you regret so much? I've been standing outside the door for a couple of minutes, so don't fucking insult me by denying it.'

Kate pushed past Neil and ran upstairs, but he followed her into the bedroom.

'It isn't what you think,' Kate lied.

'Bollocks. I can read you like a book. You've always had a problem with Ben and Lisa...you've been seeing each other, haven't you?'

'No! Absolutely not.' Kate said with conviction.

'Are you fucking him?' Neil spat.

'Jesus, Neil! How can you even think that? I love you.'

Neil left the room and thundered downstairs. Moments later, the music became louder and Kate heard laughter – the sound of people having a good time. After fixing her blotchy face, she went downstairs to find people were dancing.

Through the French windows, Kate could see Neil and Ben on the terrace, their faces contorted with rage. Bizarrely, Ludo was standing between them, his sleek head moving from left to right as though refereeing their altercation.

Kate offered a silent prayer; please don't let them start fighting.

Wide-eyed, Lisa was standing beside her now.

'What are they arguing about?' she said. 'Katie, I know about you and Ben...it doesn't matter to me but...'

'Oh Lisa, just get Ben out of here! Neil knows, and that's all I care about right now. Just go, will you?'

Lisa hesitated before going out to the garden and grabbing Ben's arm - but not before Neil landed a punch squarely on his jaw. Ben staggered back, rubbed his face and then lashed out, striking Neil on the nose. Blood spurted from Neil's face; the two men starred at each other in shock and awe.

'Stop it right now!' Kate shrieked, jumping between them. 'Two middle aged men, fighting like schoolboys...Jesus! Ben, Lisa – go home...now!'

Kate looked around at the ring of shocked faces; at Alice, appalled, clutching Natalie to her; at Nick and Charlie, both wearing the same look of perverse amusement. Tanya and Jason were pulling on their jackets and heading for the door. The others followed them out into the night, while Alice and Natalie went up to their rooms.

Then it was just Kate and Neil, standing among the ruins of the party, Neil holding a blood-spattered tea towel to his face.

'We need to go to A&E.' Kate's voice was hoarse as she fought the urge to throw up.

'The face is fine - it was a lucky punch...but Kate, you and me... we're broken. I mean... Christ. I want the truth now. I need to know what happened...all of it.'

Just for a second, Kate felt something akin to relief.

# CHAPTER 10:
## FROZEN

### KATE

In January the snow returned, bringing everything to a halt. At first, people were euphoric - liberated from going to work as the roads in and out of Eden Hill became impassable.

With a sense of pioneering spirit, the residents put on snow boots and puffer coats and went on foot to the supermarket in the town square. But after two days, as supplies began to dwindle in the shops, and children grew bored of building snowmen, people became stir crazy, marooned on their ice-island, and impatient for the thaw.

Kate could not remember a more bleak winter, the snow and ice seemingly a metaphor for her interior landscape.

'I'll stay at Jonno's for a bit...just while we work out what to do,' Neil had said, reasonably.

And that was part of the problem. Kate longed for a fight, with yelling and accusations, tears on both sides, and then incredible make-up sex that would mean everything was going to be alright.

Neil's icy calm and air of defeat withered her. And then, in one short conversation, the final nail was driven into the coffin.

'Kate; the baby...it wasn't mine, was it?' He'd asked quietly, holding her gaze.

'I honestly don't know.' Kate had hoped that her candour might count for something.

But Neil had packed a few things and left, hugging her briefly at the door.

'Take care of yourself Kate. I just need to think for a bit.'

Then it had taken Kate several days to peel herself off the sofa. She'd even walked Ludo in the dark, dragging her winter coat on over her PJs, moving through the streets like a ghost and letting silent tears fall.

'You can't go on like this,' Alice said. 'Come and stay with us – Nat's at school all day and I'm job hunting, so you'll get plenty of time by yourself. Please Katie...let me look after you for a bit.'

The irony of both of them being deserted by their husbands within months of each other was not lost on Kate.

'Thanks, Alice. But I'm better on my own for now. I'll phone you in a day or two.'

Being around anyone - even Alice - would mean making an effort and showering, eating and talking all seemed insurmountable.

Kate hadn't the energy to hate Ben and Lisa. And it wasn't their fault. Sure, Ben's big mouth had let the cat out of the bag, but he hadn't acted out of spite. There was no getting away from the fact that the buck stopped with her.

Phone calls between them were measured and hesitant.

'Kate, what do you want? I know you're hurting but I just can't be around you at the moment. It's a trust thing – surely you understand that? We'll need to make proper arrangements soon, but I'm not equal to that yet,' Neil said.

Proper arrangements? Kate had held it together, and then howled after hanging up. Neil's infrequent visits home, which were prompted by the need for clothes, books and other personal effects, were perfunctory. They'd exchange small talk for a while, and then Neil would play with Ludo – and leave. It was extraordinary how remote and self-contained he'd become in such a short space of time. By contrast, Kate would be a gelatinous, tear-stained mess for days afterwards.

On Valentine's Day, Kate waited for a sign - but none came.

'He'll come round; he loves you,' Moira said, after Kate had leaked tears and recriminations all over her kitchen table.

'But it's been six weeks - and I can't get through to him...he's just shut me out, Moira. It's hopeless.'

'He's shocked and hurt, lovie. Male pride can be a very powerful force. Keep talking; keep telling him how sorry you are and how much you love him.'

There were practical considerations, too. Neil had always been the bread-winner, with Kate's meagre freelance income providing a top up for treats and luxuries. It was scary to contemplate supporting herself – which would certainly be the case if Neil made their separation formal. The house would have to be sold and then they'd divide the spoils and go their separate ways.

'You can't let it get to that,' Moira said. 'Beg Neil's forgiveness and get him to come home for the weekend, remind him what home feels like – what you feel like, Katie love.'

To her astonishment, Neil had agreed and Kate's heart swelled as his car swung into the drive on Friday night. He had bags with him.

Throwing caution to the wind, Kate opened the door and hurled herself at Neil, unable to speak for the mysterious wad of cotton wool that seemed to be blocking her throat.

She'd made lasagne for supper and opened a bottle of Shiraz.

'My favourites – thank you.' Neil said, absently stroking Ludo's silky head.

That morning, Kate had been to the gym, had a facial and then had her white roots coloured. It had been a much-needed boost.

Neil frowned: 'You look well – there I am, thinking you'd missed me and that I'd find a wreck.'

'You know I do - every day. Thank you for coming home. I just want us to talk, properly – it's been a long time. And...we can't just leave things as they are, in this horrible holding pattern.'

'I agree,' Neil said, topping up Kate's glass, before switching the subject to work and the various back-biting machinations at Harrington's. It never ceased to amaze her just how childish and competitive adults could be in the workplace.

'Have you seen them?' Neil said.

'Who?'

'Ben and Lisa.'

'No - and I don't want to, but I expect I'll bump into them at some point, they're practically neighbours.' Kate began to clear the table. 'Neil, I just want to say, whether you forgive me or not – and I am praying that you will find it in your heart...I will never forgive myself. It was wrong on every level and it wasn't anything to do with Ben – he's an idiot. It was about my own stuff; loneliness mostly.'

'So it's my fault then,' Neil said 'For not being there for you.'

'No, of course not! I have never blamed you, Neil.' Wanting to be held, Kate put her arms out, but Neil swerved into the next room.

'Shall I take the mutt out while you clear up, or vice versa?' Neil said, stretching his arms over his head. He looked tired.

'I'll clear up quickly and then perhaps we can both go for a walk,' Kate said, not wanting to let Neil out of her sight.

Outside the air was damp, but the temperature was surprisingly mild. Perhaps the worst of winter is over, thought Kate.

Picking his own route, Ludo led them towards Regents Place and past Lisa's house. Visible behind the gates and neatly trimmed evergreens, Ben and Lisa were curled round each other on the sofa; in the golden lamplight, it was a cosy tableau.

'See that?' Kate said, 'If we split up, we've got nothing. Please don't let one stupid mistake change our whole lives.'

'That's a big ask,' Neil said.

⟡

## LISA

Manager, muse, PA; from the moment Ben's album was released, Lisa found herself with more new hats than Ascot.

Not that she minded. By the third time she'd booked a day off work to support Ben, going with him to TV and radio interviews and holding his hand right until he walked on-set, it felt right and natural for her to be there.

'We could make this proper you know...if I left work. I mean, we're alright for money and I love my job, but I love being with you more. Ben, this could all disappear in a puff of smoke, and I don't want to miss anything,' she said, eyes shining.

Her colleagues at the clinic had been sweet, throwing Lisa a small leaving party and clubbing together to give her spa vouchers.

On her last day, Rupert Dale had made her blush.

'You're a smashing girl, Lisa. No wonder you bagged yourself a popstar. Ben's a lucky man. We'll miss you – I'll miss you...very much.' Then he'd kissed her on the cheek with real affection. It felt like the end of something good.

⟡

The record label's PR and marketing team had pitched Ben just right. Launching the album two weeks before Valentine's Day had been a stroke of genius, along with an ad campaign that painted Ben as the great romantic he'd never actually been. Or so he said, but his sweet, loving gestures told a different story.

'Yeah...well, don't tell anyone. I've got my bad-boy image to keep up,' Ben said, after Lisa had accused him of being a softie when he'd given her a beautiful cashmere sweater.

At the behest of the record company, he'd made a few personal upgrades, getting his teeth whitened, seeing a personal trainer - and spending a fortune on facials, manicures and a bunch of other 'poofy' treatments, as he called them.

It was paying off in spades. An appearance on Loose Women followed by an interview on the Lorraine show, ramped up album sales exponentially; it was uncanny.

'But why now, Leese?' he'd asked her.

'Because, my love, you get better with age – look at you, you're bloody gorgeous.'

The following week, an interview in *'At Home With...'* magazine put them firmly on the map as a couple. There in a spread that had been shot in their 'exclusive and gracious home' (as the mag put it), Ben and Lisa's smouldering chemistry and youthful looks were splashed across pages five to seven.

And when the interviewer asked them about marriage, Lisa's coquettish response had upped the ante.

'It's early days, but neither of us can imagine being apart...so... watch this space.' She'd snuggled closer to Ben and they'd giggled like teenagers.

The photographer caught the moment and the caption read 'marriage is on the table for this sizzling pair'.

Sponsorship opportunities began to trickle in, some for the 'grey market'; Ben was having none of it.

'Bollocks to it. I'm not endorsing cheap insurance for the over-50s. It's not very rock and roll, is it?'

Lisa had laughed at him, but not unkindly. He was living proof that age was just a number; he was her Peter Pan, her sun moon and stars and she could scarcely remember life before him.

♘

The day Lisa had run into Kate in the supermarket, she had woken up thinking she might, and tempting though it was to sprint for another aisle, Kate looked so fragile and forlorn that Lisa felt genuine concern for her old friend.

'Katie – how are you?' she said.

Kate sighed; 'I'm okay, you?'

'Oh, fine... are you shopping for Neil's dinner? I never know what to cook for Ben these days...one minute he's...' Lisa trailed off, aware she was babbling.

'We're not together anymore – not since New Year's Eve.'

'Oh god, Katie. I'm so sorry. Can I do anything? Look, I know we've...lost touch recently, and-'

But to Lisa's amazement, Kate dropped her basket and walked out of the supermarket.

Lisa followed, calling out to her.

'Kate! Wait, please!' Breaking into a jog, she caught up with Kate as she reached her car.

'Katie! Don't go like this. Talk to me for Christ's sake!'

'Why?' Kate's eyes were flinty.

'I'm worried about you. What happened with you and Neil?'

'Lisa, I know you're blonde, but you really can't be that stupid. You know what happened – you were there. Neil found out about Ben and he can't hack it. He's staying in London with a friend. I hardly see him and when I do, we're like strangers.'

'Oh god! That's awful.' Lisa said, rising above Kate's rudeness.

'Yeah, well....we'll be putting the house on the market soon, so we can separate properly.' Kate got into the car; 'So now you know,' she added, before pulling away.

'Don't get involved, Leese,' Ben said over dinner. He'd devoured a huge steak, while Lisa had picked at hers; the encounter with Kate had quite killed her appetite.

'But don't you feel even a teeny-bit guilty? She's on her own now – and she looked awful.' Lisa said.

'Not really,' Ben belched. 'I mean...I feel bad for her, but there's nothing I can do, is there? I think her old man overreacted. After all, it was only...'

'Spare me the details,' Lisa said, collecting up the empty plates. 'Anyway, there's something I want to talk to you about.'

'I'm all ears, baby,' Ben said, patting his now rounded stomach.

And then she'd explained about wanting to do something good with some of 'Justin's money'.

'Ben, I've felt like this for ages. That money was never mine, and that's why I've hardly touched it. And I don't want to just give it away to charity; I'd like to actually do something... of my own. I even talked about it to Kate once – but the moment passed. The thing is - people listen to us now...we're kind of...famous.'

Lisa grimaced; they'd never be A-Listers, but while they were enjoying their fifteen minutes of fame, they had people's attention.

'I'll get my guitar out and pass the hat round, shall I?' Ben joked.

'That's not a bad idea, actually,' Lisa said. 'Yes! What if we organised some kind of event...like a village fete, but bigger and with music as the central theme?'

Ben nodded; 'Sounds like a festival to me.'

'No, too big – it would take us months, years even, to organise

- and anyway, I'd be completely out of my depth.' Lisa paced, her mind whirring.

'We'd have to hire an event management firm; it would ramp up the cost but it would guarantee a good job and they'd help us handle all the health and safety stuff...permission from the council and so on.' She said, warming to the idea.

'But Leese, you can't finance something like that yourself – it would clean you out.'

'Not if we can secure sponsorship from local businesses,' Lisa said, 'babe, it would be brilliant. We can get local schools and colleges involved... art students, street dance troupes, young musicians – and guess who'd be the headlining act.' Lisa paused for a reaction, but Ben shrugged.

'You of course! You'd have to put a band together, but I know you can do that. Baby, you can do anything. Oh Ben, this is so exciting - I've got a good feeling about this!'

That night, Lisa couldn't sleep; instead she lay plotting, imagining an extravagant and flamboyant event that would put her on the map as a gracious philanthropist, fundraiser and kick-ass businesswoman. She'd get on it tomorrow; treat it like a job and start doing some research. She would bloody well make it happen; she would own it!

The next day, Lisa rang her ex-brother in law.

'Sean, it's Lisa. I'm sorry it's been a while...' It had been over a year; she braced herself for a cool reception.

'Hello, gorgeous. Long time no speak. How are you, Leese? Me and Debs saw you in 'At Home With...' magazine. You look happy – I'm chuffed for you.'

'That's so kind of you - I wondered if you'd even speak to me after all this time.'

'Don't be daft. How long were you married to my brother?'

'Bless you, Sean – you're a good man. How's Debbie... and George and Eileen?'

'Debs has got a new fella – seems nice enough; they're trying for a baby. Mum and Dad are okay...getting old...you know, like the rest of us.'

'Sean, the reason I called, I'd like to meet up. Can we get together in the next week or so? There's something I need to do - something I should have done a long time ago.

# CHAPTER 11:
## GREEN SHOOTS

MARTIN

A card in the newsagent's window yielded three customers within a week. It was a promising start.

'The thing I like about dogs,' Jan said, 'is that they don't judge - and anyway, being outside will get me a bit fitter.'

Dog walking had been Jan's own idea – and one that Martin had warmed to instantly. He'd read that being with animals – particularly dogs, with their soulful eyes and their wagging tails – could be helpful for people suffering from depression. And being out in sun, wind and rain would put some colour in Jan's cheeks and change her perspective.

So Martin had treated her to a hooded jacket from the country store in Crabton High Street; Jan had gone back the next day and bought wellingtons to match. Then she'd been to the pet shop in the next village and bought various dog treats and toys in shiny packets, and a strong collar and lead.

'Jan, I'm so proud of you,' Martin said.

Things had been different since what Jan now referred to as her 'holiday' at Russell's. Life had become more structured; they were a team now, like other married couples.

'I know I was wrong about that lady, and I'm sorry.' Jan said, when she'd decided to stay following a surprisingly upbeat Christmas.

'But even with all that embarrassing business out of the way, we still need to make some changes. I want us to be a proper couple. Maybe we should have a few more sessions with Nigel; we'd made some real progress before that misunderstanding – don't you think, Mart?'

Martin remembered the tiny wren and the lingering kiss in the lane. It seemed so long ago.

'If that's what you want, my love,' he said.

'There's something else,' Jan had that stubborn look on her face; 'I've played second fiddle to that shop for years, and I'd like you to start taking a day off a week, so that we can spend more time together.'

Martin had promised to sort something, but it was easier said than done and he'd need to speak to Trina about it.

Then he'd made a few demands of his own; it seemed only fair.

'I want us to make more of an effort – you know, smarten ourselves up a bit. Let's treat ourselves to some new clobber...and you can get your hair done regularly. We should go out more, too... for dinner and so on. And Jan, I want to play a bit more badminton again. What do you think?'

She'd kissed him on the cheek and made them both a cup of tea.

'Good idea. You need to do something for yourself, love.'

Terms and conditions had been renegotiated – it was a fresh start and they'd gone out for a pizza that night.

'Start as we mean to go on,' Martin said.

He rang Hayley; 'Well, thank god for that,' she said when he told her that Jan was home for good.

'You'll both need to make an effort though - you know that, don't you? No more taking each other for granted. And dad, you've got to stop babying her and bossing her about all the time. Let mum take some responsibility for a change.'

Martin smiled into the receiver; when had his daughter become so wise?

♂

## KATE

The daffodils and hyacinths in Kate's garden came and went, and as the days grew longer, all hope of Neil returning began to recede. They'd agreed that if either of them met someone else, they'd own up and tell the other. Now Kate was beginning to suspect that Neil was seeing another woman, possibly a colleague who'd hooked her claws into him – but it was pure speculation on her part.

'Katie, you've got to move on – it's been over three months,' her sister said.

'Al, I can't. Neil's still paying for the house, and there's been no mention of divorce or anything else more permanent. I'm not giving up on him.'

Alice harrumphed; 'I had to – you didn't see me mooning about waiting for Pete to come home and take it all back, did you?'

'Alice, that's not fair; you were grief stricken for months, just like me.' Kate was adamant. 'And anyway, Pete was having a baby with someone else – Jesus, Al, there's no comparison!'

'Alright, I'm just saying. Look...this limbo-land you're living in isn't doing you any good. It's time to get up off your knees, Katie. Tell that husband of yours that you've apologised for the last time and that if he can't forgive you, you want a divorce so you can both move on.'

'What if it backfires?' Kate said.

'Then you've lost nothing – and to me that says that Neil was just looking for an excuse in the first place. Katie, if you're not ready to have the conversation, at least start living again. Get a job, start looking after yourself, and get back out there. Honestly, I've never seen you like this. This sack-cloth and ashes routine has got to stop!'

Kate called Neil at work.

'It's me. Neil, I've apologised until I'm blue in the face – I still love you, and I couldn't be clearer about that, so I think now...'

'I'm sorry, I can't do this here. I'll ring you tonight,' Neil cut in before hanging up.

That went well, she thought, deflated.

By ten thirty, Neil hadn't phoned, so Kate sent him a text before crawling upstairs to bed.

'Apologised for last time (it said). Gutted our marriage meant so little to you. Time to move on'.

She'd expected her message to galvanise Neil into texting or phoning; neither happened.

Too numb and exhausted to cry, Kate fell asleep with Ludo sprawled on Neil's side of the bed; the one male she could always count on.

⚫

In the morning, Kate woke up feeling fresh and energised. Something had shifted during the night and after some tea and a brisk shower, she walked Ludo along the bridle path near the orchards.

It was peak dog-walking time and after fifteen minutes or so, Kate fell in step with a familiar looking woman whom she could not place at first. Waddling beside her was a rotund, old Staffordshire bull terrier.

'Ah, he's nice,' Kate said, bending to stroke the dog, who wagged his tail so hard that his whole rear end went with it.

'He's called Storm,' the woman said, 'He's fifteen. He's not mine, I just walk him.'

'Bless him; he looks well on it,' Kate said. 'We've met before, haven't we?'

Kate recalled first the pharmacy incident, and then pictured the woman in a black dress at the Hunters' summer party.

'Yes, I know your face. I'm Jan.'

'Of course - sorry. I'm Kate – and this beautiful boy is Ludo. It's a gorgeous day, isn't it? Shall we walk to the end of the track?'

Kate remembered Martin-the-carpet-man, and his emotional outburst and obvious despair months earlier. Now, it was clear from Jan's conversation that they'd managed to overcome their differences. If only she and Neil could do the same.

'Do you have a card or something,' Kate said, when they arrived back at Jan's Fiesta.

'No, I haven't been doing this long, but we can swap numbers if you like,' Jan said, heaving Storm into the back of the car, and settling him on a plaid blanket.

'Thing is, I'm looking for a part time job so I might need some help with the boy soon,' Kate said, before waving good-bye to Jan.

She'd said it out loud – which made it real. She'd get a job, crank up her earnings, and start living again. It was ridiculous how lame and dependent on Neil she had allowed herself to become. When he'd met her, she'd owned her own flat in South London, had been a copywriter in a marketing firm, and had been out on the town five nights a week; what the hell had happened?

Mug of coffee in hand, Kate went to her laptop and begun trawling job sites; getting someone to employ her would be a challenge given her age and the fact she'd been freelance for years, but breaking free of the crippling inertia she'd felt since Neil's departure was half the battle.

It was fight or flight now – and Kate was going nowhere.

ঙ

## BEN

Ben was struggling to give a rat's arse about Lisa's ex in-laws. What possible bearing could they have on her life now? But, if it mattered to her, it mattered to him; partly because he loved the bones of the woman – but also because he just wanted a quiet life.

Lisa had been vague, saying it was 'a financial matter' and something she needed to do. Ben had offered to go with her but she'd given him that old fashioned look she sometimes wore when he said something crass or off-beam, and told him it would be 'tactless'.

So she'd gone out, looking a million dollars, in a short knitted dress and boots, but had come back looking pensive and with half her eye makeup missing.

'Baby – you've been crying. What happened?' Ben asked as Lisa went straight to the fridge and opened a bottle of wine, although it was only five thirty.

'I'm fine, hon, but it was…emotional, you know? They were my family for years.'

Then she'd gone upstairs to wash her face before dropping the bomb.

She'd given away a hundred thousand pounds.

'Jesus, Leese! For a minute there, I thought you said you'd given away a hundred grand,' Ben was shocked.

She'd only smiled serenely.

'Ben, it's done now. And I'm glad; it was a very…illuminating meeting. I gave Sean and Debbie £50,000 each. Babe, it was meant to be. Debbie's going through IVF at the moment; well now she can go private, can't she? And I...I found something out – and I got upset, but it's all sorted now.'

'Come here,' Ben said, gathering her up in his arms; 'Is there any wonder that I'm so mad about you? That was very generous, and you know what? Your old man would have been proud, too. Justin was a lucky man – wish I'd known you half as long.'

'Hmm, not sure 'lucky' is the word you're after...but thank you, sweetheart, I know what you mean. But Ben, for god's sake, don't tell my mother, will you?'

There was no danger of that. He'd met Rita once and was not a fan. Lisa had pulled out all the stops to make her feel welcome and relaxed, putting fresh flowers and scented candles in her room, and baking a cake from scratch. Unimpressed, Rita had spoken to Lisa like rubbish all weekend when she thought Ben was out of earshot, but had flirted outrageously, becoming quite the coquette to his face – it had grossed him out.

Lisa had been the very model of tact and patience.

'She's not a happy woman; you have to make allowances,' was all she'd said.

🍏

Diplomacy was only one of Lisa's ample talents. He had to hand it to her – she could be dynamic; making things happen at a rate of knots. No sooner had she voiced an idea – Bam! It was game on. She'd been deadly serious about putting on a summer event in Eden Hill, and had hired an event planning company to take care of the legals and logistics. Now it was all getting very real.

Incredibly, she'd even managed to get a handful of local businesses on board, putting together sponsorship deals worth thousands of pounds. He'd seen her in action, the way she handled people; the woman was irresistible – all proposals and spread sheets up the sharp end and then, to clinch the deal, she'd fix some hapless suit with those incredible eyes and hypnotise them into signing on the dotted line.

They'd trawled local charities together for days, deciding which should benefit, finally picking two that were niche, but brilliant; a sports camp for disabled children where the kids could have a blast, and the parents could take a break, and a drop-in centre for young people with drug and alcohol issues.

Ben was choked and humbled in spite of himself.

♉

Ben didn't mind that they'd inadvertently become local celebrities, attracting attention just going about their daily routine. The album continued to sell steadily, and the record label had earmarked a follow-up single for release in early summer – perfect timing for the fund raiser, which was planned for the first Saturday in July.

The only blot on the landscape was Kate. He'd seen her around town and walking past the house with the mutt – always alone, and with that hang-dog, martyred expression. Come to think of it, what was that saying about people looking like their dogs?

He knew that Lisa missed her friend and had tried to build bridges, but Kate was having none of it. It was a classic case of Kate cutting off her nose to spite her face; she'd always had a stubborn streak.

Ben pushed any residual guilt to the back of his mind. Shit happened – it was how you handled it that mattered. It wasn't his fault that Kate's marriage couldn't weather a little dalliance.

♉

Sometimes Ben would catch himself, enjoying the feeling of his bare toes sinking into the deep pile carpets, or smiling smugly over a cappuccino he'd made with the shining Italian gadget that Lisa had installed; he loved watching Match of the Day on one of their massive flat-screen TVs. And then he'd remember the way he'd judged Kate for selling out – for his contempt for Eden Hill and all that it represented.

Well if that made him a hypocrite, then so be it; there were worse things he could be.

Until he met Lisa, Ben had always spat the word *suburban* as a pejorative term; now it just felt like home. He revelled in the comfort, the peace and the order of their daily lives. He liked that people were so damn decent and chatty, always out walking their dogs or cleaning the car, or back slapping each other at the gym. It was all so wholesome.

Ben chuckled to himself; who'd have thought it? He'd be taking up gardening next.

ॐ

## LISA

Lisa gasped, shocked to see how like Justin Sean had become since she'd last seen him.

'No bad thing, if you ask me – he was a good looking bugger, my bro.' Sean grinned.

Debbie hung back, brushing cheeks when Lisa bent to kiss her former sister in law.

'You look so well, Lisa - doesn't she, Debs?' Sean said.

'Well...thanks. You both look lovely, and just the same – it's so great to see you. I booked a table in the atrium - shall we go and sit down?'

'We'd like a bottle of house champagne, please - while we're choosing,' Lisa told the waiter as soon as they were seated.

'Special occasion,' she added with a beaming smile before studying the menu.

'It's smashing to see you, Leese. But we were a bit surprised to be honest – weren't we Debs?' Sean raised a glass, 'Good health, ladies,' he said.

'So Debbie,' Lisa began, 'Sean tells me that you've met a wonderful man and you're having a baby together.'

'We're trying for one anyway. You'd like Andy; he's such a good man, kind, you know? Anyway, I'm forty in a few weeks, so we need to crack on – and we're looking into IVF...but it's...complicated and bloody expensive. Anyway, Lisa; how about you?'

'I'm well and life's pretty good at the moment,' Lisa said, mindful of sounding smug. 'Ben's lovely...we get on so well, and he makes me laugh, the daft sod.'

They continued to swap news and small talk throughout the main course, until Lisa could no longer contain herself.

'There is a reason I arranged today,' Lisa leaned forward looking from Sean to Debbie and back again.

'Thought there must be,' Sean said, nodding.

'Look, before I say anything else, promise me you'll go with the flow, okay?' Lisa took a deep breath. Then reaching into her leather clutch, she pulled out two pieces of paper, and handed Sean and Debbie one each.

'You're shitting me. Fifty grand? What's this for? No, I ain't taking that.' Sean laid the bankers' draft face down on the white table cloth.

Debbie was staring at hers as though trying to work out what it was.

Lisa giggled. 'I knew you'd say that, Sean – well, both of you.

Look, no arguments – I want you to have it...I meant to give it to you ages ago. Justin loved you both so much; I know he'd approve. I'm also putting on a charity event in July, in Justin's memory – it's scary, but it's all coming together now.'

Debbie's eyes were glassy with tears.

'Bless you, Debs, I don't mean to upset you. I know you must miss him so much. But I...' Lisa began.

'It's not that...well it is...but... excuse me...' Debbie got to her feet and went briskly to the ladies' room.

'Shall I go after her?' Concerned, Lisa got to her feet.

Sean shrugged.

No one else was in the mirrored cloakroom. Lisa tried to put an arm around Debbie's shoulder, but the younger woman shook her off.

'You don't understand. Don't be kind to me, Lisa – you'll make things worse.'

Lisa frowned; 'What are you talking about?'

'I can't take the money, Lisa. I don't deserve it...not after what I've done.' Debbie's mascara was beginning to blur.

'Debs, what are you saying?'

'I'm sorry...I was just so upset...grief stricken – and I blamed you, Lisa. Justin still loved you - he always talked about getting sober and getting you back and I...'

'What? It can't be that bad!'

'Yeah, it is...it's really bad, Lisa.'

Their eyes locked in the mirror.

'It was me,' Debbie said, her voice almost a whisper; 'all that rubbish in the papers...the rumours that Justin had killed himself because you destroyed him.'

The penny dropped; 'Oh god, Debbie...you fed them all that nonsense?'

'Yeah, I did...and I'm so ashamed now. And it was me who contacted that horrible creep Andrew Anson. I didn't do it for money, Lisa. I was just so...so sad...my big brother meant the world to me, and I blamed you...and I don't even know why now. I'm sorry - I'm so sorry.'

Lisa was stunned; how could Debbie have hated her so much? Tears were welling now.

'Does Sean know?'

''Course not - he'll be furious when he finds out.'

'Okay, you listen to me, madam,' Lisa said, sounding braver than she felt; 'This ends now, alright? No one needs to know – especially not Sean. On one condition, Debs...and I mean it. You take that money and you use it to make a baby...for IVF...whatever you need to do. Justin was never a dad, but he'd have made a lovely uncle.'

Debbie sniffed; 'I can't – it wouldn't be right.'

'You can – and you will. It's settled. Now, let's sort our faces out and go and have the biggest dessert on the menu. I friggin' need one after that!'

🍎

The weeks were passing at an alarming speed. There was so much to do if the fund raiser was to hit the mark. It became all consuming – more so after Lisa sacked the events planning firm, before hastily appointing Liberty, a freelancer from Tunbridge Wells.

'I had to fire them,' Lisa complained to Tanya during an early morning workout at the gym. 'The budget just kept going up and up – every task seemed to cost extra! I'm already run ragged, so I might as well do it myself - with Liberty's help of course.'

'I wouldn't know where to start, Hon. I couldn't organise a piss-up in the proverbial, but you've got a real talent for this,' Tanya said, brushing her hair in the locker room mirror.

'Believe me, Tanya, it's not about talent. It's about being organised; making dozens of lists and sticking to them. Thank god we've cracked all the local authority stuff, sorted the health and safety and equipment hire and so on...honestly, there's so much to think about. The logistics are a nightmare - car parking, porta-loos, insurance...'

'Bloody hell, I'm exhausted just listening to you. Can't Ben help?'

Lisa scoffed. 'He means well, but by the time I've taken him through what needs to be done, I could have done it myself...so honestly, no. It's fine - as long as he comes up with a great set for the finale, I'm happy.'

Ben had at least done that much; five songs from the new album – including the effervescent track from the Helium campaign, a couple of covers, and Seagull (the original version) to close the show.

Other acts already booked included a street dance troupe from the local performing arts school; Ozzie Davies, a rat-pack singer, who'd dragged his heels about performing for expenses only – until Lisa had flattered him into submission; a ladies choral group from East Sussex, who sang rock anthems with all the angelic sweetness of a cathedral choir, and a boy band from Maidstone that had made the short list of a TV talent show.

The stage set was to be small and slick, and came with an army of techies and roadies, all donating their time for free.

It was touching how the community had got behind the event. Dozens of companies and locals had offered time, know-how and equipment for free; keen to do their bit for the two kids' charities – in exchange for goodwill and some local PR.

The PTA at Eden Hill Primary school had amazed Lisa by taking a raft of food stalls, offering to make and sell cakes, biscuits, burgers and bangers; there was something for everyone.

But it was local farmer Mike Millard who had come up trumps, by turning his fields over to Lisa to stage the whole shebang. He'd even given her a barn for 'Creature Corner' - a make-shift petting zoo, where children could meet and stroke lambs, goats, rabbits and other small furies.

Mike's farm occupied a strip of land that ran between the edge of the estate and the outskirts of Crabton. He'd approached Lisa directly after the event company had sounded him out and she'd been grateful enough to overlook Mike's hand grazing her breasts and bottom at every opportunity, during her first recce.

She'd mentioned it to Ben - which had been a mistake.

'I'll knock his block off if he does it again, cheeky bastard. That's the last time you go there alone - next time, I'm coming with.'

Lisa rolled her eyes.

'Babe, I've been dealing with his sort for years,' she said.

# CHAPTER 12:
# UP

## KATE

Kate had expected a dismal concrete exterior, housing magnolia walls, carpet tiles and dusty filing cabinets. The reality was a barn conversion with floor to ceiling windows and a bright comfy reception area where two pretty young women were fielding calls from the busy switchboard.

'Hi, how can we help?' said a smiling, freckle-faced redhead.

'I'm seeing Dominic Reid; my name's Kate...Kate Stone.'

Just saying her maiden name aloud made Kate feel more in control. To all intents and purposes, she was a single woman now and with any luck, she'd soon be a working woman, too.

At least ten years Kate's junior, floppy haired and brown eyed, Dominic Reid loped into reception. Kate shook his hand before following him through an open plan office buzzing with activity and into a small meeting room.

'So, what brings you to our door?' Dominic said, once they'd cut through the pleasantries. Feeling matronly in her charcoal trouser suit and candy-striped blouse, Kate mouthed the answers she had rehearsed in her head over and over; it was time for new challenges; she didn't want her skills to atrophy through lack of use; she missed the interaction of working with a team of gifted creatives - clichéd stock-phrases that were all code for the fact that she needed the money.

Dominic smiled; 'I see. What's the real reason?'

Something about his open expression touched her. Kate took a leap of faith.

'Dominic – those things are all true, but if you're asking 'why now?' after being in the freelance wilderness for so long, I'd have to say that it's about my change in circumstances.' Kate twisted her wedding ring unconsciously.

'I'm getting divorced and I need to be financially independent. I've blown my cover, haven't I?' Kate held Dominic's treacle coloured eyes for a moment.

He nodded; 'Now that I can relate to. Let me tell you what we need here...'

Kate found herself listening intently to Dominic's warm, honeyed voice. The job was well within her remit; writing blogs and website copy, with the occasional requirement for product literature - all standard fare. But there was something appealing about the place – and certainly about the man sitting before her.

'Look, I'm not going to mess around here. I've read seven or eight examples of your work online, and you're a very competent writer. I've been interviewing all week and nobody of your calibre has come through the door yet. So Kate, the job's yours if you want it. I'll drop you a line before close of play regards salary and terms etc., then sleep on it and let me know tomorrow.'

Had he just offered her the position? She'd been so nervous about the whole thing, now it seemed too easy - where was the catch?

'I don't need to think about it, Dominic. Thank you so much! I'd be delighted to come and work here.'

Stepping out into the afternoon sunshine, Kate felt a bolt of pure joy shoot through her. She reached for her mobile and dialled

Neil's number – then changed her mind and hung up before he could answer.

This was the first step towards standing on her own two feet; she didn't need approval from her soon to be ex-husband.

Ć

Relenting, that evening Kate rang Neil.

'Wow, Kate...okay...are you sure? What about Ludo?'

It was not the reaction she'd been hoping for.

'God, Neil. You might at least be happy for me.'

'I am happy for you. It's just... I don't know – it's been years since you did anything like that and I'm surprised, that's all.'

'Look, if you're worried about Ludo, it's only three days a week and I've met a great dog walker, Jan – I told you about her... and anyway, don't make me feel guilty. It's not as though I have a choice.'

'What does that mean?' Neil sounded hurt.

'Love, we've been separated for months. You can't go on paying for everything here...we've got to make proper plans now. This job is a step towards that.'

'Have I once complained about supporting you?' Neil said.

'No, but why should you? When we were married, you were the bread winner and it was fine then, but...'

'Kate, we still are married...well, we were the last time I looked.'

'Then come home. Be with us. We miss you.'

It was a stupid argument – but one that stirred hope in Kate every time they had it.

'I can't, Katie, I'm sorry. I just keep picturing you and Ben...at it,' Neil said.

Ć

Kate had seen the flyers in Crabton, and the ads in the local Gazette. Ben's grinning face had grabbed her attention, compelling her to read the whole thing, in spite of her irritation.

She remembered fragments of a conversation with Lisa, about putting on a fund-raiser. Well hats off to her; she'd made it happen. On a whim, Kate emailed Lisa, with the words 'Olive Branch' in the heading.

'Am available to pour tea, man a stall, bake cakes or write press releases,' she wrote, adding 'Hope life is good for you and Ben.'

She needed to forgive them both if she was to move on with her life, which had been improving by leaps and bounds since starting work. Kate had slipped seamlessly into a weekly routine of three days spent at the barn, a day at home freelancing, and a blissful day of freedom, during which she indulged Ludo and herself if the mood arose. She was missing Neil less, and had started to feel strangely detached from the house, which now felt like a glorified wardrobe.

'Neil, we have to stop treading water. You're renting with a colleague and I'm rattling around this show-house with a small dog. It's ridiculous. I think we should put the house on the market and split the equity – it's the only way.' Kate's words had tumbled down the phone one Saturday afternoon in May – and this time without the tears and recriminations that usually followed.

'Okay. If that's what you want, Katie,' Neil said.

'It isn't. I want us to be a family again, but as that ship has sailed, I need a home of my own...and to start again.'

'Oh, I get it. You've met someone haven't you? Neil was gruff.

'I haven't met anyone. But you know what, Neil? For the first time – I feel that I might like to.'

Neil's reluctance to move forward was baffling to her. At first, Kate had seen his cock-eyed, juvenile living arrangements as a ray of hope - but as time went on it irritated her beyond belief. How could he be so passive?

'Kate - I'm working twelve hours a day as standard, and getting on a plane some weeks. Where I'm living is not a priority right now,' was how Neil had justified it.

Ć

Lisa's familiar, breathy voice sounded harassed but happy.

'Katie, so great to hear from you,' she said.

'Thanks – you, too. How are things with you and Ben?'

'Really good, thanks. Mad busy though...there's so much going on, what with the fund-raiser and Ben's career. He's playing a couple of small festivals this summer, can you believe it?'

'That's brilliant, Lisa - I'm happy for you. Look, I meant it about helping out. If you need an extra pair of hands – I'm your woman, okay?'

They'd chatted for ten minutes before Kate raised the subject of Neil.

'We're over, Lisa. It's sad, but we both need to move on now,' Kate said, before adding 'Hey, I've got a fab new job and I've made friends there. You'd like my boss, he's hot!'

It felt good talking to Lisa again. Her taste in men might be dubious (not to mention embarrassing) but her warmth went a long way.

# CHAPTER 13:
## A BIG DAY OUT

One-Two...One-Two! A searing whine emanated from the stage as the sound check got under way. Mike Millard covered his hairy ears and hoped he wouldn't regret hiring out his land for this shin-dig.

He'd expected a bit more gratitude from Lisa Dixon. He'd managed to cop a feel of those magnificent boobs of hers – and make it look like an accident, but now that long-haired grinning idiot always seemed to be about, stuffing up his chances.

What the hell? It was all for a good cause; those kiddies' charities needed all the money they could get, and Mike's cronies on the council had duly noted his act of generosity, which would no doubt come in handy at some point.

By noon, a queue of vehicles had formed at the parking field; other people were arriving on foot, cutting across the fields from Eden Hill, carrying rugs, cool boxes and picnic bags.

'Nice day for it, lovely,' Mike said to Lisa, as she hurried past wearing a radio head-set and a tight vest emblazoned with the words: 'Eden Fest'.

Lisa paused in her stride; 'Hi Mike - you mean the weather? Yes, it'll be brilliant if it stays like this all day. As long as it doesn't get too hot – we don't want people passing out from heat stroke.

Thanks again Mike – you're a darling – I won't forget this.' Lisa turned her eyes on him full beam, before joining Ben at the side of the stage.

'You did it, babe. I'm so fucking proud of you,' Ben said, his face splitting into a huge grin. Lisa looked about her. Months of planning, of endless lists, phone calls and meetings, and several weeks of broken-sleep had finally come together.

In a clutch of white tents erected as dressing rooms, half-a-dozen nervous acts were warming up, getting ready for the nine-metre stage, where sound and lighting rigs were being rigorously tested by incumbent crew.

Over twenty stalls, selling everything from cakes to candles, were being given their finishing touches, while local businesses made the most of their sponsorship packages, posting flags and flyers on display boards, and unpacking merchandise to give away.

In the kids' zone, a face painting stall and a bouncy castle competed with the petting zoo, from which emanated grunts and whinnies, and the pungent smell of urine on straw. Stewards in red dungarees were on standby, poised to mop up tears and tantrums - and potentially vomit, judging by the amount of confectionary on sale.

Lisa took a deep breath; 'Half an hour to go; I feel sick...I must have been to the loo five times in the last hour. Are you nervous, babe?' She said, steadying herself against Ben.

Ben laughed; 'A bit...it's not exactly the O2 is it? But I think you've done an amazing job to sell 400 tickets in advance.'

'The sun will bring more people out, you watch,' Lisa said; 'Ooh...I'm needed in the performers' tent,' she said, pressing the headset to her ear, before charging off on her mission.

Ben spotted Kate arranging flyers on the raffle stall - he waved; Kate smiled and waved back. She looked fit today, in T-shirt and combats; a tight top had always suited her, he thought.

☾

Martin and Jan bickered about whether to take a blanket or a couple of folding chairs.

'It'll be me that gets lumbered carrying them,' Martin said; 'It's been dry all week, so a rug will be fine – and it's not for long; it finishes at 18.00 hours.'

'Or at six o'clock,' Jan said, rolling her eyes. He was a funny bugger, always so precise. She'd put on a summer dress and flip flops with Star-Fish on them. Her limbs were lightly tanned for the first time in years. The dog walking had done that; out in all weathers with Storm, Ludo, Basil and Barker - which had amused her; 'I ask you, Martin – who calls their Pekinese Barker?'

Jan's list of fury charges was growing, and the more Jan walked, the more robust she became – halving the number of tablets she took within a few months.

'There's something about being outside...seeing all the trees in bud and the flowers pop,' she'd explained, 'And the way the dogs look at me; it makes me feel full up - here.' Jan said, placing a hand over her heart.

☾

At one o'clock, parking as close to the entrance as possible, with Jan holding the rug and Martin lugging a cool-bag stuffed with sandwiches, a bottle of pop and a box of French Fancies, they found a spot near the front.

'Not many here, are there?' Jan remarked, spreading the blanket.

'We're early,' Martin said, studying the printed flyer; 'Must be twenty years since I went to a pop concert.'

'Is that what you'd call this then?' Jan said, rummaging in her bag for sunglasses.

A constant stream of people were coming through the gates now; all ages, in colourful clothes and carrying picnics.

'Do you mind if I have a wander, Mart?' Jan said, setting off in the direction of the cheerful white awnings and trestles where people chatted to friends and neighbours, or looked for an excuse to spend money.

'Hello, Kate,' Jan said, spotting Ludo's owner.

'Jan – you look well. Do you want to buy a raffle ticket? They're £5 each, but the prizes are fantastic – no bath salts here! You can win a flat screen TV, a spa weekend, designer clothes...there's all sorts - we've had some brilliant donations. Ooh, hello - we're starting.'

A piercing shriek from the PA system caught their attention as Lisa walked to the centre of the stage.

'Go on Lisa!' Kate whooped, clapping hard.

Polite applause and a few wolf whistles rippled through the audience.

Ben beamed with pride: 'That's my bird. Am I punching, or what?' he said to one of the techies and anyone else who was listening.

 &#63743;

'Good afternoon everyone,' Lisa breathed into the mic.

'Ooh that's loud, isn't it?' She giggled before going on with her speech. 'My name's Lisa Dixon - and I want to welcome you all, and say a massive thank you to everyone. Whether you've bought tickets, given time so generously, provided goods to sell or raffle... however you've helped – thank you so, so much.'

People whistled and clapped while Lisa named and thanked the sponsors, before plugging the two children's charities that would benefit, and welcoming their respective founders to the stage.

'Okay,' Lisa beamed, 'you didn't come to hear me banging on, so without further ado, will you please welcome, from the Hollywood Road performing arts school – Synced In!'

Lisa jogged off set as the music thumped into life and a troupe of dancers sprang onto the stage. Bursting with pent up energy, the street dancers' moves were slick with precision power. The audience roared its approval.

'Was I alright?' Lisa asked Ben, who'd gone decidedly quiet.

'You were great, babe – you looked amazing up there. Think I'll have a beer; take the edge off my nerves.'

He'd rehearsed his set in the studio, with Steve on keyboards, Ricky on lead guitar and a drum machine as their fourth band member; none of them had arrived.

'Where the hell are you, man?' Ben had called Steve – to learn the boys were stuck in traffic.

'Thank god we're on last...just means we'll have to set up in full view of everyone.'

'Alright mate - that's no biggie. See you in about forty minutes.' Steve said, hanging up.

Ben had been hugely relived to see Ricky's van rumble into view, and then he'd corralled the guys into the performers' tent where they made minor tweaks to the set.

'I've had an idea,' Ben said, 'I'm doing the first verse of Seagull unplugged – and then you come in for the chorus and on we go. What do you think?'

'Hello, Kate. Is this your good deed for the day?'

Kate blushed to see Dominic, super cool in battered jeans and a faded black T-Shirt looming over her.

'Dominic, hi. I didn't know you were coming. Is anyone else here from work?' Kate fluffed her hair, instantly wishing she'd made more effort with her appearance. Poor Dominic always had that effect on her, even in the office.

'Yes, Maddie and Jo-Jo are somewhere around. How come you're involved?'

'I'm friends with the organiser – Lisa. And it's not exactly taxing, I'm selling raffle tickets - there are some fab prizes...'

But before Kate could launch into her sales pitch, Dominic produced his wallet and peeled off two twenties.

'Go on then – however many that buys me. You look great by the way. See you later, Kate – perhaps we can grab a drink...or something?'

Had he been hitting on her, or merely making conversation? It was an important distinction to make when it was your boss asking.

ტ

Nobody spotted Danny Burden as he slipped through a narrow gap in the fence. Nobody ever noticed him; certainly not his mum, who, by most afternoons, was too drunk to care where her boy was. Nor his teacher; classes were altogether more pleasant without the pimply, whey-faced youth disrupting others - he'd actually overheard Mr Stevens say that. Even his big brother Jake had blown him off, since he'd gone and got himself a girlfriend, bloody-Bridie, as Danny thought of her.

Well today, just for once, being thin and small for his age would be an advantage.

He looked around. Bloody do-gooders. All this for a few spazzy kids? Well, boo-hoo; nobody had ever helped him – even when he'd asked for it, at the drop-in centre in town. They'd been too busy to see him, so he'd sat in the car park round the back and smoked weed until he puked behind an old Datsun.

Well today he'd help himself.

Starting with something to eat - the smell of fried onions was driving him insane with hunger.

'How much is a hot-dog?' he asked a white-haired woman in an apron.

'£2 for this one - and £2.50 for a big 'un,' she said, reaching for her tongs.

'Large,' Danny said, pretending to count out change while his bun was being assembled.

'Please,' the woman said, passing Danny the hot-dog.

'Ta,' he said, holding out his hand as if to pay, before running like the wind, as the woman shouted after him.

It was a start, he thought, wolfing bread and sausage and beginning to feel better.

🍎

One by one, the live acts took to the stage, performing their hearts out to varying degrees of approval, and in between a DJ kept everyone fizzing with a mixture of rock and dance music. Buoyed up by sunshine and alcohol, the crowd, which to Lisa's delight had swelled to over 500, sang and danced on a tide of goodwill.

They were all there; friends, neighbours, people from nearby villages – and hoards from Maidstone. It seemed that the boy-band she'd booked in all innocence, had quite a following – evidenced by the screaming that ensued when they leapt on stage, in low-slung denim, caps and chains.

'These lads are brilliant,' Ben conceded; 'Two of them can actually sing. Youth Inc. could be next year's big thing – stars of the future.'

'Well the young girls certainly like them - but don't forget who's headlining,' Lisa said.

Ben spread his arms wide; 'Leese; you did all this. You've raised thousands of pounds today – and given people a bloody good day out that they'll remember for years. You're amazing, babe. I just want to make you proud when I go on.'

Danny pretended to browse the stalls. He had no money to speak of; some change jangled in his left jeans pocket (he'd counted out £4.27), and in his right, another metal object felt cool to his bony fingers. The screwdriver had been just lying there, on the table, hard and shiny. He'd palmed it easily, right from under some geezer's nose, without breaking his stride.

It was all very well thieving hot-dogs and tools - but he wanted cash. He'd hung around a jewellery stall for a bit, but when he'd looked at the earrings, necklaces and other hippy-shit for sale, he'd seen it was all junk – like the rubbish his Mum wore...which made him think it wasn't worth robbing either the jewellery or the money-belt round the sales woman's waist.

But some of the smug rich bastards from the estate were worth a mint, thought Danny, restlessly doing another lap of the place. So he'd wait; see what occurred and in the meantime, he'd watch the show and nick some beer – it was better than being indoors.

By five o'clock, the sky had turned a dull sulphurous yellow.

'Oh, you are joking,' Ben said, 'don't tell me it's about to piss down, just as we go on.'

After speedily setting up, Steve and Ricky took up their positions. Ben swaggered on stage to mild applause.

'Good evening Wembley,' Ben boomed into the mic. It was a tumbleweed moment.

'I'm Ben Wilde; this is Rick...and Steve. And this is from the new album; No Surrender.' Ben launched into the title track, an upbeat single that people seemed to recognise, instantly surging forward and shuffling in time.

'Woo-hoo! I love you, Ben Wilde,' cried Lisa, watching from the wings.

Ben ostentatiously blew her a kiss; he'd get her on stage before the show ended.

For their second track, Ben cranked up the volume and launched into the Helium theme, buoyed up by the vibrating crowd before him.

'He's good, isn't he?' Martin said, nudging Jan. 'I've seen him around Crabton. Did you know he goes out with Lisa Dixon?'

They were on their feet, trampling the blanket, swaying and gyrating along with everyone else.

'He's handsome in a grubby sort of way,' Jan said, taking Martin's hand and twirling towards him.

People of all ages were clapping along now, even though rain had begun to leak through the clouds.

Ben reached down to brush hands with a few people at the front, the showman in him emerging. He could even pick out a few faces; Tanya, her model boyfriend, a couple of neighbours and

SEEKING EDEN

several ladies from the gym; hey, they'd be looking at him in a new light after this, for sure.

Finishing a gutsy rock number, Ben took a swig of water, before plucking his acoustic guitar from its stand.

'If you're of a certain age, you might remember this,' Ben paused for effect; 'This is Seagull – and it's for an old friend.'

Kate knew at once that Ben had dedicated the song to her and as olive branches went, it was a big one. Ben was a good man after all, she decided, as a tiny, hard nugget broke inside her chest.

Feeling wistful, arms swaying above her head, Kate sang along to the chorus. She spotted Dominic nearby, and had decided to make her way towards him when she felt someone standing too close.

'Give it here,' the boy said.

Suet-faced and feral, his hard eyes were fixed on the money belt tied around Kate's waist.

'What?' Kate stepped back, her hands clutching the wallet.

The boy moved towards her.

'Fucking give it 'ere,' the boy's cigarette and onion breath made her flinch, but it was his dead-eyed expression that frightened her.

'Take it off, or I'll cut you, bitch.'

'Get away from me. This is for charity...you should be ashamed. Does your mother know where you are?' Kate was stalling for time now, quite sure she wasn't giving up her stash. She searched the crowd for a protector, but all eyes were on Ben as Seagull soared to its climax and people waved mobile phones as torches, even though it was still light.

'I warned you,' the boy snarled.

With something glinting in his right hand, the boy struck like a viper, ripping the belt from her. A second later, Kate felt searing heat and wetness on her thigh. Blood oozed freely through her combats, turning her fingers red when she felt for the source of heat. The pain was visceral now, sucking the breath from her lungs. She saw the boy's legs merge into the crowd, before feeling the cool damp grass on her face.

⌘

At first, Ben ignored the commotion erupting in front of him. Seagull had ended and people were applauding and shouting for more. Feeling ten feet tall, he beckoned Lisa who was sashaying her way across the stage towards him.

He'd joked about Wembley, but it was amazing how much energy and love a few hundred people could give off; he was flying.

But the crowd was beginning to look fractured; a scuffle had broken out – a fight perhaps, or an accident, but something looked very wrong out there.

Still wearing her headset Lisa reached Ben, but instead of leaning into his open arms, she froze, a look of abject horror on her face.

'Oh my god, Ben. Someone's been stabbed.'

Mindless of the audience, who were still high on a wave of nostalgia, Ben left the stage, dragging Lisa after him.

⌘

'Stop right there, young man,' Martin had seen the lad weaving ferret-like through the rows of people – it was obvious he'd been up to no good. He grabbed at the boy's clothing, making him stumble.

'Fuck you, grandad,' the boy said, shoving Martin.

'Oh no you don't - you little...' Martin took a clumsy swing with his fist and stuck his foot out; the boy went down.

'My brother'll fucking kill you – ya tosser!' the boy spat, before letting out a scalded wail, as people came to Martin's aid, and two marshals in high-vis bore down on him.

Gripping Lisa's hand, instinct drove Ben towards the back of the field, as people starred after them, and got out of their way.

'It's Kate,' Ben shouted, moving a gaggle of people aside and dropping down beside her.

'Katie...are you okay? Can you hear me, love?'

Kate's eyes were closed as two first aiders worked on her inert body - one woman methodically creating a tourniquet for the wound, the other had wrapped a blanket around her upper body and was trying to rouse her.

Oh god, there's too much blood, Lisa thought, beginning to shake.

'Has anyone called an ambulance?' Ben said, clutching his phone.

'They're on their way, but there are sheep on the bypass and they can't get here for a while. We're First Aid trained and I've...'

'Sheep? Sod that. I'll take her myself,' Ben phoned Steve's number, and to his relief, his band mate answered after a couple of rings.

'Steve. It's me. You and Rick...get the van – quick as you can; we're taking a mate to hospital...yeah, man...just do it...then ring me back and I'll talk you in.'

It seemed like an age before Rick's van bounced across the grass towards them – but in reality is was a few minutes; the boys knew when to take Ben seriously.

⚡

Ignoring all protestations from the first aiders, Ben and Steve had gently lifted a semi-conscious Kate into the back of Rick's van. They'd made a stretcher from blankets and cushions, sweeping aside the cables, beer cans and other muso debris – it was far from ideal.

'Ben, look after her – I'll follow on as soon as I can.' Lisa said, remembering she had a show to close; today had been her baby and she had to finish things properly.

In the van, Ben knelt beside Kate, holding her hand, repeating that everything would be fine, just fine, to convince himself as much as Kate.

Then at Ben's insistence, Rick put his foot down - even running a red light – and within ten minutes they'd arrived at the hospital, stopping right outside A&E.

Ben ran inside, shouting for attention.

'We've got a lady here who's been stabbed – she's lost a lot of blood.'

Adrenalin had powered him on, but when the medics took over Ben slumped in a plastic chair, trying to makes sense of it all.

The weird stuff just keeps coming, he thought – wondering if it was the same for everyone.

⚡

After finding Neil's mobile number in Kate's phone, Lisa repeated the words, gently and slowly, waiting for his ears and brain to fall in sync.

'Christ, no! Is she going to be alright?' Neil shouted. Why hadn't he been there for her?

'Katie's stable,' Lisa said 'but she's lost a lot of blood and she's a bit weepy as you can imagine.'

Then Neil had driven across South London like a man possessed, daring anyone to stop him, and after doing ninety miles an hour on the M20, he'd arrived at Kate's bedside within the hour.

'I turn my back for six months and this is what you get up to.' Neil said, with a weak smile.

'You came...' Kate rasped. 'How are you?'

'How am I?' Neil said, taking Kate's cool, limp hand. 'Oh, you know... fine...for someone who's been acting like a complete moron all year. Can I get you anything, my love?' Neil's voice was tender.

She looked so vulnerable in her hospital gown; it reminded him of the last time she'd worn one. It didn't matter now - nothing mattered except that Kate recovered.

'God, Katie – you could have been killed. I wish I could get hold of the little shit that did this.'

'He was just a kid. They caught him though... and the money's safe.' Kate attempted a smile.

'I'm so sorry, Katie...for being such an arse - and for not being there for you. But I'm here now, and I'm going to look after you.'

'That's nice,' Kate said, before drifting off to sleep.

ᕯ

Ben, who was pacing the corridor, stiffened when Neil emerged from Kate's room.

'I don't want any trouble...I've no beef with you, mate,' he said, backing away.

Neil shook his head and put out his hand.

'We're cool as far as I'm concerned, Ben. You saved Kate's life... you and Lisa – I've everything to thank you for. And, I'm sorry...

about…you know…before.'

Ben grasped Neil's hand and they shook.

'Pleasure, man; I'm sure you'd have done the same for Lisa.'

She appeared then, carrying a cardboard tray of coffees.

'I hope you two are playing nicely,' she said, before taking a sip of the tarry liquid. 'Hey, not quite the Saturday night we were planning, eh? Some after-show party this has turned out to be.'

ᘓ

Martin re-read the front page of the gazette. Usually he hated the way these rags liked to sensationalise everything, but for once he didn't mind. He'd been called a hero, community spirited and a model citizen - all in the space of a page. Martin didn't agree; all he'd done was trip the lad up, but he'd rescued the money – and that was before he'd even realised that the little thug had stabbed Kate Farleigh with a screwdriver.

'I'm so proud of you, Martin – you're my hero,' Jan said for the third time that morning. 'You can have anything you like for tea tonight…go on, you choose.'

Martin looked at his wife - eyes shining, cheeks flushed with pride and pleasure. She even walked taller these days – or did he imagine that?

He returned to his paper; pages four and five were also devoted to the festival – but the spread focussed on the acts that had played, and the money that had been raised. Amid action shots of the performers on stage, a photograph of Lisa smiled out at him; 'event-director and philanthropist' the caption said. It seemed like a much more fitting label than WAG.

And then Lisa herself had come into the shop, wearing a yellow summer dress and tortoise- shell sunglasses, looking like a film star.

'Lisa, hello! What can I do for you on this sunny day?' he said.

'Nothing - you've done enough, Martin. I came to thank you for everything you did. You were very brave,' Lisa said, stroking his arm lightly and opening her eyes wide.

'Well, I don't know about that.' Martin blustered.

'It's true. You're a good man, Martin – I've always known that... and if your wife can forgive me for that daft mix-up, Ben and I would like to invite you both to dinner at ours on Saturday night. Does eight o'clock suit you?'

Martin beamed.

'Ooh, get you, boss - mingling with the stars,' Trina said, after Lisa had gone.

♋

Charged with aggravated robbery, Danny Burden had confessed, spewing out his story through thick choking sobs, while he waited for his mum and brother to arrive at the police station. The officer in charge had given him tea and biscuits, thinking the poor skinny kid probably needed the calories.

With the legal fall-out cut mercifully short, locals soon forgot about Danny Burden. People on the Parish Council – as well as several local entrepreneurs - suggested making it an annual event for good causes.

'I'll think about it,' Lisa said, not sure she could go through it all again.

'Babe, go for it; you're a natural. You should start an event planning business of your own – you've got a gift for it. As long as you can still manage me as well,' Ben said, grinning at his own cheek.

## KATE

Moira had been the first of the neighbours to mention the For Sale sign.

'I'll be ever so sad to see you go, Katie, love. What are your plans for the future?'

It was a reasonable enough question, but one for which Kate had no answer.

Neil had returned, but after a few weeks, he'd admitted that home didn't feel like home anymore.

'Jesus, Neil – don't do this,' Kate said, the words turning to ice in her throat.

'Oh darling, that's not what I meant at all. It's not about us. I feel so lucky that you've taken me back, after everything. No, it's this place, Katie. It's all wrong for us now.'

Kate thought back to them fleeing London after the burglary and it felt like a lifetime ago; when they'd been seduced by the peace, the countryside, and having a big house, with all mod-cons.

But then came the depression, the loneliness, seeing Ben again, the abortion, Neil's exit – the stabbing, for god's sake. Their mishaps read like a Penny Dreadful.

'You're right. We need a fresh start. We can put everything behind us and just begin again. You, me and Ludo,' Kate said, stroking the dog's silky ears.

'Darling, are you sure? You've made a life here... walking the boy, going to the gym, your girlfriends...'

'No, I haven't; that's the thing. I've tried so hard...and being happy shouldn't be this much effort.'

'What about your job? I thought you liked it,' Neil said.

'I do, I like it a lot – and the people are great, but if we move,

I'll get something else – or even commute, depending on where we go.'

They'd gone back and forth then – talking through the pros and cons - but both of them quite adamant that they would not (could not) return to London.

The following week, Jeremy Hunter had carried out a valuation personally. Kate and Neil had been aghast at how much their house was worth.

The money didn't matter; they would move, regardless. It was time.

And then fate had intervened in the shape of a job offer when Neil was headhunted to start up an ad agency in Bath.

'Wow, really? Bath is so...so cool and vibrant; all that heritage and culture! You have to say yes, darling. When are we leaving?' Kate was laughing and jumping on the spot.

'If that's what you want - but we can still play hard ball...maybe negotiate a relocation package to be thrown in, and some freelance work for you, my love.'

Then they'd drunk wine to celebrate, and had gone to bed, giddy with hope.

Kate winced; 'Be gentle - it's still sore,' she said, as Neil moved carefully around the puckered stab wound.

'Sorry,' Neil said, lightly kissing its roughness.

Like the purple scar on Kate's thigh, they were healing.

## THE END

# ACKNOWLEDGEMENTS

A huge and heartfelt thank you goes to all the people who helped me to write Seeking Eden.

Thank you to friends Gill, Jo, Jayne, Mandy, Lucy, Bob & Sue, for taking me seriously. Thank you to Nick Winter for suggesting my first creative writing course in Tonbridge (many more followed), where I met tutor Beth McNeilly, who fizzed with encouragement as the book took shape: thank you, Beth. Thank you Samantha Rice for insisting I press on with looking for a publisher, when I was almost ready to throw in the towel.

Which leads me to Urbane Publications: Enormous, fluffy, cream-filled thanks go to the fearless Matthew Smith, owner and founder of Urbane, to whom I am deeply grateful. Thank you to my fellow Urbane authors for their kindness and support - too many to name...you know who you are.

A massive thank you to my family; to David Harvey (who inspired much of Ben Wilde's cheeky badinage); to Ali Gooderham, and to Lyn Beer - bless you for all your love, kindness and support.

Finally, deepest love and sincerest gratitude goes to my wonderful partner Mark Payton – who endured Seeking Eden as a bedtime story for a whole year; thank you from the bottom of my heart, AP - you never doubted me.

**Beverley Harvey** (Bev to her friends) hails from the corporate communications world. She worked first in advertising in a variety of support roles, before moving to PR where she trained in a London agency before becoming freelance in 2001.

After threatening to write a book for years, Bev finally swapped PR campaigns for plot lines with the completion of her debut novel 'Seeking Eden'.

When not writing – or reading, Bev enjoys listening to rock and indie music, cooking, baking, and keeping fit. An animal lover and part-time dog walker, she is inspired by nature, art and life's daily trials and tribulations.

Born in Yorkshire, and raised in South London, Beverley now lives in Kent with her partner Mark and their naughty Terrier, Brodie.

http://www.beverleyharvey.co.uk/
@BevHarvey_

Urbane Publications is dedicated to developing new author voices, and publishing fiction and non-fiction that challenges, thrills and fascinates.

From page-turning novels to innovative reference books, our goal is to publish what YOU want to read.

Find out more at
**urbanepublications.com**